BJ JAMES
A WOLF IN THE DESERT

D0047556

SILHOUETTE *Desire*®
Published by Silhouette Books
America's Publisher of Contemporary Romance

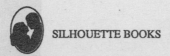

SILHOUETTE BOOKS

RECYCLED PAPER

ISBN 0-373-05956-6

A WOLF IN THE DESERT

Copyright © 1995 by BJ James

Books by BJ James

Silhouette Desire

The Sound of Goodbye #332
Twice in a Lifetime #396
Shiloh's Promise #529
Winter Morning #595
Slade's Woman #672
A Step Away #692
Tears of the Rose #709
The Man with the Midnight Eyes #751
Pride and Promises #789
Another Time, Another Place #823
The Hand of an Angel #844
*Heart of the Hunter #945
*The Saint of Bourbon Street #951
*A Wolf in the Desert #956

*Men of the Black Watch

BJ JAMES

married her high school sweetheart straight out of college and soon found that books were delightful companions during her lonely nights as a doctor's wife. But she never dreamed she'd be more than a reader, never expected to be one of the blessed, letting her imagination soar, weaving magic of her own.

BJ has twice been honored by the Georgia Romance Writers with their prestigious Maggie Award for Best Short Contemporary Romance. She has also received the *Romantic Times* Critic's Choice Award.

Prologue

"Yes . . . We have a renegade."

There was silence after the reluctant admission. In the solitary darkness of his Spartan office Simon McKinzie braced the telephone between shoulder and jaw. His face was wooden, one fisted hand rested on his knee, the other clenched a crumpled message. A message delivered by special courier, intended for his eyes only. With his back to a window that commanded an impressive view of Washington by night, his bleak stare looked blindly at a barren wall.

As he listened to the pedantic lecture of a power hungry bureaucrat wielding what the foolish creature perceived as his own special bit of authority, only the creak and groan of the chair warned of the veiled tensing of Simon's formidable body. In what could have been misconstrued as a languid gesture, a massive hand lifted from his knee, blunt, square-nailed fingers captured the receiver in a bearlike grip. No hint of change flickered over his features, but deep in his hooded eyes seethed cold, barely leashed rage.

"Of course I know it's an explosive situation." The damning scrap of paper drifted to the floor as he snarled into the receiver in response to a repetitive statement of the obvious. "He's my man. I know better than anyone what he's capable of."

Reining in his anger Simon leaned forward, eyes like lasers now, scanned his office. Once, twice, then once more, his gaze lingered here, there, probing his memory of his sweep of critical niches. With a curt nod, pleased with his last discovery, he picked up the lighter that occupied a place of honor on his desk. As the voice at the other end of the line droned on, he flicked a broad thumb over it and a flame danced and swayed in the invisible currents of climate control. A small light in the darkness of his soul.

"I have admitted we have a renegade." Heavy shoulders taut, a frown wrinkling his forehead beneath a closely cropped silver mane, his words were dangerously spaced as he looked into the calming center of the flame. "Where and why is our concern and no other's. The Watch takes care of its own."

Distaste supplanting anger in his hooded eyes, Simon listened again. A calculated stratagem more than respect for the speaker's political authority. The covert organization for special investigations had been instigated by a past president. The monumental task of making the dream of fail-safe protection above the vagaries of politics a viable reality had been given to Simon. Through sheer willpower and stubborn dedication he made it reality, he made it viable. Without him it could not have existed. He *was* the organization, and the organization was his.

In twenty years that had not changed. The rigid rules and guidelines were set down by Simon. The extraordinary men who lived and worked by them were chosen by Simon. The assignments were accepted by Simon. The Black Watch was still his.

Simon McKinzie was a powerful man. There were those among his acquaintance who thought too powerful. Those who coveted and those who feared the ungoverned control. Such acquaintances had no concept of the true man. The man of honor and truth, without personal ambition, whose loyalty to his men was superseded only by his loyalty to his country.

Simon McKinzie had and would walk through hell for his men, and twice for his country. He knew his men, singled out for constancy as well as individual talents, would do the same. There had been mistakes over the years—agents who failed, who couldn't cope, or simply opted out. But never many, never an agent trusted above all others. And only once, the threat of a renegade.

Until now, only David Canfield.

Cradling the lighter in his hand, Simon remembered.

David, the first, best of the best, a young idealist with a heartbreaking smile. Fifteen grueling years in the field robbed him of the smile, a final tragedy drew him to the brink, a step from disaster. There were enemies who wanted to hunt him down and, in destroying him, destroy The Black Watch. Simon fought for David and won. His ally, time and Raven McCandless.

Gentle Raven, master potter, creator of beauty. A woman who brought love to a bitter, heartsick man, and at long last, salvation and peace.

Simon had no gentle ally in this circumstance. He had only himself. Only he would be champion of the man and keeper of the secret. He could give his renegade that.

And time.

Balancing the telephone again between shoulder and chin, with a low growl rumbling at the base of his throat, he retrieved the yellow document. In a slow, deliberate move he dragged a corner through the fire, watching as the flame crawled the length of it to lick at his fingers. As heat singed the hirsute back of his hand, with a great sense of satisfaction and apologies to the meticulous cleaning crew, he dropped the crumbling ash into an immaculate garbage can.

Time, Matthew, he thought, keeping a careful silence as a coil of smoke drifted in an eddying current of air and disappeared. *All the time you need.*

The taut angle of his shoulders eased, grim lines that bracketed his mouth softened as he snuffed out the flame and set the lighter in its place. The bit of potter's clay fashioned in a misshapen ball around a two-bit lighter was a six-year-old child's first effort at his mother's craft. A gift from Simon Canfield to Simon McKinzie, and the elder Simon's greatest treasure.

A child. A very special child. Proof that circumstances weren't always as they seemed, and no man was beyond redemption.

No man.

"Casper." The name began as a growl and ended an intimidating bark. "Shut up." The preening monologue that poured in a torrent through the line halted abruptly.

His patience at an end, smiling the infamous rictus of a smile that sent any sensible opponent running for cover, Simon set the record straight. "There will be no manhunt. No one could find the Apache unless he wanted to be found, no one could bring him in. No one except us. This is our problem, we'll handle it."

More stupidly dense than most, Casper chose to argue. Simon cut him short in a low drawl that left no room for underestimation. "There will be no search and destroy. I repeat, none! The

Watch will handle this in its own way. Consider this a personal warning—if anyone disregards what I've said, you will answer to me." Simon paused to let his promise and what it entailed register in Casper's slow-moving mind. "You, Casper. First, last, always."

Protests and denials spewed over the line. Simon ignored them, speaking into the outburst so softly there could be no mistaking his meaning. "How you control your cohorts is your problem. How I deal with my men is mine."

As the pedantic voice turned shrill in babbled promises and denials, Simon's smile grew colder. "Good," he said at last. "I'm glad we understand each other.

"By the way, Casper, there's one more thing." Simon listened to a ragged breath caught and held, and knew he'd truly won. "As a show of my good faith, I won't ask how you came into possession of this information."

The receiver clattered into its cradle. "Have a good evening, Casper," he muttered. With the first real smile of the day beginning in his eyes, in blatant disregard for the microphone tucked beneath the rim of the immaculate trash can, he added, "If you can."

Wearied by the tensions of the day, Simon leaned back in his chair, allowing himself only a moment to rest. There was more to be done, much more. Not one precious moment would be squandered savoring his victory. The crucial point was time. Time he'd won for his renegade.

Time for Matthew Sky.

One

Beauty sighed. Beauty died.

In the first shade of nightfall, as darkness crept over a bloodred sky, her thundering heart stopped. Death came so swiftly Patience O'Hara had no time to think, none to comprehend. In one perfect moment they were barreling westward, racing at breakneck speed into the ebbing light of a fiery sunset. Patience sang. Beauty hummed, leaving a trail of boiling dust in her wake. Then nothing.

Zero. Zilch. *Nada.*

No power, no lights, no music.

Nothing.

On an obscure track in the middle of nowhere and no sign of life for miles, all three hundred, thirty horses under Beauty's pretty aristocratic nose dwindled to a puddle of nothing. The whole herd of them, gone, in a heartbeat, without a second peep or whinny.

"Beauty! No!" Patience cut short her gusty off-key rendition of "Ghost Riders In The Sky" one note past failure of all systems. "You can't do this to me. Not now. Not here."

As she pleaded her lost cause, ingrained instincts overrode the inertia of surprise. In a conditioned response she mustered the last of Beauty's dying momentum to wrest the Corvette's cumbersome, unresponsive weight to what passed for the shoulder of what could only laughably be called a road.

Bumping to a halt, her hands resting loosely on the steering wheel, she sat nonplussed, dazed, feeling the void, the nothingness closing in. As one would feel at the loss of a friend.

The silly car, an impractical gift for her journey through the west from her ever-impractical family, had become her companion and confidant, assuming a personality in the long, solitary hours they shared on the road. She'd come to know and anticipate the growing list of idiosyncrasies of this sleek work of art in fiberglass. Even to regard them fondly as she would the endearing and often annoying quirks of her eccentric family. Of whom there were seven. Family, that is. Mother, Mavis; father, Keegan; brothers, Devlin, Kieran and Tynan; sister, Valentina; and lastly, Patience. Prudent Patience. Practical Patience. Boring Patience.

Seven O'Haras true to the breed, with thoroughly O'Hara quirks far too changeable and numerous to calculate. But Beauty's idiosyncrasies? A different matter.

Patience had chronicled them, investigated them herself, and had them investigated in each new place, after each new occurrence. There was never anything. Neither she, nor any service center, or shade tree mechanic, no matter how competent, discovered a problem. After weeks of ignoring dozens of smug male smirks insinuating the peculiar and transient difficulties were in her imagination not the splendid Vette, after fending off a dozen and one too many passes, she stopped looking for trouble and coped.

Beauty had a problem; several problems, actually. Or maybe, as Mavis who was Irish to the core might say, she was inhabited by a leprechaun bent on a bit of mischief.

Whatever the cause, all the little transient problems had finally ceased being vague and transient, coalescing into catastrophe. And in that single soft sigh Patience heard the portent that this time the trouble wouldn't be going away.

"Why now?" She glared at an ever-darkening sky. "Why here?" Turning a bleak gaze at the desert she gripped the steering wheel tighter, muttering, "And where the hell are we?"

She couldn't remember a sign giving either name or road number telling where she'd been or where she was going. She couldn't remember the last sign of life. She was alone in the middle of nowhere and not even a cow for company.

"So, Beauty, you got me into this, what do I do?" An unfair accusation Patience admitted, for it was she who had left their charted route on a whim. She who, in typical family fashion, had tired of the expected and opted for this little adventurous ramble.

"My mother's youngest daughter." Continuing her muttered harangue of all things O'Hara, she rummaged through the console for The Handy Dandy Tool Kit, Tools For All Occasions. A parting gift from brother Devlin.

"There you are." Pulling the fine leather case from its spot of repose, she prepared to see what she could do about getting herself out of what she'd gotten herself into. If her gut feeling was right, attacking Beauty's problem with The Handy Dandy Tools would be as effective as attacking a rhinoceros with a hairpin.

Climbing out of the Vette one slender, denim-clad leg at a time, she stood barefoot, feeling the rising heat of the ground and the descending chill of the night. In another hour she would be shivering. In less than that the last of the light would vanish from the sky. Since she didn't relish holding a flashlight between her teeth while she delved beneath Beauty's hood in the dark, she snatched her boots from the car, stamped her feet into them with the mastery of a seasoned cowhand and addressed the task she'd set herself.

Twenty minutes later, with a swipe of her forearm over her sweaty brow, she backed away, defeated. Whatever ailed Beauty remained a mystery, no more evident in extremity than before. This strange malady was far beyond the small knowledge imparted to Patience by brother Devlin whose life and love focused on family, especially his baby sister, fast cars, fast planes, fast motorcycles, and fast women. But not especially in that order.

After putting the tools away and closing the hood with a sense of regret, Patience leaned against a fender, absently scrubbing her hands on the thighs of her jeans as she considered her options. She could walk out, but which way should she go? How far back was the last settlement? How far ahead was the next? One mile? Two? Fifty? A hundred? The road was so poorly distinguishable from the desert itself, could she be sure she wouldn't wander away from it?

Patience stared out at miles of nothing. The desert seemed static at a glance, a rendering in stone, the keeper of ancient secrets. But she knew there were creatures there, nocturnal creatures she couldn't see. Since she didn't know where she was, she wasn't sure what creatures. Birds, mice, a sure bet. Javelinas, perhaps.

Snakes.

Suppressing the shiver rippling through her, she crossed her arms beneath her breasts, her fingers clutching at the shirt pulled taut over her ribs. Snakes. She hated them. Animals were her business, she'd studied them, learned how to care for them and treat them. Her purpose for coming west, beyond distancing herself from her beloved madcap family, was to find that perfect place to establish her fledgling veterinary practice. But snakes!

Unconsciously she shook her head. She'd never managed to conquer an almost paralytic fear of them. Her unreasonable response made no sense, but it served her well for once, tipping the scales to a more prudent decision. Snakes or no snakes, only a tenderfoot would venture into unfamiliar territory at night.

Patience hadn't been a tenderfoot since she was seven and her first horse refused a fence, sending her flying braids over bootheels. She remembered the spill and how frightened she'd been as if it were twenty minutes ago instead of twenty years. In the expected tradition, after picking herself up and dusting herself off, she'd hobbled back to the horse, conducted a little heart-to-heart talk and climbed back on. He never refused a fence again. Once again, in family tradition, she would climb back into Beauty for the remainder of the night. At first light she would face any fears she must, do whatever she must to accomplish her return to civilization.

Decision made, she gathered up The Handy Dandy Tool Kit and in her long-legged, confident stride, circled to the door. Her hand was at the latch when a drift of sound made her pause. Head up, she turned, searching for something that would explain the disturbance.

Nothing.

The desert was still under the rising moon. Yet there was something, Patience knew she wasn't mistaken. Executing a slow turn she looked out over the barren land once more, her stare probing, searching, then probing deeper. Nothing moved among clumps of stunted desert grasses. No shadow skulked about the prickly saguaro, pious giants of the desert with arms raised eternally toward heaven.

She could feel the stillness permeating the air.

And yet...

Stooping swiftly she gathered up a handful of pebbles and flung them into the brush. In a nearly silent flap of wings, so slowly it seemed in stop-action sequences, an owl lifted from the scrub, a snake writhing in its beak. Patience flinched and ducked, bumping her elbow against a mirror. Pain radiated down her arm, followed by a tingling numbness, but she hardly noticed. When the shock subsided she felt only profoundly relieved, chiding herself softly for a momentary revulsion for the owl's dinner.

She was turning again to the door when some nuance, a portent, had her whirling around. Teeth clenched against an outcry, she turned cautiously in place, making another circular sweep of the land.

Saguaros stood as piously as before, grasses perched as tenuously in the sand. Above them the sky was an undisturbed expanse. Frightened and replete, the owl hadn't returned.

What then? she wondered. What had her so spooked?

Had she heard something or only sensed it? Had she been disturbed on some subconscious level by the precursor of sound?

"Ah!" She shook her head in disgust. "God help ye, Patience, ye've been in the desert too long to fall prey to such buffoonery. Mayhap 'twould be best to head back east at first chance."

The parody of her Irish ancestors dropped like a stone from her lips as she felt it. At first it was only vibration, the subtle, immeasurable shaking of the earth in response to pounding sound. Like an electrical charge lancing through her, the vibration raced to her ears, becoming sound. Deep, pulsing sound. Sound she knew.

"Two," she muttered, listening, her hopes rising with the sound. "Four." Her heart raced a bit, a frown barely creased her forehead. Her hand pawed nervously for the latch, but her gaze never wavered from the direction of the invisible sound.

"Six!" The number sent terror racing through her like a ravenous fire. Her hand shook, her numb fingers wouldn't obey as she fumbled with the latch. Frustration fed by fear erupted from her.

"God help me!" The cry was a muted scream as blinding lights rose out of a dip made invisible by the shadows of sunset. Patience wondered desperately what other secrets were hidden in the crude road that had appeared to be as perfectly level as it was straight. Spurred by the strength of panic, her nearly paralyzed fingers responded. The latch engaged and released.

Catching back a sob of pain, scrambling, stumbling, nearly falling in her frantic haste, she flung open the door and threw herself inside the dark interior of the Corvette. She managed to drag the door shut with her good hand and slap down the locks with her palm an instant before six motorcycles, six chromed and polished machines, riding in pairs roared around the car.

Savages of the modern world on modern steeds with throbbing V-twin motors circled a crippled wagon. Around and around in darkness that was complete, Harleys, Fat Boys, Electra Glides reared and spun and skidded, executing tight, sliding turns. Headlights flashed, one illuminating the one in front of it, a battery of monstrous machines, tattooed arms and brawny bodies revealed in their glare.

Patience sat woodenly, seeking refuge in a secret place of oblivion, ignoring catcalls and grinning faces leaning close to leer. Refusing to cringe as gloved fingers stretched out in their circuit to trail over the surface of the car and the windows, stroking them, caressing them, as they would the flesh of a woman.

Fighting back a shiver, she tried not to see, tried not to think. Pebbles clattered against Beauty's smooth sides, dust spewed over her in grainy plumes, and spewed again. The air churned with it, fell thick and heavy with it, and in the flaring light, turned to suffocating haze. Patience was mercifully blinded, the riders, she was sure, would be more so. With all her might she willed them to tire of the choking dust and their game, prayed they would leave her to find her way from the desert in peace.

But the bikers weren't so easily discouraged. In eerie silence, as engine after engine shut down and dust fell through the glare of headlights like settling fog, only a naive fool wouldn't have realized this was far more than a bit of roadside hazing. Her body tense, woodenly stiff, in darting glances she watched them swagger toward her, strutting through blinding brightness in leathers and boots and shining chains, with thumbs hooked in the pockets of jeans, elbows bent, biceps bulging, and six smirking grins.

These were outlaws, the incarnation of every cliché. Mean-to-the-bone, born-to-be-wild, live-to-ride bikers. If she'd been lucky they might had been one of the many rubes like Devlin. Yuppies with deep pockets and gold cards living on the cutting edge. Clean-cut, clean-living country boys fulfilling dreams. The richer, older, gentlemanly urbanite out for a fashionable spin in the desert.

But she hadn't been lucky. These weren't rubes of any sort, and she knew she was looking at more trouble than she'd ever imagined.

"Hey, baby." The first rider, a wiry man with a tumble of golden curls and goatee to match, slapped a palm on the window, jolting her from her thoughts. Rigid control kept her from cringing.

"You in there." He bent near to peer at her through the window, a sudden grin splitting his face as he called out, "Jackpot! We got us a redhead this time."

"Red?" a voice asked.

"'S what I said."

"For sure? You ain't joshing us, Custer?"

"Red-gold and curly," the biker called Custer assured them. "And lots of it."

Patience stared straight ahead, her gaze fixed, focused on nothing. She refused to turn, refused to acknowledge him.

"Hey! I said." Custer slapped a hand against the window again. The report rivaled the sound of a gunshot in the murky interior of the car. "What's the matter, Red?" He bent closer, his goatee brushing the window. "Are you deaf? Blind? Cat got your tongue?"

Another rider joined him. Another face to peer at her. Patience didn't turn, didn't look.

"Funny," the second observed, "she don't look deaf."

"How can you tell?"

"She's wearing earrings. Deaf people don't wear earrings."

"Who says?"

"I dunno, me, I guess."

"Maybe she's not blind, either." A third rider, a gross giant of a man running to fat, leapt to the hood, draping himself over it as he pressed his forehead to the windshield to smirk down at her. "Nah. She ain't blind, I saw her blink."

"Of course she's not, dummy," a fourth voice interjected. "Who do you think drove out here?"

"Who you callin' dummy?"

"You, dummy. Who else?"

"That's it." Custer snapped his fingers, interrupting the budding altercation as if an idea just occurred. "She's crazy. Gotta be. Only a crazy woman would drive in the desert alone at night."

"Yeah, who knows what might happen?"

"Why she could even have trouble with her shiny new Vette."

"And meet up with bad guys."

"Or, if she's lucky, good guys."

Keeping her determined silence, Patience heard but couldn't match voices to faces. She didn't try.

A beer bottle glinted in the moonlight as it was sucked dry and tossed away. The drinker hitched his pants and smiled blearily. "Hey, Snake, are we good guys or bad guys?"

"That depends on what Red here wants."

Another chorus rose in concert. Obscene speculations echoed, one after the other. In them Patience heard the howl of roving wolves stalking the first kill of the night.

She felt sick, her eyes burned in the unrelenting blaze of lights pouring at her from the darkness. She was afraid, but, oddly, fear had become a source of false strength. Like a spotlighted doe she was paralyzed, frozen in place, too frightened to tremble or cry for their pleasure.

The rider on Beauty's hood squirmed and turned, sliding his massive body over the glass, craning his neck to see inside. "I don't care what she wants," he declared with a lecherous grin baring broken teeth. "I'm in love. Sweet Red has skinny hips. I love red-haired women with skinny hips."

Patience clung to the steering wheel. Her palms were sweaty, her throat dry as she fought dread and despair. There was no way out. If she had a chance, it was to outlast them.

"Hear that, Sweet Red?" Custer's voice was soft, cajoling. "Blue Doggie loves you. Why don't you come out to play with him?"

Patience sat as she had from the first, rigid, unresponsive.

"Hot damn!" Blue Doggie giggled and pounded the hood. "I love it when a skinny-hipped woman plays hard for me to get. Makes it so much better when I do."

"Sweet Red," a new voice wheedled. "Come out, come out." The singsong wheedle took on a hard edge. "If you don't we'll just have to come get you. Be nice, save us the trouble and save yourself the wear and tear on this nice shiny car."

A fist slammed the car. "Dammit, Red, do you hear me?"

The vicious undercurrent in their banter was surfacing. Her time was running out. Feverishly she thought of the derringer in the console at her side. It was loaded and ready. The rifle lying in its case beneath her luggage would be better. The bikers wouldn't expect a rifle, but she hadn't a prayer of getting to it, taking it from the case and loading it before they got to her.

Maybe she hadn't a prayer, but she would fight. As hard as she could, for as long as she could. But not until she had to.

Blue Doggie squirmed on the hood, trying to catch her attention. She stared blankly, her vision focused on a distant point through and beyond his bulging belly. Angrily he reared over her, arms spread, bare chest filling her vision, a snarl hissed through jagged teeth as he planted an obscene kiss on the glass.

Patience bit down on her lip to keep from turning away. He hadn't touched her, yet she felt as soiled as the sweat-smeared glass. A coppery taste of blood was on her tongue. She ignored it, returning her stare to that distant point in her war of wills.

In frustration or anger, she didn't care which, the giant slammed a ringed fist into the glass. Cracks radiated from the point of impact in a crazed star. The ruined glass held. Blue Doggie snarled a coarse promise and swaggered away for another beer.

She saw him then.

The seventh rider.

An ebony shadow caught in a swirling haze, etched against the paler darkness of the night. A remote figure, as watchful and mysterious as the desert. Only the bike he rode gave back the light of the rising moon. Not even the churning dust of ancient and forgotten trails could dim the subtle gleam of the excellently maintained Electra Glide. Were it not for that reflection, a small light in the blackness of the moment, she wouldn't have seen him.

Riding alone a distance behind, the sound of his single engine masked by the throb of paired riders, his coming had been virtually silent. In her panic and in the frenzy of maniacal heckling she'd neither seen him nor sensed his presence.

Seeing him now, a rider apart, a man on the fringes and uninvolved, sent a frisson of something she could only call hope rushing through her. Like a blush it bathed her cold body in a glow of warmth. It made no sense, one more rider would not alter her fate. She was still a woman lost and stranded on a little used desert track. A woman with evil tearing at the door of her last sanctuary.

No, she thought as cold reality swept foolish hope from her heart, there would be no help from that quarter. No help from anyone or anything but herself.

Gripping the steering wheel tighter, without regard for cramping fingers and the mounting ache in her elbow, she stared vaguely ahead, denying her tormentors the pleasure of panic.

She didn't intend it, didn't want it, but he was there in the line of her unfocused vision. The seventh rider.

She couldn't see his face, nor his eyes. But she knew he watched her. She felt the power of his stare keeping her from the oblivion she sought, forcing her to focus on him. Caught up in the erratic moods of terror, she hated him then. More than the others. More than anything. For the frisson of hopeless hope, for watching dispassionately and uninvolved. For engaging her emotions, intruding on her thoughts, and stripping away her one refuge.

She hated him most for destroying the last precious moments of sanctuary before the wolves tearing at her fortress destroyed her.

The slap of a palm against the windshield should have torn her from her bitter thoughts, instead she discovered newfound hate brought with it newfound strength. She was done with hiding. Tearing her gaze from the shadowy apparition, she stared coldly at Beauty's assailant, her eyes seething with anger.

"Hot damn!" a new heckler crowed. "There's life here, Blue Doggie. She may be dumb, but she ain't deaf or blind. She moves, she hears, she sees. If looks were lethal, I'd be road kill."

Wearied by his prancing and crowing, Patience turned away, her attention drawn again to the source of her strength.

As the moon chased across the sky, beneath its canted light the desert came alive, shifting, hiding, revealing, leaving nothing ever the same in the eye of the beholder. Only he hadn't changed. Only he was as before, sitting astride his bike, legs bent, feet braced in dust. His hands lay lazily across chrome handlebars, his shoulders were back, his head up. Eyes hidden in shadow were turned to her. Watching.

"Hey."

Patience didn't react to Blue Doggie's return.

"Hey! Look at me," he demanded.

She didn't turn.

"I said look, damn you!" Spreading his feet and bracing his hands on the top of the door, he rocked the car as he spoke. "You look at Hogan, you look at me."

Which was Hogan? Was he the dwarf? The silent one with the scarred throat? She didn't know, she didn't care as she clung to the steering wheel to keep her balance.

Abruptly Blue Doggie stepped back, hands raised in an air of surrender. Startled by the conciliatory gesture and mistrusting peripheral vision, she turned to him in time to see his face contort into a rictus of rage. That slight turn saved her eyes, her face, perhaps her life, as a chain crashed down on the damaged windshield.

Glass cracked, breaking free at the point of impact, sending great deadly shards flying into the car. Before the chain whipped down again she scooped the derringer from the console, palming it with cool-headed expertise.

Curbing his swing, Blue Doggie deflected the path of the chain, letting it fall in a clatter over Beauty's hood. He peered through the gaping hole. First he scowled, then he laughed. "The lady's packing. A two-shot peashooter, no less."

"Back off!" Patience warned, ignoring his mockery. As threat became true peril, fear gave way to unshakable resolve. The derringer was steady in her hand and aimed precisely at the center of the hole in the glass and the point between Blue Doggie's eyes.

"You've had your fun. Now it's time to crawl back on your hogs, or whatever you call them, and disappear."

"Now, why would we go away and leave a pretty young thing like you alone in the desert?"

"Maybe because it's the wiser thing, Blue." The answer was low, the masculine voice composed. A voice of reason drifting out of the night.

"Wise?" Blue Doggie wheeled around, speaking to the darkness. "What's wise about leaving now?"

"Because the lady asked." A reasonable argument, a reasonable tone, lacking the indifference Patience would've expected. "Because even you would lose an argument with a derringer."

"Hell, Indian." Blue Doggie gestured impatiently, the chain dangling from a leather band at his wrist glinted in the headlights of the circled cycles. "She won't shoot."

Muttered agreement and more catcalls rose from the others, urging Blue Doggie on.

"If you believe that, you're bigger fools than I thought." In a cultured tone so unlike the others, he might've been dressing down a troop of Boy Scouts, not a band of cutthroats with wolf heads tattooed on their arms.

Shocked by the calm ridicule, Patience turned instinctively toward him, probing beyond the lighted circle, seeking to know what manner of man waited and watched in the dark.

"That's what you think, huh? That I'm a fool?" Blue Doggie snarled. "Then we'll just have to see, won't we?"

She recognized the threat too late. A murderous backhanded swing brought the chain down over the glass again, an instant before she turned and fired. The bullet went wide, creasing the top of her attacker's ear, fueling his rage rather than ending it forever. The glass imploded, shattered splinters became minute daggers. Patience only had time to shield her eyes and face. The derringer slipped from her grasp and tumbled to the floor. Even as her hands were stinging from minute cuts, she whirled, reaching between the bucket seats, groping for the rifle case.

Another second and she would've had it, but there wasn't another second. A fist buried in her hair, lifting her through the open door of the car. Through a haze of pain she watched as Blue Doggie smiled down at her. He shook his head as if he were dislodging a worrisome fly, a halo of blood arced from his torn ear. His fingers closed tighter, drawing her neck to an impossible angle.

"You'll pay. Before I'm through, you'll wish your aim had been true."

Grabbing his wrists, her hands slick with her own blood, she clawed at him, trying to break his hold. One nail broke, then a second; his grip tightened. "Let go, you cretin," she demanded, too wild with pain and anger to fear retribution. "Let me go, I say."

"Whooee!" Blue Doggie shook her like a terrier might shake a kitten. "The Wolves has got theirselves a redheaded wildcat, and I got a nicked ear and claw marks to prove it. She marked me," he said with no little satisfaction. "That makes her mine."

His claim sent up another rumble of protest. The loudest among them, Custer, Snake and Patience.

Catching Blue Doggie in an inattentive moment, she hacked his wrist with the side of her hand and pulled free of him. But her freedom was short-lived.

A second pair of hands seized her shoulders. Beer-laden breath was hot against her skin, a moist kiss missed her mouth as she was jerked away. She spun in the dust. Hands clutched, fingers clawed. Like starving creatures quarreling over a bone, bikers pushed and shoved. Each staking claim. Each challenged by the next.

Patience was fondled and kissed, pinched and bruised, and tugged from the grasp of one by the next. On and on, in a circle, still spinning, still turning until she was disoriented.

Snake, the youngest, pulled her from the crowd, drawing her hard against him. His body molded hers, leaving no room for question of her effect. "You're beautiful, Red. Play your cards right and I'll spend some time with you."

"Play my cards?" Patience wedged an arm between them to gain breathing space. "You have to be—"

"Kidding." Custer finished for her as he snatched her from Snake to repeat an embrace that threatened her ribs. "He's kidding himself. Snake always kids himself." Custer buried his face in her neck, biting the tender flesh, ignoring her flinch of agony. "You're mine, I found you first."

"You found her." Blue Doggie peeled Custer away, the look in his eyes signaled the banter had ended. Custer led with cunning and quick wit. But cunning and wit, quick or slow, were no match for the assurance of the giant's brutish strength. "But we ain't playing finder's keepers." His grin reminded Patience he had a score to settle with her. "No, sir," he mused. "Not today, and not for a while."

There were protests, the most vocal from Snake. A look from Blue Doggie cut them short. He had just enough beer in him to be crazy. No one in his right mind challenged the giant when he was sober, and certainly not when he was drunk and hurting.

One by one the protesters drifted away. Some to their bikes, some to Beauty to plunder and steal. Patience stood passively in Blue Doggie's grasp, wondering what to do next. When he rocked back on his heels enough to stagger, and listed to the side as he righted himself, she realized just how drunk he'd become.

She knew then she would try to escape. Her chances of making it were slim, but she'd rather face an inevitable fate knowing she'd tried, rather than regretting that she hadn't. And if she made it? Being lost in the desert was better than being found by these creatures. Snakes that crawled were preferable to those who walked and called themselves wolves.

Her chance came sooner than she expected. In the flush of victory Blue Doggie's confidence bloomed, making him careless. His hand rested at the nape of her neck, his fingers curled only loosely around the slim column. As he herded her into the darkness he stumbled again, losing his tenuous hold as he fell to one knee.

A second taste of freedom spurred Patience into action. Before he could climb to his feet, she planted her feet, locked her hands in a club of flesh and bone, and swung with all her might. The double-fisted blow that shattered her watch caught the kneeling Blue Doggie under the chin, the fragile bones of his throat absorbing the brunt. With a quiet wheeze he went down face-first like a felled ox.

Patience waited only long enough to strip the chain from his wrist and cast a quick glance to be sure no one had seen. No one had. They were too interested in plundering the Corvette. She turned to run, and had taken three steps when a hand captured her arm in an iron grip.

"Leaving us so soon, Red? When the party in your honor has just begun?" a familiar, melodious voice inquired.

The seventh rider. The one she'd forgotten.

She opened her mouth to scream, then clamped it shut. Scream? For whom? Who was there to help her? Silently, counting surprise as her best weapon, she launched herself at him. Battering with her free hand, scratching, biting, she fought wildly and desperately to escape the imprisoning hold.

"Stop. You're only going to hurt yourself." The command was a quiet entreaty. When she didn't obey, she found herself enveloped in a close embrace. Her captor held her surely but gently against his bare chest. His arms were taut, his body hard and lean. He smelled pleasantly of wood smoke and evergreen. For a moment Patience was lulled by a strange sense of security.

"I have you now," he murmured against her hair as she quieted. "I mean you no harm."

"Liar!" she snarled, rejecting the kindness she heard. She could trust no one, would trust no one. In a resurgence of angry desperation she clawed at his chest and kicked his shins, taking bitter satisfaction in his nearly silent grunt of pain.

"Dammit, wildcat." He caught her in a rib-crushing hold. To take a deep breath would crack bones. "Do you want me to give you back to the others?"

Patience couldn't move, couldn't breath, still she wouldn't surrender. Lifting her head, she glared up at her captor. In moonlight he was the most handsome man she'd ever seen. But even evil could be pretty. "Let me go," she demanded. "You're hurting me."

"Only because you make me hurt you." He bent nearer, eyes that could only be black bored into hers. "Listen to me, believe me. I mean you no harm." He searched her face. "Will you believe me?"

She was off-balance, unsure. "I don't know."

"If I let you go, will you not fight me?"

Patience didn't answer. She looked at Blue Doggie lying in the dirt, at the others squabbling over her possessions. What choice did she have but to give a conditional agreement. "Let me go, I won't fight you."

He didn't release her. "Tell me your name."

"My name?" She looked once more into the handsome face. "What does it matter?"

"Tell me your name," he insisted softly.

"Patience," she snapped. "Patience O'Hara."

"Give me your word you won't fight me, Patience O'Hara."

"What is this? Honor among scum?"

"Honor, yes, between you and me." His gaze was a black laser, leaving no hint of expression undiscovered. "Your word, Patience?"

Her ribs hurt, she couldn't catch a deep breath. In another minute she would be swooning in his arms. Even a stubborn O'Hara knew when she'd lost. Patience shrugged and agreed. "You have my word."

Once again the dark eyes searched her face, seeking the lie. "Good," he said, and released her. "I think you're a woman who keeps her word."

She stumbled away from him, folding her arms around her ribs as she sucked in hungry breaths. He made a concerned move toward her. When she jerked away he stepped back, murmuring, "I'm sorry I hurt you."

"Think nothing of it," she flared. "I knew there were snakes in the desert, until now I didn't realize one was an anaconda."

He didn't smile. She hadn't meant it as a joke. For a long moment he stared at her, his arms hanging at his sides. A trick of the moon painted his face in sadness. "I won't hurt you again."

Patience straightened, her breathing an even rhythm. Her head was back, her chin tilted at an angle. "Do you have a name?"

"I am called Indian."

"What kind of name is that?"

"Mine."

"Indian and what else?"

"Just Indian, no more."

It wasn't his real name, she realized, nor his only name. But, perhaps, it was enough. Certainly it was fitting, even too fitting among this cabal who found anonymity in flamboyant and garish aliases. Custer was no soldier, and Snake no reptile that crawled. Blue Doggie was an animal, but not blue until she'd battered his larynx. This man, who walked the desert as if it were his home, looked the part of his name. With silvery black hair clubbed at his nape and his chiseled features, he could have stepped out of the pages of history.

"All right," she said when her study of him was done. "If that's all there is, it will have to do." Her eyes narrowed, her gaze locked with his. "Give me your word, Just Indian."

He smiled then, a smile that did wonderful things to his striking features even in the garish shadows of the moon. Another time, another place, another person, Patience would have been astounded, but not now. Not here. "Give me your word."

His smile vanished. "I think you will prove a formidable adversary."

"Count on it."

"In that case, you have my word." He offered his hand, when she took it his fingers closed over hers in a strong clasp. A flash of anger crossed his face as he looked down at broken nails and bruises and the drying blood of cuts from splintering glass. But when he spoke again the anger was hidden. "Come, there is more we have to do."

"What might that be?"

"You'll see." When she resisted, jerking away from him, in the same quiet voice he'd used to reason with his companions he said, "You have a choice. Indian, or the rest of them, which will it be?"

She hesitated, weighing choices that weren't choices. When she put her battered hand in his again, it was her life, as well.

"No matter what I say, no matter what I do," he said softly, "remember I will never hurt you."

He led her then to the center of the road, waiting in silence for the revelers to attend him. Slowly, one by one, they turned, curious looks on their faces. When all was quiet he spoke. "Blue Doggie lies there in the gutter, felled by the woman. She would have escaped, I stopped her. By our law that makes her mine to do with as I wish."

"Law! What law?" Patience whirled on him, her protest lost in the roar of complaint from the bikers.

Indian ignored them, he ignored her. Keeping her hand firmly in his, he addressed Custer, the leader, with the stilted formality of a declaration. "She is a woman befitting a warrior. From now and for as long as I wish, she will be my woman."

Patience stared at him, for once she was speechless.

Turning to her, meeting her stunned gaze, into a hostile hush he declared, "Only mine."

Two

"All right, Just Indian, what the devil was that all about?"

As they moved beyond the hearing of capering, beer-guzzling revelers, Patience ripped away from the grasp that guided her over a nearly hidden stretch of rough terrain that separated his bike from the others. A grasp, if she could believe her own muddled perceptions and trust this man called Indian, that was solicitous rather than restraining.

But she didn't trust him. She wouldn't trust anyone until she walked out of the desert, free and unharmed.

Spinning around in front of his bike she faced him, bootheels digging into crumbling soil, fisted hands at her hips. "What was that gibberish about laws?"

"Sticks in your craw, doesn't it? Being called my woman," he asked quietly. Before she could lash out again, he added just as quietly, "It isn't gibberish."

"It isn't gibberish when a pack of lawless morons prattle about laws?" The moon was fully risen. A perfect leviathan ball hanging in the sky, half as bright as the sun, painting the desert in sharp silvered edges and inky pools. In an eerie moonscape he loomed over her, as somber as the land in the night shade of a saguaro. More than half a foot taller and an easy sixty pounds heavier, he was an intimidating figure, but she was too indignant to be intimidated. "Law," she snarled. "From creatures who give themselves animal names and play at being human?"

His hands shot out of shadow, catching her shoulders in a firm hold. "I brought you out here to talk to you, not quarrel, you hotheaded little fool. So shut up and listen before you make matters worse than they are already."

"Worse!" Patience flung back her head, her eyes blazing. "What could be worse? Stranded in the desert. Harassed, attacked. Pawed and fondled. Fought over by mad dogs. Parceled off like a . . ." She cast about her mind, searching for the ultimate insult.

"Like a squaw?" Indian supplied.

"Exactly." Patience's breath hissed through clenched teeth. "Why don't you explain what could possibly be worse than being your squaw."

"Hush! Now!" He shook her, just once, but it was enough to signal how near he'd come to the end of his tolerance. "Put a check on your Irish temper and shut that pretty little mouth or I'll . . ."

"You'll what? Hit me? Ravish me? Or do you plan to threaten me to death?" Her chin lifted a notch, her voice was laced with contempt. "So much for Indian's word."

"Damn you!" His fingers bit into her shoulders, driving closely trimmed nails into her flesh as he moved closer and into the light. His chest heaved in controlled anger, his body was as unrelenting as stone. "I'm not going to hit you, or ravish you. And anything I say will be fact or promise, never threat. Yes, I gave you my word on it before. I've kept my part of the bargain."

"And I didn't?"

"You promised you wouldn't fight me."

"I'm not Cochise." She pulled away from him then and was surprised that he let her go. Crossing her arms at her breasts in a belligerent attitude she glared up at him. "I didn't promise I would fight no more forever."

His look moved over her in grudging admiration for her defiance, her courage against impossible odds. "No, you didn't, did you?" Something akin to a smile ghosted over his lips and vanished. "It was Chief Joseph."

"So?" Patience shrugged her indifference, neither understanding nor caring to understand the cryptic remark.

"You were quoting Chief Joseph of the Nez Perce. The correct phrase is 'From where the sun now stands, I will fight no more forever.'"

"That's just lovely." Her drawl was saccharine. "I doubt there were six bikers and one Indian threatening him with every conceivable indignity."

"No," Indian answered thoughtfully, "there were no bikers."

"Lucky man."

"An intelligent man, who knew when to fight and when to stop."

Her head moved abruptly side to side, rejecting the subtle overture. "I'll stop fighting when one of us stops breathing."

He sighed heavily, threads of frustrated tension frayed as he struggled against the urge to break his word and throttle her. If there was ever even a ghost of a smile it was forgotten and buried. His face was somber, a startlingly tantalizing mask of stark lines and planes. "The only good Indian is a dead Indian? Is that it?"

Patience should have heeded the savage undertone in his words, but she was too lost in her own hostility to hear. "Considering that you're the only Indian I know, yes, that's precisely it."

He moved, then, like a striking snake. Quicker than the eye could focus, or the mind comprehend, he swept her into his arms. One hand locked around her waist, the other cradled her head in uncompromising control. Her head was yanked back, her face lifted to his. If the moon had been a strobe, the disgust he felt couldn't have been clearer. "Considering your reckless mouth and your ungoverned temper, I'm surprised you survived this life long enough to lose yourself in the desert. Since you have, and since it's my misfortune to be stuck with you, we have to do what we must and make the best we can of a bad situation."

"Your misfortune?" She struggled against his embrace, but he was far too strong for her. "Yours!"

"Yes, mine. There are things you don't understand. Things you can never know." The words rumbled deep in his throat, a whispered growl rather than spoken. His hand tensed in her hair as she fought to turn away from a quiet anger more frightening than savage rage.

Suddenly he was silent, as motionless as the saguaro. As inscrutable. His posture did not change, nor his manner, his relentless black gaze never strayed from her face. Yet he seemed to be waiting. Waiting and wary, listening to sounds only he could hear. He held her, his body coiled and ready, yet his thoughts seemed drawn to some distant place.

His head lifted, barely a fraction. So little even Patience couldn't have seen it if she hadn't been staring at him from less than a foot away. Slowly, as if the smallest shifting of an eye could be detected by some secret cabal, he lifted his covert gaze to the terrain at her back. For a second that could have been forever, he studied the desert grasses, the mesquite, the creosote, the paloverde, and no one but she would have witnessed.

A strange word, harsh and nearly silent, tore from his lips. A word she didn't understand, in a language she'd never heard. Yet she recognized regret in it, and anger unlike before.

"Indian?" She was bewildered and confused, and the unbearable fear that never truly left her for all her bravado, added another weight. "What is it?"

"Be quiet, woman." His voice was unnaturally harsh and loud, unlike the low melodious tone he'd spoken in before, even in anger. "I tire of your prattle."

He bent nearer, so near she couldn't see him clearly, yet his breathy undertone meant for her ears alone barely reached her. "I won't ask your forgiveness for stooping to clichés, but it isn't just your cookie that crumbled tonight, and not just you who wishes you were anywhere but here. Believe me when I say I'm not going to like this any better than you will."

She realized too late what he intended. Too late to do more than cry out. "No-oo!"

He ignored her protest, silencing it with his kiss. His mouth closed over hers, quickly, expertly, catching her lips parted in a startled gasp. He held her closer, clasping her body forcefully to his. In startling contrast his lips moved softly over hers, seducing her into stunned submission. As he swept her with him to a dark place of utter helplessness, her muted cries died in her throat. Her wounded hands ceased their fruitless resistance to lie woodenly against his chest, as wooden as she, as she steeled herself to endure his intimate conquest.

She was dangerously lifeless in his arms, a mannequin without a spark of resistance or even outrage. Indian pulled away. Only a hairbreadth separated their lips, and only his cool stare filled her vision. "What's the matter? Are you all talk? Is that it, you only talk a good fight? Where is that Irish temper now?" He smiled crookedly down at her, a triumphant look in his eyes, yet edged by something she didn't understand. "Could it be you wanted my kiss after all?"

"You're mad!" Patience stared up at him. "Stark, raving mad."

"Am I?" He pushed her hair aside to brush his lips down the curve of her throat. "I don't think so."

"Indian, don't do this." She strained away from him, trying to evade him, trying to reason with him. "Please."

"Please?" He laughed, a low sound that would have seemed oddly forced if she'd been conscious of anything beyond her struggle. "I like that." He moved his hand from her hair to stroke her cheek. "You know you want me. Admit it, admit that you want me."

"Want!" In abject fury, Patience came alive. Tearing one arm free from the iron circle of his embrace she delivered a vicious, openhanded slap to his temple. Burrowing her hand in his hair, her fingers closed over the beaded leather thong that held it back, with all her strength she pulled, wishing she could scalp him. Instead the tie broke free and she clutched it in her fist as she pummeled him wherever she could. "Damn you." She panted in her struggle against his hold. "I'll show you what I want."

He dodged a blow that would have blacked an eye or chipped a tooth and he laughed the same strained laugh once more. "That's it. Fight," he muttered. "For your sake and mine, fight every step of the way."

Reining in the little freedom he'd deliberately allowed her, he took her mouth then. His kiss was deep and hard, expertly thorough, and completely without passion.

Her mind was reeling. Her hands hurt and her head. His long, lean frame thrust against her, his hands were in her hair, on her body. The taste of him was on her lips, the scent of him in her lungs. He was everywhere. He was everything.

Danger.

Survival.

Life.

There was no escaping him.

In bitter denial of the truth she opened her mouth, clamped her teeth on his lip and bit him, wreaking what havoc she could, drawing blood at last. His smothered grunt of pain was a symphony to her ears, the taste of his blood was one small victory. Then, incredibly, he laughed as he pulled away.

"Fight, wildcat. Fight as hard and as well as you can." Bending, he kissed the side of her neck, leaving a trail of blood on the collar of her shirt. "The harder you resist, the more pleasure for both of us when I tame you."

"Never," Patience declared, thrashing and straining, trying to distance herself from him. She was so intent on pushing him away she almost fell when he released her. Only his hand at her elbow kept her from falling in the dust.

"Easy," he muttered as he helped her keep her footing. "The ground is unstable here."

Patience whirled on him, peeling his hand from her arm as if it were scabrous. "Let me go. Don't touch me."

Because they were alone again he let her go. As he watched her walk away a little distance into the desert, he listened to a stealthy retreat. Snake's step was familiar, and Custer's slight limp unmistakable.

Taking little pride in his performance, he waited until the sounds faded completely before he went to her. "O'Hara." He stood at her back, waiting for some sign, some reaction to his brutal burlesque of Jekyll and Hyde. "O'Hara, look at me."

She didn't turn. Her back seemed straighter, more rigid.

"This wasn't what you think." Indian touched her shoulder, meaning to turn her into his arms to justify, to comfort. "Let me explain."

She shrugged him off, swayed with the effort, then straightened again, assuming the ramrod posture. Drawing a shuddering breath, with the back of a shaking hand she wiped her mouth viciously. Her hand dropped stiffly to her side as an unnatural stillness enveloped her.

Indian knew she was in pain, the silent, gut-wrenching, tearless pain of humiliating helplessness. Pain he caused her.

Cursing himself and the world, he turned her into his arms. When she fought him, he let her, stoically suffering the claw of broken and unbroken nails, the pummel of poor, sore hands. He knew it wouldn't be for long. She'd fought him hard and well, as he'd wanted, but she was near the end of her strength. He waited for this last spurt of rebellion to end, speaking softly to her in a nearly wordless murmur as he waited.

When the inertia of mind-destroying fatigue overwhelmed her, when she was still again and quiet, he gathered her nearer. That there was not even token resistance proved how close she'd come to total collapse, how complete the despair that sapped the last of her vitality. Repulsed by circumstances that brought her to this, and for his necessary role in it, Indian tucked her head into his shoulder, stroking her hair, offering what respite he could.

He suspected this was a rare occurrence in any circumstance. An uncommon moment when this spirited woman faltered, in need of restoring peace to her ravaged mind and body.

She'd weathered more than he'd thought possible. When he'd caught his first glimpse of her pinioned in the glare of unmerciful headlights, she was small and fragile, her delicate heart-shaped face almost overwhelmed by a lioness's mane of hair like flame. He wouldn't have given a penny for her chances of outlasting the savagery he knew was coming. Yet he couldn't intervene, not then. The odds in her favor escalated when she'd proven immune to the head games his fellow riders were so adept at playing.

The derringer was a surprise. He didn't expect it, but from the moment she'd palmed it like a pro, he knew this woman was a breed apart.

The pièce de résistance was Blue Doggie. No one in his right mind would have believed that before Indian could reach her, this scrap of a woman, brutalized physically and mentally, could fell a man more than twice her size in one two-fisted uppercut.

She'd endured beyond human endurance and hadn't broken, until Indian took it upon himself to see to her welfare. Until Indian, in his own inimitable style, brought her to the brink. To this silent suffering.

"I'm sorry," he muttered into her hair, and the hard shuddering that shook her finally stopped.

With the flat of her palm, Patience pushed away from him, her face was bleak. "No, I'm sorry, for being weak. It won't happen again."

"This isn't weakness, it's being human and civilized. But if it were a matter of strength, I've seen men who considered themselves far stronger than you could ever be break under less."

"You misunderstand me, Indian." She turned a diamond-hard gaze at him. "I make no apologies for this. I've seen enough and done enough in my life to know that there are situations beyond our control, and times when the spirit and body fail us. My weakness was believing in you even a little. I won't make that mistake again.

"I'm not a complete fool." Her arms hung tensely at her sides, her fingers flexed, a scrap of rawhide tumbled to the ground before they curled again into tight fists. A mouth made for laughter thinned to a grim line. "As mercurial as you are, I do know what you've spared me."

"Do you?" he interjected quietly. "Do you, indeed?"

"Yes." She spat the word at him. "I know."

"Such confidence," Indian mocked. "Such blind certainty." He took a step closer. With a finger beneath her chin he lifted her face to meet her gaze again. "They were out there, Snake and Custer, the worst of the lot, watching, slavering over a tempting morsel."

Patience swung around to look to the road where six bikers lounged on Beauty's hood, or hunkered around her on the ground. Bottles flashed in the light, drunken laughter spilled over the desert. Stumbling across her misfortune offered the perfect excuse for a binge.

"There are six by the car," she said. "No one was here. No one was watching."

"They were here."

"How do you know? How could you?"

"I knew."

"Ah! You're psychic? Telepathic, perhaps? Superhuman?" The latter was drawled contempt.

"Neither." He refused to rise to her baiting. "I'm a simple man, with simple skills."

Regarding him, she remembered how he held himself aloof from the others. How no one challenged his claim. He rode with them, lived by their laws, but he was not one of them. She was sure of it. Even in rage and terror she'd perceived him as separate. Different.

Six bikers and an Indian.

"Who are you?" she whispered. "What are you?"

"A simple man called Indian. No more. No less."

"No," she denied emphatically. "Not simple. Never simple."

"All right." He nodded. "If you wish, not simple."

She recalled when she thought him as inscrutable as the saguaro, now she decided the saguaro lost, hands down. "Tell me how you knew these men were watching."

Indian shrugged a shoulder, bare beyond the edge of his vest. "I'm a tracker. A good one. My grandfather taught me to see things others don't see, to hear things they don't hear, to know things they will never know.

"Custer and Snake came, not as secretly as they thought, seeking an excuse to take you from me. They will if we don't play this right." He stroked her hair. Mesmerized, he watched it glide through his fingers, glistening like dark fire in the moonlight.

Red hair was prized by the bikers. Because of it she was a trophy coveted by too many men. Regretfully his fingers tangled in silk, holding her, keeping her, ignoring her hand at his wrist. "I can't fight them all."

Patience ceased her silent rebuff of his caress. With her hand at his wrist and the steady throb of his pulse beneath her fingertips, she stared up at him. "Take me from you? They would do that?"

"Yes."

"But your laws, your precious biker laws, what happens to them?"

"They apply, but only if we are believed."

"You mean they have to believe that I'm truly your woman." She caught a ragged breath, her tongue moved nervously over dry lips. "They have to believe that you're my lover. Rapist, if you must."

"Yes."

Patience jerked her hand from his wrist as if contact burned her. In horror she backed away, ignoring the crumbling soil of a tiny wash. Whirling around, she stepped over the groove carved by some long ago rain. Her boots scattered coarse sand as she walked. Mesquite and creosote brushed at her jeans. Thorned ocotillo tugged at the sleeve of her shirt as if it wanted to hold her back. She ignored them.

But she couldn't ignore the footsteps that echoed her own. She knew she heard them because Indian wanted her to hear. In a moment of distraction she stumped her toe on the exposed roots of a creosote bush. His hands circling her waist kept her from falling.

She jerked away, staggered on a few steps, and stopped, searching beyond her. There was nothing. Neither light nor living thing. Not to the east, nor the west. The south or the north.

"That's right." Indian stood a pace behind. "There's nothing out there. Nothing for miles. You can't walk out."

Patience spun around, and in the moonlight her hair was a veil of gossamer. "I don't believe you."

She wasn't speaking of the obvious desolation of the desert. Neither pretended she did.

"I can't give you proof." He stood stolidly in front of her, making no effort to touch her. "Proof could only come from Custer, or Snake, or one of the others. Then it would be too late."

"You could let me go. Just turn around and go back to your bike and leave me to take my chances in the desert."

"I can't."

"All you have to do is walk away."

"It would be certain suicide. You wouldn't last a day."

"For that day I would be free and my own person, not a piece of property." She'd stood stiffly in front of him, now she made a gesture of entreaty, or anger, or both. She didn't know herself. "Have you ever been a prisoner, Indian? Made to be a lesser person?"

"I've always been free," he said. "Different degrees of freedom, at different times, but free, nevertheless."

"That's what I'm asking for now, a different degree of freedom. The right to choose where I live and die, and how."

"I can't. You wouldn't have a chance, and you wouldn't have a choice. You would be hunted down."

"Then I would have tried, that counts for something."

"You wouldn't think so if Snake got to you first."

She gestured toward the road, so far away Beauty looked like a toy and the bikes like pawns of a board game. Even the bikers seemed innocuous from this perspective. Comic, toy soldiers scattered by a petulant child, waiting to be put away at the end of a hard day of play.

Appearances were misleading, the handsome man standing in front of her was proof of that. "Snake, Custer, Blue Doggie, the one called Hogan. The others." Her arm fell heavily to her side. She returned her gaze to him. "You. Why would it matter?"

He showed no reaction to her scorn. "Then consider this. When all choices are evil, isn't it wise to choose the lesser?"

"Something else your grandfather taught you?" She sneered.

"No." His grandfather would have fought to the death. It was his way. The Apache way. Indian didn't want that choice for her. He wouldn't want it for any innocent, but especially not for Patience O'Hara.

"Then you thought up this tidbit of wisdom all by yourself?" Patience taunted recklessly. "In your tiny, screwed-up little mind?"

A muscle flickered in his jaw, his teeth clenched as he silenced a reply. "We will discuss the size and condition of my mind another time," he said instead. "And, yes, the tidbit was mine."

"Let me guess. The lesser of the multitude of evils I seem to have attracted would be..." She pointed a finger at his chest, as if it were a gun. "Of course! You."

"For a woman who has more guts than brains, yes."

"My choice is a man who gives his word, most solemnly, then waffles and bends his promise to suit his needs?"

"Enough!" The command underscored an imperious gesture. "It's no wonder you have no husband! You would talk a man to death."

"You don't know that I'm not married," Patience lashed back at him. "You know nothing about me."

"You wear no ring."

"Neither do you and for all I know, or care, you could have a dozen wives."

"I have no wife. When I do, there will be only one."

"Only one, huh? And you would wear her ring?"

Indian didn't hesitate. "If she wished, yes."

"Have you, in your great wisdom, considered that perhaps my husband is a modern man? A man not bound by ancient symbolism, who doesn't wish it?"

"Never." He wondered if she knew how mysteriously beautiful she was in the half-light. How magnificently courageous. "The man who becomes your husband will put his ring on you," he said thoughtfully, "to show the world that such a woman is his."

The response startled her, catching her with no caustic reply. "But you said—"

"I know what I said." He cut her short, exasperated with himself. He wasn't a man who revealed his thoughts, a natural trait and habit that had saved his life many times. He would need to watch carefully with this woman. She had the skill to draw from him more than he wished. More than was wise.

"Come." Catching her by the shoulder, he pulled her to his side. "We've wasted too much time. By now the last of the beer from the saddlebags will be consumed. I should see that they move along before their mood turns ugly."

When he meant to return to the road with her in tow, she resisted, digging her heels into the sand. "No!"

He spun around, his face a dark visage. "Don't try me more. You've pushed your luck as far as it can go."

"So?" She glared at him when he would not release her arm. "What do I have to lose? What have I ever had to lose?"

"A fight, then? To the bitter end?"

"It's what you wanted, isn't it?"

"At given and appropriate times."

"On cue?" She laughed, a sound completely lacking humor. "In your dreams, chief."

He raised a sardonic brow. "I've been promoted? Good. Perhaps you'll be happier with a chief than a lowly Indian." He pulled her along the trail with him, ignoring her opposition.

"Wait." She clutched at his vest, her fingers brushing the heated flesh beneath. "I haven't made my choice."

He stopped, turning to catch her in his arms as she bumped into him. His face was fierce, his eyes narrowed. "I made the choice for you."

She gripped the supple leather as if she would tear it. Through gritted teeth, she spat, "You have no right."

"I have every right, and you have none."

When she would have lashed back at him, he silenced her with a look so savage her protest died in her throat.

"What? No grievance?" he taunted. "Has the wildcat finally sheathed her useless claws?"

She looked up at him, seeing a man she hadn't seen before. "Who are you? What are you?" she asked, bemused. "How many men are you?"

Though he spoke sternly, the anger in him subsided. An anger addressing his weakness as much as her stubborn strength. "I'm one man. Who I am isn't important. What I am, what I became the moment you chose to travel this path, is your only hope. With or without your cooperation I'm going to find a way to get you out of this. Unharmed and unmolested by anyone."

"Does that little declaration include you?" The caustic gibe slipped from her tongue before she could recall it.

"Yes, especially me." His expression was impassive. "There is one choice you have. We're going to your car. If you have luggage—" a shocked and angry look confirmed his instinctive guess that she did "—you will select the clothing and necessities you might need at our camp. You can cooperate and come willingly, or I'll carry you."

"Like so much garbage."

"Like a willful squaw."

Patience knew the leeway he'd allowed her had ended. Painfully she admitted "allowed" was the proper description. Given his half-foot advantage in height, and the extra sixty pounds on his ruggedly muscular physique, allowed was *exactly* the right word. Now he was allowing her to make a choice. To do what she must with grace and dignity, or to be done with gracelessly as he wished.

She had few weapons, and dignity could be one of the few. She'd seen it happen. When needed, Mavis, her usually happily undignified mother, could dig deeply for an icy dignity that intimidated the surly as well as the arrogant.

Dignity, a weapon to preserve and protect. Uncommon and effective, perhaps even against Indian. She released her hold on his vest and stepped past his reach. "I'll walk."

He wasn't a man to exult in his mastery, one lone, spare move of his head acknowledged victory. "I thought you might."

The path he chose to return wandered through shrub and grasses. He didn't look back or offer an assisting hand. He knew she would follow, that the oblique surrender pledged she would. He knew, as well, she would accept no helping hand.

"Indian."

He didn't slow or turn. "Yes?"

"I don't trust you."

His step didn't alter.

"Indian."

He didn't answer.

"I never will." Her defiance evoked no response. She expected none, suspecting taciturnity, rather than heated and lengthy discourse, was his true nature. She watched him, his honed body, his sure and easy step. He moved through the desert as if he were of it, an integral part, and all else was intrusion. And she wondered what manner of man held her life in his hands. Engrossed in thought, she put a foot wrong. The step jolted, but she righted herself with only little effort.

Indian slowed imperceptibly until he heard her steady step again. He smiled, visualizing her frown in her concerted effort to keep him from knowing her passage was not without difficulty.

Their trek continued, Indian leading, Patience following, saguaro lining their path like spine-encrusted sentinels. The scent of beer, peculiar smokes, and drunken mutterings reached out to them before the refracted light of headlights still burning.

"I won't stop fighting, Indian," she declared in a hushed tone. "Not ever."

Indian stopped at the shoulder of the road, keeping his back to her. His shoulders lifted in a long, drawn breath, a breath exhaled in a resigned sigh. "I know."

As he stepped into the light, a haggard Blue Doggie looked up at him and beyond. Virulent hate burned in rheumy eyes.

Indian reached back, pulling her to him. "Go to the car. Choose what you will need. Sturdy serviceable clothing as you're wearing now, and no more than a couple of changes. A hat if you have one, but don't bother with a bag, bundle everything in a shirt. When you've finished, tie your hair back and wait until I come for you."

Patience nodded. When she moved toward Beauty, without looking away from Blue Doggie, Indian stopped her with a hand tangling in her hair, detaining her.

"Stay there, until I come," he repeated.

"I will."

"Promise." There was a new, watchful tension in his voice, arcing through his body.

"I promise."

"Thank you."

Patience was surprised by the courtesy but wasted no time thinking on it. Beauty had sustained more damage, clothing and toiletries were scattered inside the car. Even that garnered little of Patience's attention.

The rifle. She wanted the rifle. Where was it?

To the sound of revving engines, she picked her way gingerly through splintered glass. Her luggage lay in the back as it had. It had been opened and riffled through, the clothing tossed in all directions, but the bag had been moved little. Hoping against hope that the rifle remained undiscovered, she threw the bag aside, scattering clothing and glass more.

"Thank God!" Miraculously the case was still strapped in the special niche created for it by brother Kieran.

The sound of motorcycle engines was fading. She was alone with Indian. This was her one chance to escape. Hurriedly she attacked buckles and straps. Too hurriedly. Haste made her injured hands clumsy. She'd barely managed to yank the case from its place and slide the rifle free when she heard his footsteps circling the car.

There was no time to retrieve bullets and load. When he stopped at the broken window at her side, she faced him, the empty rifle pointed squarely at his chest. "Back off, Indian."

"Ah." He acted as if it were common to face a rifle. "The rest of the arsenal?"

"Don't be cute. Cute doesn't suit you. Do as I say, back off."

Crossing his arms over his chest, he looked down at her. He was perfectly calm and at ease. "You're going to take my bike and ride out of the desert, and you'll shoot me if I stand in your way."

Patience shifted the rifle against her shoulder. "Precisely."

"I don't think so," he murmured.

"Are you fool enough to challenge a rifle?"

"Yes." He reached inside, closed his fingers over the barrel, taking the rifle from her. "When it isn't loaded."

She didn't resist, there was no need. Burying her head in her hands, she faced failure and accepted it. Wearily she dropped her hands to her lap. "How did you know?"

"The derringer. If the rifle had been loaded, you wouldn't have wasted time with it before." He laid the weapon aside and extended his hand. "It's time to go."

The rifle was her last stand. The adrenaline that bolstered this last hurrah, vanished. She was hardly aware of leaving the car; like a puppet she walked mindlessly through gathering the clothing he felt suitable. All of it no more than vague perception.

When she struggled with her hair with hands grown unbearably stiff, it was Indian who bound it. As he did his own with a bit of fringe ripped from his vest.

She was astride his bike behind him when she realized she would likely never see Beauty again. "What will happen to her?"

"Her?" He glanced over his shoulder. "The Corvette?"

"She was a gift from my family. In a strange way, she had a personality. She was my friend." Maybe it was crazy to consider a car a friend, but Patience didn't care. She asked again. "What will become of her?"

"She'll be stripped. Anything of value will be sold, what's left will be pushed into a canyon and covered with dirt."

"Poor Beauty."

"There's no hope for the car. There is for you. You don't have to trust me or like me, but we must do this together. You've that choice to make. We have a couple of hours of hard riding tonight. Think on it."

The engine revved; Indian turned his bike into the desert. To a place Patience knew she might never leave.

Three

Absorbed in her own fortune and in keeping her seat as the Electra Glide sailed, then flew over inhospitable terrain never meant to be traversed, Patience spared no energy on speculating what the camp would be. As Indian climbed one last incline, cut the engine and rolled to a silent halt, she realized no amount of thought or speculation would have prepared her for what lay before them.

Shifting in her seat she stepped down to stand by the bike to have a better view of the camp. It was a well-chosen site, a walled fortress carved into the mesa by wind and water and ancient cataclysm. On the boulder-strewn floor lighted by a single campfire, there were people. Men. Women. Some sitting by the fire, others moving frenetically on the fringes.

The orgy of drinking begun on the roadside continued, as if never interrupted, in this secluded place.

"We'll wait here, until it's calmer," Indian said, his tone conveying no judgment of any kind. "In a while they'll drink themselves to sleep or into a stupor. It will be easier on you that way."

Easier? Patience wondered what about this could ever be easy as she studied the enclave. There were no cabins or tents. Nothing in the littered clearing suggested any sense of permanence. Through dry, weary eyes she looked down on a primitive and barbarous scene in a primitive and barbarous land.

"This is it?" she asked as she faced him. "This is what you call home?"

"We have no home, nor any of its trappings. Out of necessity we travel light, and often on a moment's notice."

"Leaving your litter behind." This observation followed the shattering of a bottle tossed against a sandstone dome. "A delightful welcome when you pass this way again in your wanderings."

"We never camp in the same place twice, but I try to see that we leave as little evidence of our passage as possible."

"Oh, really?" Patience drawled. "Who cleans the litter?"

"The women do a passable job." The crash of another bottle punctuated his response, the sound wafting to them on a rising current of cooler air.

Patience waited for the resonant clatter to fade. "Broken glass and all?"

"Yes."

"Figures."

Indian ignore her derision. "You'll be one of them. The difference will be that you belong to me. You will ride when I say. Eat when I say. Sleep when I say, and where. Whatever I ask, you will do."

"Ask?" Her tone was cynical.

"It would be easier if asking were enough."

"Easier for whom?"

"The both of us."

"Somehow," she observed wryly, "the rationale for that escapes me."

Indian swung off the bike, secured it and wheeled toward her. He was a darker shape, sketched against a dark sky. "I have explained." With a motion he indicated the canyon below. "And you've seen."

Patience nodded, not bothering to look down again. Sensing even from this distance, the inherent depravity. "I've seen. They're like children. Vicious children, who make no secret of what they are and what they want." She lifted her gaze to his. A gaze she could only feel. "You aren't the same. There are secrets in your eyes." She shook her head, despair rampant in her. "What do you want, Indian?"

"To keep you from their tender mercies." The answer came quickly, without need for thought. "And, one day, to take you home."

"Tender mercy." Patience laughed shortly. With the bravado of Scarlett facing Armageddon she drawled, "My, how you do go on."

"You won't think this is a teasing matter when you see what men like Snake, and Custer, and Blue Doggie do to their women. Especially Snake."

"Maybe I'll take your word for what I think it's worth," she lingered on the last, giving it a disparaging emphasis. "And maybe I'll take my chances with one of the others. Even Snake."

He took a step closer, looming over her, shutting out the waning light of the moon. "You won't."

Her defiance blazed up at him. "Who will stop me?"

"You'll stop yourself." He walked away, to the edge of the mesa. "There is a young woman, little more than a child, really. An exquisite child with hair like corn silk falling to her waist. Her eyes are that rare shining violet of a desert sunrise after rain. Her skin is smooth and translucent, and, oddly, never burns nor freckles. She's stunningly beautiful." His fisted hands flexed and curled again into fists. "She *was* beautiful, until she displeased the Snake."

"What did he do to her?" Patience stared at his back, reading horror in his posture. What, indeed, had Snake done to fill Indian with utter revulsion?

"Snake fancies himself an artist. His brush is his knife, his paint, ashes. His favorite canvas is a woman's face." He turned his back on the canyon, walking to the bike and Patience. "Tomorrow seek her out, see for yourself what Snake has done. Look at the other women. Learn who belongs to whom, and how they're treated."

His face was grim, his mouth drawn into a rigid line. "If you find one you prefer, I'll give you to him."

Another time Patience would have lashed out at him at the possessive arrogance, would have doubted what he said. But not now, when his every move and word were filled with bleak sickness. Now she could only stare up at him, imagining a beautiful girl, a knife, and ashes. Like tears, a sickness of her own welled in her eyes.

Indian felt a twinge of guilt for the heartache he saw. He'd spared her some of the story, but he wondered if it were kindness. Perhaps it would have been kinder to prepare her, but could he say or do anything that would prepare for Callie, for all that could be done to an artless child in a short, sordid existence?

The women were camp followers. Bikers' groupies. None were like Patience. None was captive against her will. In her special unworldliness, not even Callie. None had been taken, innocent and unsuspecting. Not since he'd ridden the deserts and the mountains with the Wolves.

He didn't dwell on Callie. Callie was another story, for another day. A day he'd promised himself long ago that would come. If there were any semblance of life in him when this was done, it would come.

Patience was his first concern. For now, for always. What he'd done to her was unforgivable. He'd pushed her to the end of mental and physical endurance, then pushed for more. Even in his shadow she was haggard and drawn, barely clinging to the last of her energy. Body and mind feeding on a spirit that burned like a consuming fever, at a cost that was all too easy to see. The bones of her face were more prominent, her eyes huge and seething with fear and hate. The taut, supple body beneath the flow of a clinging chambray shirt and tight jeans seemed to be shrinking, as if none-too-ample pounds melted from her in a matter of hours.

"I'm sorry." He touched her cheek, drawing a finger down the smooth curve of it. When she turned her face away, his hand followed, curling at her chin, bringing her gaze back to his. "Dear God, I'm sorry."

Again, when once she would have lashed out at him, she was silent, unwillingly beginning to believe a little what she saw and heard in him.

A night wind stirred, only a small, secret gust. Too little to feel or notice, but enough to tease a tendril escaped from the band he'd tied around her hair. Enough that the clean, fragrant perfume of it drifted to him.

He didn't recognize the scent, couldn't separate the blend of a woodsy bouquet. It was simply natural, unpretentious, honest. All things that had been missing in his life for so long.

Catching the fluttering strand, he wound it around the tip of a finger, reveling in the silken resilience, the soft strength. A woman could bind a man to her with hair like hers. Weaving a gossamer prison from which he would never wish to escape.

Stunned by the direction of his thoughts, hastily he tucked the strand behind her ear. With a mind of its own, his hand lingered to stroke her hair as he filled himself again with the scent of it.

"O'Hara." He said her name hoarsely. For no reason but that it was like her fragrance, like her.

Reluctantly he pulled away. Resignation lay heavy on him as he looked to the sky and the desert, gauging the hour. Moon shadows were long around them now, for soon it would be setting. There was little left of the night, little time for her to rest before the ordeal of her first day in camp would begin.

He repressed a flinch as an enraged roar rose behind him. The sharp report of an open palm against bare flesh preceded a shrill curse. The coarse and vicious culmination of a drunken quarrel echoed through the canyon. Indian caught back a sigh. He was taking her into this. Into a culture few could imagine. A life-style she shouldn't have to suffer.

Temptation was strong in him. The need to ride out of the desert with her, turning his back on commitment and obligation, nearly overpowered him. It would be so easy, if he were truly Indian. Truly the man she thought him.

But there was more to this than Patience O'Hara and a man called Indian. More lives at risk than hers. More than his.

He was so close to a truth that had eluded him for months. One he couldn't turn away from. Not even for her.

"Indian?"

He heard the edge in her voice and forced his thoughts aside. "Yes?"

"You were so quiet. What were you thinking?"

"Only that soon it will be time we went into camp."

She shook her head, gazing intently into the darkness that shrouded his face. "It was more than that." She looked past him to the camp. "You hate this, don't you? You hate my being here as much as I. You hate it for my sake, but for your own purposes, as well."

"I have no purposes."

"I think you do. And now you're torn between that purpose and keeping me safe."

Indian stood impassive. By neither gesture nor word did he reveal how near she'd come to the truth. Patience O'Hara was truly a woman to guard against. An intuitive woman, who saw and understood more than he would wish. He laughed, shrugging aside her suggestion as if it were nonsense. "Careful, if you endow me with such nobility, next must come trust."

"Maybe." She brushed a hand over her eyes, as if by brushing bangs from her eyes she could brush cobwebs from her mind. "Maybe I do trust you. A little, at least."

"At least." It was a beginning. He had his first concrete hope that he could make the best of this for both of them. She was frightened. She hadn't stopped being frightened. He'd seen it through her anger, when she fought with him, or goaded him.

Patience was no stranger to fear—the gut-wrenching, heart-stopping fear that could paralyze and decimate. She'd learned to deal with it and function with it. He'd guessed it from the first, when she'd faced impossible odds with stoic courage. Now he was certain.

Where? he wondered. How and why? What circumstance had given her the stamina to deal with this? She'd wondered about him, and questioned. He wondered now about her. "Who are you, Patience O'Hara?" he asked, bemused. "What manner of woman are you?"

"A cowardly simple-minded one," she answered. "If I weren't, I wouldn't be here."

"Foolhardy, perhaps, but not simple-minded." He smiled to himself, remembering a derringer and most of all a rifle that was not loaded. The bluff had taken more than courage. "Certainly not cowardly. I would say daring, even reckless."

"Daring? Reckless? My family wouldn't agree. I'm plain Patience, prudent Patience. A dullard with my books and quiet walks. Poor, placid Patience, jinxed by a placid name."

"I think not." She was anything but placid, anything but dull. "I should think your family would appreciate what you are, and love you for it."

"Oh, they appreciate me, and they love me. There's no question of it. They appreciate and love me to the point of suffocation. That's why I'm here." Patience stopped abruptly. A hand tugged at the spill of her hair tied securely by Indian. "If they could see me now, they'd think I was insane.

"*I* think I must be insane! Sitting astride a motorcycle, in the dark, in the middle of a desert, heaven knows where. My beautiful, impractical car stripped and dumped in a canyon. Ravening monsters at my feet." She looked up at Indian. "And you. And what am I doing? Babbling on as if it were teatime with an old friend.

"My Lord! I'm losing my marbles." With her fingers at her temples, she massaged muscles that ached from teeth clenched too

long and too hard. "Why else would I forget that for all your sof
words and your sweet promises, you're still the enemy?"

Indian grasped her wrists in his, holding them, forcing her
look at him. "I'm not the enemy."

She tried to pull away. When he wouldn't release her, she stoppe
struggling. "No?" She looked pointedly at her wrists manacled b
his fingers, then at him. "Then what do you call this? What do yo
call holding me against my will? Taking me where I don't want
go? You keep saying you'll take me home. If that's true, if you re
ally want me to believe you and trust you, take me now."

Releasing her, he backed away. "I can't."

"Can't or won't?"

Indian considered lying. He was sorely tempted. But if she wa
going to trust him, she needed the truth. "Both."

"That makes no sense." She gestured toward the canyon. "Loo
at them. Who's to stop us from riding out now? Right this min
ute. Not one would be sober enough to follow. We could go, In
dian." There was a wistful note in her voice, a note of entreaty
"No one would be the wiser before morning."

"I can't." Indian raked a hand through his bound hair, nearl
tearing it free from the leather that held it. Where would he tak
her? Who was out there in the sparse settlements that dotted th
fringe of the desert? Who could be trusted to take care of her? I
the Wolves came looking, bent on taking back their booty, wh
could keep her from them? Who would? Who was innocent an
uninvolved? And who among the innocent did he dare put at risk

There was only one, but he was far from the desert. And India
had too much to lose to go the distance. "I'm sorry," he mut
tered. "Sorry I can't take you, and sorry I can't explain. There ar
things you can't know. But if you could just trust me."

"Trust you! You ask too much."

"I know, yet you told me you did before. Only a little, but it wa
a start."

"Yeah, well I also told you I was losing my marbles. Trustin
you to any degree is proof."

Indian sighed, a low, weary sound, discovering he was tired a
well. Before the gang stumbled across Patience, he'd ridden for ha
a day. A hard, taxing ride, adding one more name, one more cor
tact to a growing list. Only one, when there were so many.

Yes, he was weary. Weary of living on the edge, of running an
hiding. And too weary for more of this. "We've been over this tim
and again. We take one step forward and two back. Then two fo

ward and three back." He touched her hair only briefly, but in that brief moment she didn't move away. "How many more times will t take? When will you trust me unconditionally?"

He asked too much, too soon. More than she could give to a stranger, even one who had taken her from crueler hands. Perhaps more than she could ever give him.

Silence grew intense, a tarnished web spun by evasion and unanswered questions. A howl rose out of the distance, the melancholy cry of a rancher's dog. A descendant of the wolf that once hunted this land, roaming where it would in tightly knit packs, until t was hunted into nearly total extinction. A creature of civilization, returned by the night to the wild, mourning the passing of his kind. A lost and lonely creature. As lost and lonely as she.

Tears gathered in her eyes, she blinked them back. She never cried. She wouldn't now. But nothing stopped the ache in her heart. Nothing eased a growing, desperate need to believe in this man she knew only as Indian.

"How can I trust you?" Her whispered cry was as mournful as the solitary dog.

"Follow your instincts. Listen to what they tell you."

"No!" She inched back a step, stopping when the fender of the bike brushed her hip. "I don't even know your name."

"You will," he promised, "when the time comes. That and more."

Patience neither rejected nor accepted his conjecture. Her heart and mind were in conflict. One saying, *Yes, believe him.* The other insisting, *Never.*

"Life isn't always clear-cut choices. Everything can't be black or white with no shades of gray. And things aren't always what they seem." He lifted his hands as if he would take her shoulders. To shake the obstinate opposition from her? To make her believe what he wouldn't if he were she?

God! What he was asking of her. What he asked her to do. His hands shook. His fingers flexed into impotent fists at all he couldn't say. With a ragged sigh, he dropped his arms to his sides. "People can't always be what they truly are, but there's faith. Faith in what we can't see, or don't really know, and we believe."

He wheeled around, returning to the rim of the mesa, rather than waiting for a response. He didn't want one yet.

The sky to the east would soon be paling, the stars fading. The fitful night wind was dying, only creatures of the dark roamed the cloaked and hidden land.

The camp at the base of the mesa was quiet. They were intrud
ers, these men and women who desecrated the canyon floor lik
flotsam washed from a sandy sea. Intruders who would never be
long and would never know as the desert dweller knew, that her
was a place to be revered. A place of secret life and rare beauty.
place for contemplation and reverie, where in distance and stil
ness there was peace.

The campfire burned in smoldering embers. As the man they ha
named Indian looked fiercely down on them, they slept at last.

A wave of bitterness welled inside the Apache. For what ha
been done to a land that once had been the land of his people. Bi
terness that pulled him back to the desert after many years awa
from it.

He wanted to take Patience away from this. He wanted mor
than he could say, to spare her what lay ahead. But he couldn't. H
couldn't go. Not yet. Not with consuming rage in his heart.

Not until the task he'd come to do was done.

For her safety he'd delayed entry into the drunken orgy of th
camp. Now that immediate danger was past and delay served n
purpose. He swung around, facing her, feeling her cautious gaz
on him. "Are you waiting for me to shed my mask and turn into
brute?"

"Maybe." She didn't turn away. In the darkness he was a shad
owy figure painted in bold, somber strokes, more handsom
phantom than man. Yet when he touched her he was flesh an
blood. Indian was no specter created in the mind of a frightene
woman. But was he part of the nightmare?

Beneath the desert moon she knew only that he was tall, sler
der, broad in shoulders, lean-hipped. His hair and eyes were lik
the night, his features of carved stone. The nuances that were th
essence of him, the truth, lay shrouded in mystery. If he wore
mask, it would be revealed by the light of day.

Indian crossed his arms over his chest, the fringe at the hem c
his leather vest rippling with the move. He looked back at he
meeting her intent stare, holding it. After a moment, he smiled. "
won't happen, you know," he said in an even voice. "There is n
mask. I'll be the same in the light as I am now."

"No mask," Patience murmured, her eyes shifting to look pas
him toward the canyon. "But a masquerade? Could it be tha
you're not really one of them?"

Indian was staggered once more by her shrewd perceptions, realizing, as before, that she was a dangerous woman. A risk to herself and to him.

Shrugging in a dismissive gesture he hoped would mitigate her suspicions, he refuted them with a stolid insistence. "There's no masquerade. I ride with the Wolves. That makes me one of them."

"No."

"Yes."

"If a hawk flies with crows, he doesn't become one."

Indian laughed, with false humor. "O'Hara," he mused with deliberate drollness in his tone, "Irish to the bone. Yet you speak like an Apache."

Patience wouldn't be diverted. "I'm no more Apache than you are vagrant biker."

"Dammit, Patience." With a shake of his head he bit back what he would have said, refusing to be drawn into contention, and sorry he'd let it go so far. "It doesn't matter," he said with a return of stern forbearance. "Believe what you will."

"I'll believe what I see as the truth, Indian."

He heard a strange serenity. It didn't mean she wasn't frightened, nor that she wasn't filled with rage at the indignity and the loss of freedom. It didn't mean truce or compliance. She'd reverted, instead, to powerful and primordial instincts. The most basic and powerful element of survival.

Patience O'Hara, with her flaming hair falling to her waist and Irish blood flowing through her veins, was more Apache in her heart than she knew.

"Watch with more than your eyes," he told her thoughtfully, "and see."

He lifted his face to the sky. Little had changed, but dawn would come too soon. "We must go. We've delayed long enough."

"Your good and true friends are sleeping."

"Yes." Ignoring her mockery, he moved past her, his curious, rolling, moccasin-clad step no more than a whisper over the ground. Mounting the bike, his face without expression, he waited for her to follow.

"We'll wake them."

"Nothing will wake them, they sleep like the dead. Only the sentries know we're here. Only they will know we're coming in."

"Sentries?"

He shifted on the seat to face her fully. "They've been watching. Two of them, beyond hearing, but watching nevertheless. You

will always be watched. Guard yourself well when I am not with
you."

"Who will guard me from you?"

"I will. You have had my word on it."

He expected a response. Another trenchant evaluation of the
worth of his word. But there was only thoughtful, unbroken silence. As the hush deepened he lifted a hand to her, waiting.

Patience looked past him to the vast expanse beyond him. There
was nothing, no light in the darkness, no sign of human inhabit-
ants, no avenue of escape. Yet in the throes of its death, hope demanded one more probing search. One more assurance there was
no hope.

"There's nothing out there."

"You wouldn't let me go in any case?"

"No."

Something almost like a smile tugged at her lips for a second. "I
had to try, one last time."

"I know." He would have done the same. He would keep on
trying, as he knew she would.

"Dammit, Indian! Why did this have to happen to me?"

"The wrong place, O'Hara," he answered. "The wrong time."

"The right time will come." She took his hand. Her clasp was
steady and strong. "My time. I promise."

Indian said no more. With unspoken words of hate and the
pledge of vengeance ringing in his ears, he took her down into the
netherworld that waited below the rim of the mesa.

It was morning. When Indian had taken her down a pitch of
track strewn with potholes and boulders without regard for waking those below, she hadn't thought she would ever sleep. Yet she
had. Dawn broke and the sun was warm on her face before she
woke. With waking came instant recall and alarm. Scrambling
from a blanket laid by the separate fire he'd made, she looked
frantically around, sure there were dangers lurking at every turn.
But little differed from the scene that had greeted her in the night.

By ones and twos, the bikers and their women slept in the
comatose throes of alcohol. The fire was cold, gray ash. Clothing
littered the ground, discarded where the mood struck. Bottles lay
where they were thrown, some intact, some shattered. In the pale
light of morning the camp was suspended chaos, waiting to begin
again.

With her face a mask of disgust, Patience listened to the titter of birds foraging for a first meal. Overhead a black hawk, with white-banded tail flashing in the sun, surfed a rising thermal. Life in the canyon continued little changed, as it had for a millenium, as it would for another. The Wolves were a passing intrusion, a blight endured.

In her unsettled sleep she'd dreamed that when she woke they were gone. But only Indian's place by their smoldering fire was empty.

The one constant in her life for hours was gone.

Her first thought was of escape. Freedom. But escape to where? Where would she go? How? She gauged the face of a cliff rising thirty feet to the top of the mesa. An incline too sheer to climb, the mixed layers of tawny volcanic tuff and blue-black basalt too rough.

Yet beyond the tawny walls of her prison lay civilization. Close enough that a howling dog could be heard. Close enough that she could reach it. If she could wend her way undetected through the canyon. If she knew which direction to walk.

If.

Pushing a hand impatiently through her falling hair, she considered her options. Spinning around, seeking a hidden trail that might be her secret path to freedom, she found herself face-to-face with Indian.

"I wouldn't if I were you." Only his lips moved as he spoke in a low voice.

"What?" He was so close, Patience could see her reflection in eyes that were as dark by day as by night. "What do you mean?"

"You were thinking of escape. Even a tenderfoot could see the cliffs are too steep and too rough. That leaves a path." He swung around, gesturing in the direction he'd come. "There's one of sorts, with sycamores and junipers enough to conceal your passage, and somewhere out there lies a ranch." He turned back to her, his dark face unreadable. "You wouldn't make it. They'll sleep for hours yet, but even with a head start, you wouldn't.

"I would come after you." There was neither anger nor threat in his words. Only fact.

"I know," she admitted.

"But you had to try, or think of trying."

Her chin tilted a telltale inch. "Wouldn't you?"

He looked down at her for what seemed a long time, then he smiled. An action that, as it had the night before, did more wonderful things to an already handsomely constructed face. "Yes."

Patience waited for more, but there was none. She realized she should have known. He never said more than one word, when one was enough. Somewhere in the camp someone snored, coughed and sighed, and slipped again into the heavy, rhythmic breathing of deep sleep.

Indian turned his head, found the source of disturbance, then returned his attention to Patience. "It's better not to disturb them, better to let them sleep off most of what will be monumental hangovers. But if you're hungry..."

"No," Patience assured him quickly. Then again. "Not at all."

As if he would erase the bruises of fatigue from her, he brushed the tender flesh beneath her eye with the pad of a thumb. "I'd hoped you would sleep longer."

"I'm an early riser." She didn't dodge away from his touch, didn't flinch when his palm curved at her cheek.

"Every minute of every day is too precious to waste. Even the bad ones? Even days like today?" He didn't wait for an answer. Taking his hand from her, he stepped back to pick up a slender stalk of mesquite lying at his feet. Pausing a moment, he squinted at the sun, judging the time. "Desert heat is tricky. Until you're better acclimatized, I'd like you to stay in the shade as much as possible, and drink as much as you can."

"I can take care of myself," Patience shot back. "I've been in the desert before."

"Maybe you can, and maybe you have. But not like this." He stopped gathering up the rest of the brush he'd collected. When he straightened there was a sheen of sweat shimmering on his face and throat. "There isn't an air-conditioned hotel within a hundred miles, O'Hara. No dude ranch. No swimming pool. The only cooling the canyon can offer is the shade of a sycamore or juniper. On its best day, at its fullest, the creek wouldn't cover the top of your feet."

Patience stifled a retort in the sudden intuitive knowledge that it might be to her advantage if no one knew just how familiar she was with the desert. The less anyone knew of the lessons taught her by her fey, adventurous family and their madcap expeditions, the better. With parents whose concept of education was living life to the fullest, in as many places, in as many ways as possible, there was little she hadn't tried and accomplished. For most of her twenty-seven years, she'd roamed the world with her parents, her brothers, and her sister. Before she entered the university, the one glaring lack in her education was the classroom.

But no one need know. Especially Indian. All the better to find a way out of this, if she could lull him into a false sense of security in the certainty of her incompetence.

"Maybe I will," she mused, almost laughing out loud at the ironic simplicity of her plan. It might not work, nothing might, but this was worth a try. To Indian, she said, "Maybe you're right."

Indian paused as he was, his hands filled with brush and his eyes with doubt. "I am?"

"Of course you are." With a helpless gesture completely foreign to her nature, she said, "I was foolish to suggest my vacation in the west could qualify me as anything more than a tourist. I shouldn't presume that it did."

"Foolish, huh?"

"Exactly." Patience was uncomfortable under the laserlike scrutiny of his searching gaze, but felt no qualms at lying by omission. After all, what concern was it of his if her vacations in the west had actually been many, and not really vacations in the truest sense of the word?

He needn't know of her Gypsy father's penchant for wandering the world exposing his children to varying life-styles. Nor that one of those ventures included two years her father managed a ranch in Arizona, with his family serving as cowhands. Those years, with another spent on an archaeological study in the petrified forest, might not qualify Patience as an expert, but she was anything but a novice.

"You think it's best I rest in the shade?"

"Yes, Patience." There was amusement in his voice, her change in temperament didn't fool him. He didn't for a moment believe she'd suddenly become the acquiescent female resigned to her fate. Only time would reveal what her resourceful mind had concocted. In the meantime it would be up to him to ensure that she didn't make her circumstance worse. In spirit of her game and because he admired her determination, he added innocently, "I'm glad you've come to terms with what has to be."

"This isn't exactly a case of 'if you can't lick them, join them,'" she warned, certain that sudden and total capitulation would only fuel his evident doubt.

"I never thought it was."

"I'm not embracing Chief Joseph's philosophy."

"That, either," he agreed.

"It's just a matter of being practical."

With a mockingly gallant bow, Indian murmured, "Of course."

For some reason that small bit of gallantry and its mockery infuriated her. An angry retort burned on her tongue, but she bit it back. She was talking too much, saying more than was needed. For the security of her plan, she'd best do as she'd agreed. "I assume you have plans for the brush you've gathered, so I'll just sit in the shade, while you do whatever it is you plan to do with it."

"That's a good idea, Patience. You sit in the shade, and I'll do...whatever."

For the next hour Patience lounged beneath the branches of a sycamore, occupying herself with straightening her sleep rumpled clothes and brushing her hair. All the while, her attention was riveted on Indian.

He'd shed the vest he wore without the complement of shirt or tee. His bare shoulders were broad, with ironlike sinews and muscles rippling beneath skin the color of pale cinnamon as he worked with limbs and shrubs. Faded jeans cinched with leather thongs rode low on his hips. She noted again that instead of the boots de rigueur for most bikers, he wore moccasins laced to the knee.

Shoulder-length hair that gleamed like polished onyx was drawn severely from his face, accentuating the utter and complete masculinity of his classic features. His face was a study in concentration, sparing only an occasional flashing glance at her as he worked. Every move was with purpose and sure, in a task he'd performed many times.

The camp was stirring with the first signs of life when he backed away to survey what he'd done. Turning to her, magnificent with sunlight gleaming over his sweat-burnished torso, he bowed with the same mocking gallantry. "Night quarters." One corner of his mouth lifted in a rakish smile. "Yours and mine."

Speechless for once, Patience glared at the perfectly constructed lean-to and back again to Indian, not really sure how she felt or how she should feel. It would be a relief to be shielded from the prying eyes of the camp, but could she deal with the intimacy of the lean-to, where no camp fire would lie between them?

"This is where we'll spend our nights for the duration of our stay in the canyon. Where you'll sleep with me." There was no smile now to soften the subtle ultimatum. "You have until dark to come to terms with what the night will bring."

Sparing her the need to reply, Blue Doggie coughed and stirred and rose naked from his sleeping bag, stretching, yawning, and scratching immodestly like an old bear waking from a long sleep.

Turning away, her face flaming and confidence flagging, Patience wondered how she would ever survive the days to come.

Four

Indian sat by the fire as Custer, Snake, Hogan, and the quieter Hoke played poker again. This fascination for cards escaped him, but he never missed sitting in, occasionally playing a hand. Always watching, always listening.

He was torn now by the need to be with Patience, to ease her way, to serve as unwelcome protector should it be required. But this was a crucial time when he might discover some bit of valuable information. When all but one would be close enough to sober to speak sense, but drunk enough for loose tongues.

He'd been with the gang only a short time when he'd learned that not everyone was part of the conspiracy. These four were the inner sanctum, and Hoke, not Custer, was the voice of authority in all things that pertained to the real purpose for the Wolves existence. Hoke, who was quieter and smaller, who held himself aloof from most of the interactions of the gang, speaking little in his ruined voice, was always cold sober, and by far the most dangerous.

"Your woman keeps to herself." Hoke spoke. The rasping whisper, emitted from a mutilated throat, strained to reach across the fire that was rebuilt in the morning chill, burned in the suffocating heat of the day, and would be their only light come nightfall.

Indian looked up from his carving. Sliding the trinket in a pocket, but keeping the knife clasped loosely in his hand, he shrugged. "She isn't accustomed to the desert, nor to our ways, but she will be."

Hoke lifted a quizzical brow in a face turned to a rictus by the play of flames. "You plan to keep her long enough for it to matter?"

"She's stubborn and trouble," Indian admitted. "But, yes, I mean to keep her for a while."

"The other women are jealous. There isn't one among them who didn't hope Indian, with his pretty face and his fastidious ways, would choose her." With his observation hinting of the culture and education of a past far removed from his current life, Hoke turned from Indian only long enough to toss a card on the blanket that served as gaming table.

"They were taken," Indian said succinctly.

"We share," Custer put in.

"Or trade."

Indian's dark gaze moved from Custer to Snake, sickened by men who traded the favors of their women with no thought at all. And by the women who allowed it.

"Hey," Hogan added, "you gotta admit, your little redhead is a number to make a man's blood pump."

"What Hogan is trying to say," Hoke interpreted in his more classical speech, "is that Miss O'Hara is like wine to men thirsting in a barren land. A tasty morsel for men who hunger."

"Tasty ain't the half of it," Snake groused, irritable as he always was when conversation moved past the basics. "I've seen her at night, staring at her own special fire, acting like none of the rest of us was good enough for her." He clinched his cards in an brutal fist, crumpling a winning hand. "I get half a chance, she'll know who's good and who ain't. She needs a real man."

Indian didn't turn his black gaze from Snake, didn't glance toward the separate fire. He didn't need to look to know that Patience would be sitting alone and apart, with dusk falling around her. Her hair would be loose, stopping just short of her waist, drifting over her in a fiery veil as she brushed it. In the soft light, when there was languor in the shadows and a land ruled by the sun made ready for night, she found respite from the shocking turn of fortune in this hypnotic, healing, and uncannily feminine pastime.

The lines smoothed from her face, the taut, watchful posture of her body eased. Stroke after stroke the brush slipped through her hair, taming it, turning it to silk as she lost herself in thoughts he couldn't fathom.

Absorbed, transported to a place deep within herself, she performed the elegant ritual, innocent of eyes that lusted. She moved with an unconscious grace, unaware that the very natural qualities were foreign to others. Heedless that this intimately personal act only fueled the lust of men who would strip from her every shred of the grace and elegance and innocence, destroying what they wanted most to possess.

Caught up in her own diversion, with bright strands flowing under the rhythmic stroke of the brush, catching the light of the sky, the light of the fire, she became a tantalizing vision. An enchanting sorceress with secrets hidden in unfathomable depths. A beautiful woman, ever mysterious, ever alluring.

In days past, when the people of his great-great-grandfather Cochise rose this land on steeds of flesh and blood, she would have been revered for her quiet dignity, respected for her enduring strength. Coveted for the blaze of her hair.

She would be called Blaze by the Apache.

"Sharing has been our custom, always," Hoke whispered, and to Indian's ears it was the scratch of evil at heaven's door.

"It isn't my custom," he said flatly. In the eerie silence that followed, his gaze touched lightly on each man, lingering only a fraction longer on Snake. His point was made.

"I don't share." His stare challenged the undeclared leader, while in the quiet rang the unspoken warning, *Not with any man.*

"That ain't fair," Hogan protested as if fairness were ever his concern.

Hoke cut him off with a gesture. Folding his cards, he regarded the Indian. "A one-woman man." His laugh was too much for a throat that could only issue a series of clicks and gulps. "That explains your immunity to the much plied charms of our ladies. And answers Snake's question of your virility."

Indian didn't bother to dignify the speculations of men who understood only wantonness and brutality. To whom gentleness was weakness, and men who did not think as they were suspect.

Hoke's garbled laughter ceased as swiftly as it began. His attention was riveted on Indian. The others might vanish from his side and from the earth, and in his concentration he wouldn't notice.

This was between the two of them. Himself and the Indian. His voice was weaker, punished by the effort of laughter. "You know she can never leave us."

"Yes."

"No one can. Not you, not her. No one."

"I know. I knew months ago when I joined you."

"Never is a long time."

Indian shrugged, but his grip tightened over the hilt of the knife half hidden in his lap.

"When you tire of her, will you hand her over to the others?"

"No."

"Ah." Hoke leaned back, a low boulder supporting his shoulders. "So it's like that? Your woman or no man's."

"So long as she's in camp, she's only mine."

"Then when you're through with her you intend to put her on the block to be sold?"

In a fluid move, Indian rose from his cross-legged position. In buckskin vest and tall moccasins, a hawk's feather dangling from his bound hair, neither his striking appearance nor his masculinity could be questioned. Nor his purpose. "Patience O'Hara is mine. When I tire of her, I'll do with her what I must. When I must."

"A pity," Hoke mused. "All that courage, the good looks going to waste. Worse is the mind, the years of study." The grating whisper sank lower as if he were imparting a special secret. "Did you know our red-haired captive is not Miss O'Hara, but Dr. O'Hara?"

"No one told me."

"From personal papers found in her car, we discovered she graduated cum laude from a veterinary college in the east."

Indian wasn't surprised. Little Patience did, or had done, would be surprising. As she'd demonstrated, she was a lady of cool intelligence and innovative courage. Often with more guts than sense. "I take it the papers were retrieved shortly before the car was destroyed."

"It reposes in a canyon beneath a ton or so of rock and soil."

"She called it Beauty."

"What?" Hoke rarely missed a cue, possessing an uncanny ability to hone into the gist of the most confusing conversations.

"She called the Corvette, Beauty. I don't know why." For two long weeks they'd shared a separate camp and fought. Eaten together and fought. Shared the same lean-to for the night and fought. But never talked. Indian realized he knew everything about Patience that was immediate, but nothing of her past. He hadn't known her profession, or even that she had one. "She is, as I've said, difficult. I know little of her," he said, "but I will."

"Hey!" Snake's young face shone with ill-concealed lust as he leered up at Indian. "Maybe when you get better acquainted with your own old lady, you'll find she wants another man. A real man, one not so much prettier than she is. What then, pretty boy?"

Only a subtle shifting of Indian's body warned of his readiness. Light glinted off the blade of his knife, polished and honed to a razor's edge. He meant the attitude and the knife as a reminder, not a threat. Snake was hotheaded and priming himself for a move. One that would surely come. If not full scale across the fire tonight, then later. Only the devil knew when or where. It did no harm to let him know there would be a battle.

"What will I do? Nothing. It won't be her choice to make." Indian asked the question that needed no answer, "Was it ever?"

With a bow that mocked the younger man, he backed away. "If you will excuse me, there are matters that need my attention."

He was beyond hearing when Hoke turned to Snake. "Don't let jealousy make a fool of you, kid. With his pretty talk and pretty face, Indian is a class act and a dangerous man. Custer." The scar that crossed his throat from right ear to left shoulder contorted with his command for complete attention. "What do we know about him?"

"Not a lot." Custer braced himself for an interrogation he'd endured before. "Except he's a good man to have at your back in a fight."

"That's how he came to join us, isn't it? Saved your skin in a bar when the odds were five to one. He made it five to two and even."

Hoke knew the answer, but Custer responded as expected. "The man moves like a cat and he ain't afraid of poor odds. I was too drunk to ride and the little hick town was ready to lynch me, so he brought me back to camp."

"You showed him the way, you mean."

Custer squirmed under Hoke's hard glare. "Well, yeah."

With sleeping doubts resurfacing, Hoke's eyes narrowed, watching Indian approach the woman. "That was down in Mexico where you got too friendly with one of the señoritas, wasn't it?"

"It was a misunderstanding," Custer protested.

"One that would have ended with your liver being fed to the pigs. Indian rides in like the cavalry, plucks you out of trouble, brings you back to us, and never leaves,'' Hoke mused aloud. "He's a closemouthed son of an Indian. Three months and what do we know about him? *Nothing!* And that bothers me more now than ever. If he has nothing to hide, why is he so secretive? Who is he, really?''

Custer scratched his head. "I dunno, all I ever heard him called is Indian.''

"Did he tell you he was called Indian, or did someone here give him the name?''

Uncomfortable with the angry disgust he saw in Hoke, Custer made a groveling, placating move of his hands. "I think it was Callie.'' A light of relief sparked in his face. "Yeah, sure, it was Callie. You know how she is, calling them the way she sees them. To Callie he looked like an Indian. The name stuck.''

"So, what you're admitting is that no one here knows his name?'' Hoke's lips curled in a snarl, pulling the loose skin tighter, making the scars on his neck more gruesome.

Custer knew that if there was blame for bringing Indian among them, it would lie at his door. "Hell, Hoke.'' He laughed, making light of his worries. "You said yourself we needed window dressing. Someone to draw attention away from the four of us, characters like Blue Doggie, and Pritchard, the dwarf. Hey, who even sees us when we ride in with Indian. Can you name a better cover?'' He was talking fast now, selling his excuse. "So, we don't know his name. Who knows Blue Doggie's, or Snake's, or mine?''

"I do,'' Hoke said coldly. "Every name, except one. Three months and he still isn't truly one of us. This with the woman proves he never will be. So, one wonders why he joined us. What he's looking for?''

"He's a pretty, sissy boy looking for thrills. A rube who'll try to go back to his real life one day, to brag to other rubes that he rode with the Wolves. What else do you want to know about him?'' Snake asked.

"A better question would be, what does he know about us?'' Leaning forward, in a swift move, Hoke tossed his cards into the fire. Watching the king of spades twist and curl as if trying to escape the flames that scorched and blackened it, wondering if Indian had been a mistake, he muttered, "Maybe Snake's right. Maybe he's too soft for us.''

Hoke's look swept the camp, the refuse strewn around, the slovenly men, unkempt women. "Maybe he's too decent. So, why did he stay? What does he want from us?''

"You don't think he's trouble for us?"

"I don't know what the hell I think." The raucous whisper interrupted Custer. Suspicions that had nagged for a long while burst into full growth. "Watch him. Watch every move, day and night."

"Hoke, you've got him wrong," Custer insisted. "He's a little soft about the woman, but that don't mean he's different than he was before. It ain't just me he's helped. He's the best scout we have. Nobody finds better camps than Indian."

"Who was he helping, Custer? Us or himself?" Hoke watched Indian's distant fire grow brighter as shadows lengthened and twilight deepened. "Watch him, then we'll decide."

"Why bother?" Hogan demanded. "We can take care of him easy."

"Not before we know who he is and what he's after." Hoke spoke in a tone he would use with a simpleton. "Or before we know who else is involved."

"If he's just a regular guy with a peculiar hang-up about broads? What then?" For all his faults Custer was loyal to the man who had saved his life. He would be until there was concrete proof he'd been a judas goat. But, if the unthinkable were true, Indian would need all his mental and physical strength to survive.

"If he is what he seems then we don't have a problem, do we?" Hoke leaned back against the boulder, rubbing his thumb absently over the face of his watch. "We have time, all the time we need. Watch him. For now it should be enough."

Grumbling at the turn of events, and over their spoiled game, one by one Snake and Hogan and Custer followed Hoke's lead, tossing their cards into the fire. One by one they sauntered away, leaving their covert leader to his speculations.

Cognizant of the sudden resurgence of suspicion, but unaware of how serious the doubt had grown, Indian covered the distance between the camps in long, muffled strides. His soundless approach offered no warning. Patience's first inkling of his presence was the clasp of his hand at her wrist, stopping the motion of the brush.

She whirled to face him, catching her hair in a low, swaying limb of the juniper that clustered at her back. "Indian! You startled me. I thought . . ."

"That I was one of the others?" He knelt by her, taking the brush from her shaking fingers. "I could have been. Because of this."

"Because of a hairbrush?" Color that had flown from her face began to return pretty degree by pretty degree. "I don't understand."

Indian sighed and rubbed his temples with thumb and forefinger, wishing he could rub away the weight of his worries. "I know you don't. God help us both, I know. Just don't brush your hair by the fire anymore. Better yet, don't brush it at all."

Patience's temper flared unreasonably, burning hotter in the aftermath of shock. "You abduct me, destroy Beauty, keep me prisoner in this godforsaken land, insist that I wear this—" she clutched the thong he'd worn in his hair, crumpling turquoise and feathers in her fist "—branding me as your property. I've slept on the ground, freezing by night, sweltering by day. I haven't had a real bath in days, and now you say I can't even brush the tangles from my hair?"

"You have them catalogued, don't you?" Indian observed. "All my sins."

"I've only just begun."

"No, O'Hara, you're all through." Rising, he took her with him.

"Ouch!" Patience pulled free of him as her head was jerked back by the juniper. "Are you in such a hurry to scalp me that you're going to do it without a knife? The right way would be less painful."

Indian didn't answer. His hand rested lightly at the knife once more in its scabbard in his moccasin. As she twisted and turned, trying to see, trying to untangle herself and only making matters worse, he drew the knife, lifting it over her head.

Patience screamed and dodged again as the knife descended. "Don't you dare!"

The knife cut cleanly through the limb, sending the fragrance of fresh evergreen wafting over Patience. The clean scent she forever associated with Indian. Her sudden release from the talons of the limb sent her stumbling into him. As his arms closed around her she fought, by instinct rather than thought, clawing and scratching at every inch of bare skin she could reach.

"Ouch, yourself, wildcat." Indian held her away from him, his arms long enough to turn her fight to futile pantomime. "Be still. I only cut you free."

Patience stopped at the top of her swing. Color that had drained from her face again, was slow to return as she lowered her arm. "The knife, you were angry." She was babbling and didn't know how to stop. "I thought you were trying to scalp me."

"Scalp you?" He smiled grimly down at her. "Believe me, I was tempted."

"But you didn't."

He chuckled for real at the understatement of the obvious. "Maybe next time."

"You and who else?" Patience chose bravado to mask her turmoil.

"Only Indian, my dear girl."

"I'm not your dear, and I'm certainly not your girl," she flung back at him.

Indian drew a weary breath, his chest rising and falling beneath the vest. Angry welts left by her nails were vivid on his coppery skin. "I'm aware of that."

"Good." Crossing her arms over her breasts she continued to glare up at him. "At least we got that straight."

"Very straight." On the heels of the clipped response, he reached for her. "Come here."

"No." Patience skidded back a step, but not far enough.

He pulled her closer, forcing her down with him to the ground, fitting himself snugly at her back, his knees bent at her sides.

"What are you doing?" she demanded as she tried to turn.

Folding his hands around the back of her head, he turned her firmly to the front. "Be still, unless you want this twig to become so entangled in your hair we have to cut it free. If that's the case, I can make quick work of it. Then your only decision will be whether you want to start a trend of being half scalped and half not, or wear a crew cut."

He released her, pulling the knife from the scabbard in which it had only just been sheathed. Holding it in front of her, he turned it slowly, letting her absorb the impact of what he'd said. "There's another way. You can behave. If you do, I think I can work it free."

He turned the knife again. "Which will it be?"

Patience started to speak, but words of surrender clogged her throat. She drew a long, hard breath, cleared her throat, and licked lips as parched as the desert at midday. Her voice was barely a breath itself. "I'll be still."

"What was that?" He leaned close, his cheek brushing her hair, his lips nearly touching her ear. "Did you say something?"

"You heard me." She raised her voice a decibel.

"Did I?"

"Dammit, Indian!"

"Tut, tut." His breath was warm on her neck. "You're getting angry again."

"I'm not angry."

"If you're not, I'd like to see the fireworks when you are."

"Shut up," Patience snapped. "Just shut up and cut it."

Indian leaned away from her, stroking her hair with one hand, stealthily sheathing the knife with the other. Clasping a strand that gleamed like burnished rubies, he let it drift through his fingers. "What a shame." His hand tightened again, tugging lightly. If the edge of the other hand pressing down on the stunning mass were really a knife, the lock he held would have been shorn at the scalp.

"Wait." She caught his wrist in her healing hands. "Don't."

"Don't what?" he asked with a wicked innocence.

"Don't cut my hair. I'll be still." The words didn't come any easier from repetition.

Indian laughed and released her. "I thought you might."

"Put your knife away." If she clenched her teeth any harder they would break.

"My knife is in its scabbard."

"It has been all along." Patience finished for him. "You never intended to cut my hair."

"I'm an Indian, not a criminal. Cutting hair like yours would certainly be a crime."

"Yet I shouldn't brush it? That makes no sense."

"It would if you understood the men you're dealing with."

"If it weren't for you, I wouldn't be dealing with them."

"No," he agreed with deceptive mildness, "by now you wouldn't be dealing with anyone, anywhere. If you don't count Saint Peter at the pearly gates."

Biting down on her tongue she stopped its runaway harangue. Indian was right. He'd saved her life and more, but her abominable Irish pride would only admit it in the most private part of herself. "Oh, forget it. Just take the blasted tree from my hair."

"Please?"

Patience hesitated.

Indian waited.

She knew he would wait forever with the implacable tenacity of his kind. "Irish pride, be damned," she muttered. "Take the tree from my hair. Please."

"My pleasure." There was laughter in his deep tone.

She was tempted to make a pointedly caustic comment about fools laughing in the face of disaster, but his hands were in her hair lifting it from her neck. His fingers carefully puzzled through the intricacies of the snarl. He was gentle as he always was when there was peace between them. He worked without rancor, meticulously, long after she would have ripped the twig away, and with it any tangled hair.

She felt herself relaxing, forgetting. She heard only the sound of his breath as it whispered over the nape of her neck. There was darkness around them, sometimes she felt there was always darkness when they were at peace. The fire burned brighter and the night grew darker. Flames leapt and curled in a beguiling dance. The sky above the rim was clear. Stars, scattered over it like crystals over midnight velvet, seemed close enough to catch, to pull from the sky.

No clouds blotted the perfect panorama, yet in her pensiveness she heard the methodic and muted rush of thunder. A steady, rhythmic throb. Too steady? Too rhythmic? Too close? Not thunder at all?

Finding she was free, discovering he hadn't moved away though he no longer touched her, she bowed her head, turning until her cheek brushed his chest. The buckskin was as supple and cool as satin, his flesh hot and firm. There was no thunder. The beat of his heart filled her mind and body, singing through her blood.

She could touch him. All she needed was to turn her head only a fraction to press her lips to his chest. She felt herself drifting and wanting. Wanting his arms around her. Wanting his lips against hers. Wanting things she'd never dreamed. Wanting him.

Bawdy laughter sheared through her reverie. The inescapable call of reality that his gentle touch might ease, but wouldn't change. Pulling away, she sat stiffly, questioning the sanity of her response to him.

"Patience," he began, and there was question in the low rumble.

"No," she refused violently, "I don't want to hear." She felt the quick rise of his chest, the heat of him burned through her shirt.

"Of course." He eased away, his hands lifted in resignation. "You're right. Some things are better left unsaid."

"When you finish, we can forget this happened."

"It's finished."

"Thank you." The words rang false even to her ears.

"Por nada." He slipped away from her and stood to pace the edge of their camp. His back was toward her as he faced the inky canyon wall.

"For nothing," Patience interpreted, using the Spanish taught her by one of her many tutors. For nothing, he claimed, but when she was honest she knew it should be for everything.

Climbing to her feet, she was surprised that she wanted to smooth over their differences, to regain the rare but erratic camaraderie they shared. "I'm sorry this was such a bother. I'll be more careful of the trees next time."

"There won't be a next time." He turned on her and his face was controlled and grim. "You'll brush your hair in the lean-to, and if that isn't good enough for you, Princess O'Hara, you won't brush it at all. Is that clear?"

"Perfectly." She bristled and any desire for truce ended. "Since you were kind enough to build this castle away from the castle, I think I'll make use of it. Early to bed, early to rise, you know."

"Be careful, princess. All the early bird gets is the worm."

"Good," she quipped as she moved to the bushy structure. "Even a worm would be better company than you."

"You didn't think so a few minutes ago." He aimed his jeer at her back. "That wasn't what you thought at all."

Her step developed a hitch, she slowed and faced him. "A few minutes ago I was crazy. Given the things that have happened, I'm entitled to a crazy misstep."

"Now you've made it," he suggested in his laconic fashion.

"A doozy." She curtsied, an insolent princess in front of the king. "With your permission, or not, I think I'll retire. My friend the worm will be waiting in the morning."

Crossing the camp, she was a lady, regal in faded jeans and scuffed boots. When she reached the lean-to he called after her, "What really happened here tonight, O'Hara?"

She didn't turn. "Nothing happened. Nothing at all."

"Good." The word was a low, guttural bark. "I'm glad you realize it was nothing, and that nothing can come of nothing."

"Thank you for that profound analysis."

"Anytime." Then, because he was weary of this, of himself and of their battles, he commanded, "Go to bed. The sooner you do, the sooner tomorrow will come. Then there will be one less day before I can be rid of you."

Without waiting to see if she obeyed, he stalked into the desert, for once careless of his step. Small stones rolled beneath his feet, scrub clawed at his clothes. His escape into the dark was viciously clumsy and haphazard, and unlike him. His response to Patience was as vicious, but calculated to be so. To drive her away.

Because he cared.

He cared too much, and he knew he shouldn't.

Patience lay in the cloistering shelter, her eyes wide and unseeing as she listened to his thrashing passage. She hurt deep inside with a restless sort of ache, and didn't know why. She lay for hours, listening even after his steps faded away, too tense to rest, too bewildered to sleep.

Sounds of night in the canyon had grown familiar in the two weeks that seemed an eternity. Most familiar was Indian's hushed and tired sigh as he slipped into the lean-to to lie at her back.

She didn't speak or touch him. But as she sensed his presence, drawing comfort from the warm strength hidden in the long, lean body, the knotted ache in her slowly unwound. Her eyelids grew heavy, quivering nerve endings quieted. She slept then, and was not aware that she slept. With Indian at her side, even the nightly revelry of the camp didn't disturb her.

Indian lay beside her, a prisoner of his thoughts, every sense alert as he prepared for the inevitable, regretting what he must do.

Hoke was suspicious, Snake wanted the woman and would do anything to have her. They would be watching, along with the others, waiting for a mistake, a wrong word, a wrong move. They would begin the surveillance by coming tonight to satisfy a sick curiosity. How he acted and Patience reacted could mollify distrust or prove a point.

As he'd walked the desert clearing his head he knew, suddenly and with conviction, what would come to pass and what survival would require of him. Deliberately delaying his return to the lean-to, giving her time to sleep or be near sleep, he'd loitered where no sane man would loiter and devised his plan.

He didn't expect he would have to wait long after his return to the quarters they shared. So he lay by her, aware on an unconscious level that she sank deeper into sleep, but with his immediate attention focused on the brush nearest the lean-to. The first sound that sent alarm ranting through him could have been a mouse, a night bird, a reptile. The second was the unmistakably stealthy footstep of a man. Not so close yet, but close enough to begin.

"Forgive me, O'Hara," Indian muttered. Turning his body into hers, one leg pinned her legs to the ground, one hand clasped her hair, the other cupped her breast.

Patience woke abruptly. There was no confusion, no disorientation. She knew where she was and what was happening. All she didn't know was the identity of her attacker.

"Stop!" she cried, and began to fight, calling on every dirty tactic she'd used in fun in the free-for-alls against her brothers. But now she fought in earnest, there were no pulled punches, no sheathed claws, no tempered kick or bites. This was for real.

She wanted his eyes. Dear God! she wanted them. She struggled to see his face, to reach it, but any way she turned he was there at her back, his great, hard hands holding her, touching her. His breath was hot on her face, his hair tangled with hers. She butted him head-to-head and heard his muffled groan. In the momentary loosening of his grasp, she managed a half turn, but still couldn't see his face or reach his eyes.

Damn you. Bastard. The words were only in her mind, she wouldn't waste the energy to speak them. Silently she fought on, denying her flagging strength, straining from his kisses, growling in the back of her throat like an animal. Then he was on her, over her, as his mouth covered hers.

She couldn't think. She couldn't breathe. His body was heavy, pinning her to the ground. She tried to move her head from side to side to escape, but his hands in her loose-flying hair held her in his kiss.

She was drowning, suffocating, dying.

The kiss went on forever. A deliberate kiss, and for all its prowess and expertise, curiously without passion.

Her fingers were in his hair, catching handfuls of long silky strands, tugging with the last of her stamina. Her arms cramped, her grip slipped away. This was a nightmare and she couldn't wake up. A battle she wouldn't win.

A ragged sob rose from a shattering heart and died in her throat. Then he was gone. Rolling away from her, but not leaving.

Patience lay as he left her, gasping for air, breathing in the scent of evergreen. Her hand hurt. She lifted it close to her face. There was fringe twined around her fingers. Buckskin fringe, stained with her blood as it cut into her flesh.

No one wore buckskin but Indian.

Like an old crone she sat up, slowly, bones creaking, muscles squalling.

No one had hair like silk but Indian.

Staring into the desert, she tried to ease the horror.

No one smelled of evergreen but Indian.

"You," she said wearily, turning at last to the shadow that slumped at the edge of the shelter.

"Yes." He didn't lift his head from his hands.

"Why didn't you finish what you began?" she asked bitterly.

"Are you asking why I didn't rape you?"

"That's what it was all about, wasn't it?"

"No."

Patience needed more, but he said nothing. "That's it? Am I to believe you get your kicks out of near rape?"

He looked a her then. "Would you prefer the real thing?"

"Damn you, Indian! What do you think of me?"

"A lot more than you think of me at the moment, I imagine."

Patience absorbed the sorrow she saw, remembering that he hadn't really hurt her, hadn't done more than touch her breast and kiss her. They'd slept side by side for two weeks and he'd made no advances. Now this, something half-done. It made no sense, or it made a great deal of sense. "They were out there again," she ventured, realizing she should have guessed. "Weren't they?"

"Yes."

"Talk to me, Indian. I need more than one word answers. Explain. I don't want to..." The admission she was about to make froze on her tongue. Lamely, she finished. "Just talk to me."

"Why?" He moved closer to the lean-to, ducking the fraction needed to enter. He knelt in front of her and saw the remnants of terror illuminated by the dying fire. "What, O'Hara?" He smoothed her hair from her face, the back of his hand brushing her cheek. Sickness churned in him when he saw the effort it took not to recoil from him. Yet he was grateful for the effort, and heartened by it. "What don't you want?"

Her tired eyes were luminous, her bruised mouth trembled. She shook her head and would have turned away, but his fingers at her throat wouldn't let her.

"Why?" he asked again with a kindness that was her undoing.

"Because I don't want to hate you." Her reluctant whisper was ragged and low.

"After all I've done, how could you not want to hate me?"

"I don't know." She bit her lip and shook her head again. The attack was a sham, but an insidious dread seemed to have seeped into her bones, to dwell there forever. She curbed a shiver that had nothing to do with the chill of the desert night. "I don't know!" Her voice was rough from screams unuttered, from fears unnamed. "I don't know anything anymore."

"I'm sorry." He pulled her into his embrace, a strange tenderness in him as she tensed only a little, then lay quietly against him. "Sorry for this, for everything."

"I know."

"Do you?" He pulled away, only far enough to look down at her, the reflection of embers from the fire glowing softly in his eyes. Thoughtfully he murmured, "I wonder."

"I know all that matters. That you truly wouldn't hurt me and that you would never do this without reason."

"There was a reason. The same old reason." He pulled her down with him as he recounted the confrontation by Hoke's fire. When he was finished, exhaustion overtook her, and he held her, watching over her while she slept again.

He'd bought a little space and a little trust. The Wolves would wait for a while, but his time and hers was fast running out. And the definitive information that could topple an empire eluded him still. He needed only a little more, but could he risk her life to save hundreds? Would he?

For the first time he asked the question of Matthew Winter Sky. Matthew had no answer.

Five

Another week, their third camp. As nearly as Patience could judge, they were in the vicinity of Phoenix. Not that she could see the city, nor had she seen it. Not even its lights, except a glow that washed the southern horizon at nightfall. Which, she admitted, might not be Phoenix at all. A battered and fading sign glimpsed on the little-used roads and trails the bikers used was her one clue.

That wreck of a sign had assumed an inordinate importance in Patience's thoughts. Tattered and curling, peppered with buckshot, and leaning at an impossible angle, it had become her lodestar, not to the north, but to herself. It was her orientation, the finding of herself. It had become increasingly important to know where she was, to document it even in the vaguest of terms. A necessary exercise to keep this real.

Terror could dull the mind, nature's palliative turned reality to a nightmarish dream. Patience wouldn't allow herself that luxury. Reality she could control, dreams she could not.

The pitiful derelict standing haphazard among the mesquite could have been a prank. Some desert dweller's idea of a great joke. But for Patience it was truth. It had to be.

The little knowledge was hope. Hope for escape. Hope for a future. An exhilarating stimulus that swept paralyzing fear from the mind, sharpening muddled thought processes.

Clutching this cherished secret to her heart, Patience could look out on her movable prison with a new understanding. The sudden frenzy of moving twice in as many days, and the clandestine travel seemed confusing and more than strange after two weeks of idle days in the canyon. She realized now that the weeks had been a time of waiting, hiding and waiting, for some signal. But what? And why?

In those first days of her captivity few left the canyon, then only in pairs. Now all the men rode, and with them most of the women. Indian, who hadn't left her alone in camp before, rode, too.

Only Patience never left her prison without bars. Each trip out, two of the women were left behind and set to guard her. Given the way some of them looked at her, the silent, sullen watching, she often wondered who would guard her from her guards.

Sitting apart now, as she always did, as Indian wished her to, she became a not-so-detached observer of the latest spate of activity. That they were readying to ride was obvious. If she hadn't spent this interminable time with them she would know this was different, more than a joyride. Excitement ran through the camp like chain lightning. A spark leaping from one to another, as wanderers nailed to one place for too long made preparations for a serious ride.

Only Hoke, his triumvirate, and Indian did not see to their bikes. There was no camp fire now, with the midday heat too oppressive for it. Snake and Hogan and Custer crouched on their haunches around Hoke, listening, seldom speaking. A few paces away, out of range of their conversation, but keeping them constantly in his line of sight, Indian busied himself with the repair of a moccasin in perfect repair.

As she watched him watch them, Patience was completely convinced he knew what they were saying, as surely as if he heard them.

He's reading lips, she decided. What did the foul four have to say that was so important? And why did Indian eavesdrop in such a covert manner?

Sighing, shrugging a shoulder beneath her sweat-soaked shirt, she turned away. The broiling sun bore down through the scruffy shrub that was her meager shelter. The air was stifling, so hot it seared the lungs with each breath. The bits of shade that dappled her skin offered no relief. In this crudest of camps, the most temporary and barren, Indian had neither time nor resources to construct a lean-to. A little shelter that would be welcome now.

Subconsciously she lifted her braid lying over her shoulder like a strip of heat. Brushing her fingers over the banded tips she found herself turning again to Indian, remembering his care and his tenderness as he'd worked with her hair, braiding it, securing it against the wind that beat at her as she rode behind him.

In seeming oblivion of her interest, he knelt at the edge of their sector, one knee on the ground, one foot firmly planted. His hair was drawn cruelly from his face, a glittering fall of all the iridescences of black. His features were cast in stark relief, angular and rough-hewn, its handsome harshness unrelieved by his dark, riveted gaze and the grim line of his mouth. Beneath his right eye, a bruise she couldn't see faded to yellow as it blended into the coppery hue of his skin.

The bruise she'd given him with the butt of her head on the night that proved her suspicions. The night she knew Indian was more than he pretended to be. But who was he? What was he? And why did he travel with these men who viewed him with mistrust, if not total distrust, and afforded him only tentative acceptance at best?

As she puzzled about him, he stood, rising to his full height of six feet. He wore the buckskin vest, his chest and arms bare beyond its cut. Beneath the blazing sun, darkening skin that never seemed to burn shone red-brown. Only a light sheen of perspiration shimmered on his forehead and chest, when others, including Patience, sweated profusely. He was a being made for the desert, a man abiding with its exigencies, dealing with them in uncanny ease.

The riders called themselves Desert Wolves. A grandiose misnomer for the creatures they were. Swaggering marauders in a fragile, unforgiving land, but not of it. As Indian turned his probing, intelligent gaze to her, she knew that only he among them was of the desert, only he was the wolf.

Her thoughts faltered, her pulse quickened as he came to her in his easy, ground-eating step. With his back to the others he knelt by her, touching her face with his fingertips, smoothing a drifting tendril from her cheek. "We ride soon."

She nodded in acknowledgment. "Everyone but my guardians."

"Alice and Eva," he complained under his breath. "I hate to leave you with them."

Alice was the oldest, the roughest, the sliest. A beefy woman with tattooed arms. And Eva, a crude creature with hard, bitter eyes, who looked with evil intent at the world. A mockery of her own sophisticated name.

"I'll be all right," Patience assured him with a conviction far from the truth.

"You'll stay close?" He meant the place he'd made for her, her place apart.

"I won't budge an inch beyond our perimeter. And I won't do anything to antagonize either of them."

The promise didn't satisfy him, but it was the best he could expect. The best he could have.

"I wish . . ." It did no good to wish. There was an alternative in the beginning—to take her out of the desert to safety, abandoning all he'd accomplished, or to keep her with him, salvaging what he could of a crucial investigation. He'd made the self-serving choice and now she, as well as he, must live with the consequences. Framing her face between his hands, he looked deeply into her eyes, into her soul, the source of her indomitable spirit and sometimes foolish courage. Willing her to keep herself safe, he growled a low demand, "Take care." He pressed his lips briefly to her hair. Moving away, touching her only with his eyes, he murmured, "Please."

Then he was away to his bike without a backward glance.

Long after the predominant roar of the Harleys had been swallowed by the desert, Patience sat as he'd left her. All that moved was her hand, stroking her hair. When she realized her fingers had by their own volition found the place his lips had touched, she yanked her hand away. Folding one over the other, keeping them stiffly in her lap, she sat with dread in the silence of the camp.

She missed him already, and insisted to herself that it was because he was her only ally. Because he was her gentle protector, more than her keeper. Because the women were her enemies, with the two set to guard her now, the worst of the lot.

"Hey, Red." As if on cue the taunting call shattered the silence, drawing her almost gratefully from thoughts she wasn't ready to accept. "You gonna sit all day and mope?"

When Patience didn't answer, Eva joined her brittle call to that of Alice's. "Miss High and Mighty ain't so high or so mighty now, is she? Didja see her mooning after the pretty boy, Alice?"

Alice chuckled, an unhealthy rattling sound. "Face longer than a lonesome hound dog. Too bad the pretty one ain't here to see.

Make his heart go pitty-pat.'' A crude expletive rolled off her tongue with a hideous naturalness, as she tossed back a lock of hair too sooty black. "Do more than that to Snake." Poking Eva with an elbow, her face crinkled in a sly caricature of a grin. "That I'd like to see."

"None of us was good enough for him," Eva announced tartly. She called no names, but no one doubted that she spoke of Indian. "Only your ladyship here would do. Bet he wouldn't think so much of her once Snake got through carving on her patrician face." The way she pronounced it, breaking it into broad, derisive syllables, patrician became a parody of itself. A scornful insult.

"To my way of thinking, a little roughing up would improve more than your ladyship's looks. Tone her down some, then she wouldn't be so special, sitting over there all alone," Alice observed a little too casually.

Patience didn't like the direction their taunts were taking them. With her thoughts ranging, she searched for a way to diffuse the escalating situation. Drawing a blank, she took refuge in the only recourse left her. Passive resistance. Complete silence. If their remarks prompted no retaliation, she hoped they would find little sport in them. It hadn't proven successful on a lost and lonely trail, but it was still her best and only recourse.

"Hey, you." Eva sauntered closer, hips swaying as her boots scuffed the dust in her burlesque of the mincing steps of a grand lady. She was more slender by far than Alice, yet still bigger than Patience. When her call elicited no response, she stopped, hands on her hips, flat, cruel eyes flashing beneath a shock of close-cropped hair the color of platinum. "You!" She pointed a finger. "I'm talking to you."

Patience knew she'd been mistaken in her silence. Mistaken because there was nothing she could do to diffuse this. These women had waited nearly three weeks for redress of some imagined dishonor and they intended to have it.

Concealing a rueful sigh, she turned to these hardened camp followers bent on malicious mischief. Lifting her chin a regal inch, she addressed them calmly. "Yes?"

"Yes!" Alice snorted. "She doesn't know what you want and she's already saying yes."

Patience ignore Alice. "You were speaking to me, Eva?"

"Well, I sure as hell wasn't talkin' to myself."

"How may I help you?" Patience wondered how many times she'd heard her mother use that phrase to discourage determined gossips. She hadn't really listened then, but was surprised at how like Mavis she sounded. "Is there something you need?"

"Something I need!" Eva howled and slapped her knee. "That's a good one. What would I need from you?"

"I have no idea," Patience said as she stood to face the woman. "You came to me, not I to you."

"Oh, my, what a pretty speech. Do you think you could teach me to talk like that?"

Eva was circling her now, and Patience turned as she turned. Alice had initiated this encounter, but Patience was convinced she was only the instigator. One who liked to stir the bitter broth, then stood back and watched it bubble. Alice would be no trouble; Eva was the one she must not take lightly.

"I could teach you," Patience said, pretending she hadn't heard the contempt in the gibe, "if you like."

"And if I don't like?"

"You asked, Eva, I didn't offer."

"You really think you're something, don't you?" Eva's eyes glittered with hate, her words were filled with venom. "You waltz in here like Miss Perfect in the flesh, and have all the men panting after you. Including Indian, who wouldn't give me a look." She clamped her teeth down on a damning admission. And Patience understood at last why the woman hated her so.

Eva wanted Indian, and in her mind Patience had taken him from her. "You're wrong, Eva. I didn't waltz anywhere. I was brought against my will. I never wanted any part of this."

"You think I believe that?" Brows many shades darker than platinum lifted nearly to her hairline. "What kind of fool do you think I am?"

"I don't think you're a fool at all. Mistaken, but not a fool." Patience kept her voice steady, her face serene.

"Nothin' ruffles the grand lady, does it?" Eva sneered. "I wonder how grand you'd be with that red braid hacked off at the scalp? Or your nose trimmed like a cheatin' squaw?" The knife at her belt was suddenly in her hand.

The game was over.

Patience had no knife, but she was not without weapons. Her father had insisted long ago that his daughters not be without protection. Keegan determined that protection would be themselves and the skills learned from a great, hulking Oriental who had no speech, but moved like a dancer and taught physical mayhem with ceremony in a teahouse setting. What Kim taught Patience and Valentina was simple and deadly. With a single move either could disable or cripple a much larger assailant. But she had no wish to cripple Eva, nor to do her lasting harm. She wanted nothing more than to persuade the jealous woman to leave her alone.

As she backed away, hoping this little giving of ground would satisfy the woman, Patience readied for attack. Relaxed, her weight evenly balanced on both feet, arms at her sides as she leaned ever so slightly forward, she could move surely and quickly. Surprise and speed, and unexpected knowledge would be her forte. With regret for the need of it, she waited for Eva to charge.

Spurred by envy that was fueled by the cool composure of the smaller woman, Eva became like a wild animal guided by rage rather than thought. With a cry she launched herself at Patience, slashing savagely with the knife. She had only a millisecond to halt, glaring blankly at the space where Patience had been, before a booted heel crashed into the side of her knee. That very vulnerable and complex structure buckled, pitching Eva's weight onto it, inflicting added damage in an instant before she fell on her face.

Patience backed away. That quickly it was finished. Not with the damage she could have done, but enough. Eva would be a long while standing, and longer repeating her threats. For a moment, as the crying woman cringed at her feet, Patience felt a strange compassion for her. Compassion she dared not reveal as she lifted her head to stare coldly at Alice who gaped as if her eyes played tricks.

"You started this, now come get your friend." Patience's command was harsh. "Take her back to your own camp. Tend her."

"But h-how?" Alice stammered.

"Bind the knee, stabilize it. See that she doesn't walk on it for a while. After this, stay in your own camp." The last was flung over Patience's shoulder as she walked away, distancing herself from her own havoc. Kim's most devastating technique had served her well before. She never hesitated to employ it, but she never liked it.

When the women were gone, she returned to her seat beneath the scrub. Sunlight glinted on gray metal. Eva's knife lay at her feet. Plucking it from the sand, she wiped it clean and tucked it in her belt. Taking her low-crowned cattleman's hat from the tree limb where she'd hung it, she pulled it low over her forehead. Depleted in the unrelenting heat by the exertion of her encounter with Eva, she tugged the hat another notch lower and, with the brim shading her eyes, leaned back in the pitiful shade to wait for Indian.

She knew she couldn't sleep. Shouldn't sleep.

Not even after exhausting hours of wary vigilance, nor in the comforting assurance that Alice was too cowardly for another skirmish, and Eva incapable. As the balm of a soothing languor seeped into body and mind, she welcomed it, giving herself up to it, emptying her mind of everything but this day, this minute, the nirvana of capricious peace.

But she wouldn't sleep.

Shielded by the precious umbrella of shade, as heat swept the chill of fear from her bones, she heard the rustle of tiny leaves stirring in rising currents of heat, the cry of a bird in flight, the secret scurry of small creatures. Insects raised their chorus, a summer serenade in this beautiful land, this land she called unforgiving.

Hours spun themselves away slowly, she drowsed and listened.

She didn't mean to sleep.

Silence reached into a dreamless darkness. Silence in which there were no crying birds, no scurrying creatures, no serenading insects. Even the air was motionless, the leaves quiet. It reached for her, drawing her from the darkness to the still light.

Alarm crept into the languor of sleep, padding across tender nerves like a lazy tiger. Releasing a long breath unconsciously caught and held, Patience stirred with guarded restraint, feeling the weight of oppressive heat, the touch of an unrelenting gaze upon her. Cautiously, making no sudden moves, with the tip of one finger she pushed the hat from her eyes. The sun was a white light, blinding her, turning the world to a glittering haze. Yet she knew someone was there, watching her.

Leaning away from the tree, her back straight, she blocked the glare with a hand beneath the brim of the tilted hat. The glare swam into a pattern of hot white and sooty blur. The blur became a shape crouching at her feet. Recoiling, she choked back a cry, her eyes straining, focusing. With excruciating concentration the shape became a body, a face. Ebony eyes studied her intently.

"Indian!" The word was a croak torn from a parched throat.

He didn't move, nor turn his riveted stare. He didn't speak or acknowledge the leap of grateful recognition in her voice. Slowly, with utter care, his probing scrutiny moved methodically over her, noting grimly a tear in her shirt before returning to settle relentlessly on her face.

Patience addressed him again, to prove to herself he was real. "I didn't hear you come back. I didn't hear the bikes. How long have you been here?" Her voice faded away; he wasn't hearing her.

She stared up at him, seeing a far different man. There was a chilling light in the black depths of his piercing stare. A dangerous cast in the grim set of his features. For the first time she didn't doubt that he was far more deadly than Snake, or Blue Doggie, or Hoke.

"Are you all right?" The question cut harshly through her worried concern.

"All right?" She blinked, and shook her head to clear it. "Of course I am."

"They didn't hurt you?" There was no ease in his stare.

"Hurt me?" Her mind dulled by sleep and surprise, she could only parrot his words. "Who?"

"Alice." He spat the name. "And Eva."

The encounter with the woman came rushing back to her. Not forgotten. Repressed by the lassitude of sleep, diminished by his return, but never forgotten. "How did you know?"

"I heard the story. Their version." He shifted from his crouch to rest his weight on one knee. "I'd like to hear what you have to say."

She shrugged, at a loss to know what he wanted.

He touched the tear at the shoulder of her shirt. His voice was harsh, brittle. "Eva did this."

Shocked, Patience looked down at the tear, at the thin red line that marked her arm. She licked her lips, finding them suddenly dry. "I don't know."

"I know," Indian said softly, the savagery of his anger constrained, but not absolved as he looked toward the other camp. "They came together. Alice stopped there." A gesture indicated the exact spot Alice had stood to bait her. "Eva came closer, here, by the grass." Again a gesture that was uncannily accurate. "She waited there awhile. One would assume she was talking to Alice, and to you. She moved once more, in a walk that was unnatural to her."

Patience frowned her surprise, remembering Eva's mincing imitation of a grand lady.

"She waited," Indian continued, then was quiet, replaying the reconstructed scene in his mind. When he turned to face her again, his eyes were bleak. "Then she attacked." He touched her shoulder as if he would brush away the livid reminder left by Eva's knife. "And did this."

Patience looked down at his hand on her arm, too amazed to hear the ache of guilt and sorrow. Lifting her startled gaze to his, she asked, "How do you know all this? How could you?"

"The land tells the story. And this . . ." He smiled then, softening the harshness in him as he touched her chin with the tips of his fingers. "This beautiful, expressive face Eva would have mutilated, if the woman who wears it weren't the indomitable O'Hara."

His smile vanished, the spark of light left his eyes. "Can you forgive me? For leaving you with them? For everything?"

Patience caught his hand in hers. "There's nothing to forgive."

"Nothing?"

She knew he was recalling the night in the lean-to. The awful night when he'd been reduced to behaving as the Wolves expected. As they would behave. Gripping his hand tighter, she said in a tone that allowed no dissent, "Nothing. What you've done, you've done for me. My mind and my thoughts were too muddled to understand at first. Now I do."

"You only think you do." Turning his hand in hers, clasping it closely, he pulled her up with him. Keeping her near, ignoring the heat that rose around them in scintillating waves. He brushed his free hand down her braid, his fingers lingering at the beaded thong. "I wonder if you'll be so charitable when you know the whole story?"

"What is the truth? Who are you really? What are you? I've asked so many times!" Her fingers moved urgently within his grasp. "Tell me."

His head moved in the tiniest negative gesture. "Telling you would change nothing and serve no good purpose. For your own welfare it's better this way, for now."

"Better? You hold my life in your hands and it's better I don't know who and what you are? What good purpose does that serve?"

"It's safer this way."

"Safer for whom?"

"For you, O'Hara."

"Why?"

He laughed then, a hollow sound of little amusement. A signal the discussion was ended. "We begin to sound like a broken record. Same song, same verse."

Patience met his look levelly. "You aren't going to tell me."

"No, and you aren't going to stop asking."

"Bet on it."

"I suppose this is what one would call an impasse."

"Call it what you like." She tugged her hand from his. "We've covered every possible angle and I've had enough."

As she spun away from him, he caught her wrist, bringing her back to him. Folding her arm with his to his shoulder, he pulled her nearer. "There is one more thing."

He stroked her braid, gathering it in his palm and tugged her head back, turning her face up to his. There was something new, something she couldn't interpret in his expression.

"What?" she demanded, chafing at his unconcern for her ill-tempered resentment.

"This." His arms closed around her, trapping her. His head descended to hers. When she would have turned away, he caught the braid again, brushing it aside to cradle her head in his palm.

"Indian, no!" Her cry was only a whisper as she struggled in his embrace.

"Yes." He ignored her efforts as his lips skimmed over her face. "For the others." His mouth teased a corner of hers and drifted away. "The warrior's woman is expected to welcome him home, thus." His cradling palm guided her mouth to his kiss.

For all her resistance, her mouth was sweet and still as he crushed her body to his. Her braid tumbled down her back, a sensuous rope of silk brushing his bare arm, teasing the sensitized flesh. Indian heard his own unexpected gasp and felt the throb of his measured heartbeat as the taste of her struck fire to embers long banked. The need he'd struggled to deny sent him reeling and he held her tighter, yet more gently than he'd ever held anything in his life.

With hot-blooded perception he was aware of every nuance of her, every subtlety. Her familiar scent was the freshness of a morning breeze in the midst of high desert doldrums, the taste of her was smoky heat in his blood. Inch by tiny inch he felt the rigidness of her posture lessen. Slowly, deliciously, the satin curves and velvet hollows of her body conformed to his.

With mindless initiative his hands moved from her head to her shoulders and her back, releasing her from his kiss if she wished it. Yet she didn't turn from him. When her lips softened beneath his, it was Indian who broke away, Indian who moved beyond her touch.

He stood, as silent as the stone that surrounded them. As still. His body was taut, his dark eyes brooding as the summer sun bore down on him. He'd never felt such fear for anyone as he had for Patience. When Alice greeted the Wolves return with her tale of the encounter with Eva, he'd been mad with it. Fear was ashes in his mouth and ice in his heart.

As one demented, he'd hurried to her, the darkness in him growing darker, the cold colder, when he found her lying so still in the shade of the juniper. Even as he realized that she slept peacefully, only a will of iron kept him from snatching her from her slumber. He wanted to hold her close to his heart, to run his hands down the long bones, the soft muscles, proving what his eyes told him. Assuring that she was unharmed.

As he crouched at her feet, a black-eyed savage waiting for her to wake, he'd never known such utter anger, such utter relief. Such utter need. Until she looked at him as she did now, her eyes languorous with the lingering remnants of sleep, her mouth pouting and trembling from his kiss.

She was beautiful, too beautiful, and nothing in the world could have stopped him from taking her back in his arms. Nothing could have stopped his kiss. Pulling her nearer, quietly pleased when she made no move to resist, he leaned the little distance that separated them to brush his lips lightly over hers again. A kiss that was no more than a touch. The whisper of a promise.

Patience's thoughts were muddled. She was bewildered by him and disturbed that her response was as fickle as the wind. He was her keeper and her savior. One minute she hated him. The next she didn't know what she felt.

As if physically warding off thoughts she didn't understand, sensations she shouldn't feel, she lifted a hand to his chest, meaning to keep the little distance that could preserve her sanity and her tenuous control. But she hadn't reckoned with her own raw nerves, nor the crumbling strength that held terror at bay. The beat of his strong, steady heart under her palm was her undoing. All the horror came crashing in on her, memories as raw and fresh as this moment engulfed her. Her mind became a morass of the days past. Images flashed before her blinded sight, replaying every torment with exquisite clarity as she plummeted into quiet hysteria.

In a waking nightmare of recall, motorcycles roared out of the night, dark, shiny steeds of evil. In a pall of dust, new world savages, with war paint etched in flesh by tattoo needles, danced in the light of a thousand moons. The sound of shattering glass became the knell of a bell of doom that tolled for her. And into the darkest part of her vision strolled Eva, a knife curved like a scimitar drawn and threatening, sunlight glinting off an edge sharper and more deadly than any razor.

Patience wanted to shake herself, to pull away from this fugue of terror and found instead that she was trembling. Image after image burned itself again in her mind and wave after wave of fear engulfed her. Fear made more virulent, more consuming, in its delay.

She hadn't been so afraid since she was seven and the black water of an arctic bay closed over her, sealing her from sky and land, sucking the breath from her lungs, filling them with its own murky chill.

She was cold, as then, so cold, and not even the high desert sun could warm her. She was afraid and only the man as true and strong as the heartbeat beneath her hand could give her respite.

There was shock and agony in her face as she clutched at him. A woman clinging to the last thread of strength. A woman lonely in her fear, worn by doubt, needing him, and terrified of her need.

"Please," she whispered hoarsely, and her trembling became shivering, and shivering great racking shudders.

He saw her struggle, more costly than the first encounter when she'd stood gallantly with fear in check. She'd endured with stoic determination and pride, no matter the pressure. Never revealing more than nominal fright, never plumbing its seething depth, nor coming to terms with the toll it exacted.

She'd refused to break, refused the admission of terror that threatened to destroy her. Now it was there, all of it, in her vulnerable eyes. Flexing his fingers at her shoulders, he stood mute, not certain what she wanted. Not sure what she needed.

"Indian."

Her bare whisper was a breaking cry, calling the name that was not truly his. And his heart broke with it, for what had been done to her, for her silent suffering, and for his part in it.

Swaying on her feet, she grasped the edges of his vest, her fingers sliding over abraded seams, nails tearing at roughened nap. Her head was down, tears gathered on her lashes and glinted in the sun, but never fell. On the rush of a grating sob catching in her throat, she lifted her face to him. In a wintry voice, the terrible truth he'd always known spilled out. "I was afraid. So afraid."

"God help me." His guttural words were prayer and plea as he pulled her closer, holding her tighter, using the heat of his body to drive the brittle chill from her. Lending his strength to her strength as guilt and pain flayed him, as the tears she wouldn't let fall were

salt in invisible wounds. He should have taken her out the first day.
He should have turned his back on the investigation that might or
might not succeed. That might or might not save a hypothetical
number of hypothetical lives.

But he hadn't done what he should. Instead he'd gambled, risk-
ing one real, flesh and blood life for that vague, faceless number.
And had done this to her.

"I'm sorry," he muttered into her hair. "Hell!" he snarled in
rage, "I'm always sorry." It was sorrow more than rage he felt as
he held her tighter in an embrace that promised aching ribs. "If it's
any consolation, you can call me what we both know I am. A
cowardly, selfish son of the devil."

"No!" Her head lifted from his shoulder, her fingers sealed his
lips. "No," she said again fiercely. "I may not know what you are,
but I know what you aren't. Even when I forget, I know."

She spoke nonsense, but he wanted to hear. Needed to hear.
Recapturing her hand, holding it to the curve of his face, he asked,
"What do you know, sweet Patience? What do you believe so
fiercely?"

"That you aren't a coward. Prudent, but never cowardly."

"I should be grateful for the confidence, when you have nothing to base it on."

"I have enough. I've seen enough, heard enough."

He stroked his cheek with the back of her clasped hand. "When
did you grow so wise?"

"It doesn't take wisdom, only eyes to see, and ears to hear, and
half a brain to remember when the other half forgets."

He held her away from him, his dark gaze sweeping over her
from head to toe. The pallor that blanched the color from her lips
and cheeks, and marked her eyes with bruising shadows, had fled.
There was color in her face, her eyes were calmer, her mouth was
full and rosy, and enticing. The hand he held in his no longer
trembled. He'd wanted to wrap himself around her to shield her
from her pain. Instead she'd defended him against himself, and,
in finding her cause, garnered strength and calm from it.

"You aren't trembling."

Patience looked at her hand engulfed in his, quietly taking stock.
"So it seems."

He pulled her back a step, back to him. Twining his arm through
hers, he folded her against him, resting their clasped hands on the
side of his throat. The pulse there beat against her wrist, as steady,

as strong, but with a heated rhythm. "You aren't afraid any-more?"

"Not now." She drew a long, deep breath and gave him the an-swer he wanted. "Not with you."

"Not even when I do this?" He bent to kiss her, touching only her lips, holding only her arm twined with his.

Patience didn't react, but she didn't move away when he lifted his head again. She answered huskily, "Not even then."

He kissed her again, longer, slower, teasing her mouth with wondrous skill, and was rewarded by only the tiniest nuance of re-sponse. Only the slightest softening, the gentle curving of her lips against his. But it was enough. He pulled away, reluctance shining in his face, a secret storm stirring in his black gaze. "And now, Patience O'Hara? Are you going to turn and run from this? From what is beginning between us?"

"I have nowhere to run." She deliberately ignored the last of his question.

"Is that the only reason? That you have nowhere to run?"

"Yes. Of course. Yes," she answered a bit too adamantly.

Indian laughed softly. Releasing her hand he wound her braid around his palm, tilting her gaze to his, cupping her cheek with his free hand. The pad of his thumb traced a lazy path over her chin and the fullness of her lips, teasing as his kiss had. When she trembled, he knew it was not from fear. Her fear was gone, it was the need born of it that lingered.

"Little liar." He tugged her braid, arching her neck even more, exposing the rushing pulse at the delicate hollow of her throat. The little flutter mesmerized and pulled him down to her again as un-erringly as a lodestar. "The first was for the others," he mur-mured an inch from her mouth. "This is for me."

Binding her to him with her braid, keeping her with his em-brace, he kissed her, long and hard and sweetly. Patience sighed and slipped her arms around his neck and her mouth was honey and wine. Drinking deeply of her sweetness, savoring the velvet touch of her mouth, the wildflower scent of her hair, he lost him-self in her. There was no sun, no moon, no prying eyes, no threat. There was only Patience, and need.

As need flared into desire, he clung to a thread of sanity.

"No." Taking her hands from his neck, gathering them to his lips, he kissed them. Meeting her glazed and bewildered gaze over their joined fingers, he murmured against their heated flesh. "No," he said more quietly. Then again, "No."

He put her from him, then, blinding himself to her shock, he bent to pluck her hat from the ground. Brushing the dirt from it with his forearm, he placed it on her head and tugged the brim low. His fingertips lingered at her cheek. "I want you, Patience O'Hara," he murmured, "and I need you. But not here, not like this. Not yet."

He turned away, stopped and turned back. Trailing the back of a knuckle down her throat, he promised softly, "Soon."

Patience was still as he left her, dazed and staring after him long past the time he disappeared into the desert. She didn't feel the burning rays of the sun, nor hear the booted step that slipped stealthily through the barren dirt. A hand catching at her elbow, tugging at her sleeve, was her only warning as she whirled to face her newest intruder.

"Hurt."

Six

"Eva hurt you."

"Callie!" Patience gasped. "What are you doing here?"

"I heard them talking, sayin' Eva hurt you. I don't want you to feel bad." Tears gathered in eyes that were wonderfully blue, full and luscious lips trembled as tentative fingers brushed lightly over the tear in Patience's shirt.

"It's nothing, really," Patience assured the girl, who couldn't have been a minute over sixteen, if she were that. Clasping Callie's hand, she pulled her to her side. "Thank you for caring, Callie, but you know what Snake will do if he sees you here."

Delicate shoulders lifted in a graceful shrug, eyes as placid as a summer morning gazed levelly at her. "I know."

And Patience had heard the sharp crack of too many open-handed slaps and punches too many times not to know. Brutality and public humiliation were Snake's method of punishment for small and imagined infractions of the rules he expected Callie to follow. Indian had warned her not to intervene, for her own sake, but mostly for Callie's. He'd learned the difficult lesson that intervention only brought greater abuse when they were alone. One morning of watching her move in exquisite agony had been enough to throttle his objections.

Even Patience had come to realize that Callie accepted Snake's public punishment so unflinchingly that it was unthinkable what he must do when they were alone. But what fiendish torture waited for her if he saw her in Indian's camp?

"You know he's made this area off limits." She spoke as she might to a child, for in mind and thought, Callie was little more than that. "He'll be worse than angry if he finds out, and he might do something terrible to you."

"I know that, too."

"Callie." Patience brushed hair like corn silk from the girl's forehead. Her fingers touched the scar that marred what had been a flawless face. Carefully, regretfully, as it were an unhealed wound she stroked the twisted mark. "Hasn't he done enough to you?"

"Don't matter." Again the elegant shrug. "He can't help I make him so mad."

Patience didn't argue. She could have argued throughout eternity and it wouldn't change Callie. She'd had little contact with the girl or any of the others, staying apart as Indian wished her to, and as she wished, but one would have to be blind and deaf not to see the girl's innocence and naiveté. Only sociopaths like Snake and the Wolves wouldn't be enchanted by her fey, sweet gentleness and unearthly beauty.

Callie was an ethereal creature misplaced in time and circumstance. One who should be cherished and protected, and left to play in shady, dew-strewn glades, not snatched away to a harsh, hard land by a pitiless marauder. Sighing in frustration at what she could never change, Patience clasped the girl's hand, surprised all over again at the fragility of the tiny bones. Pulling Callie with her, she went deeper into the camp Indian had prepared for them. Stopping behind the concealing foliage of the juniper, she explained, "The least we can do is try to keep from making him so mad."

Mad was the right word for Snake. Mad as in insane. But what Snake didn't see, he couldn't use as another flimsy excuse to abuse Callie. "Sit here by me in the shade." Patience sat cross-legged on a blanket-covered bed of cushioning leaves. Indian had made it for her, carefully positioning it to catch the warmth of the early morning sun, then to lie in deep cooling shade in the heat of evening. "Come." She patted the blanket. "We can visit awhile out of the sun."

Callie rubbed her peeling nose. "That would be nice, I never burned before yesterdee, when I lost my old cap. Snake says I just must toughen up. But I do believe the sun is closer and hotter here than in Carolina."

"You're from Carolina, Callie?"

"Yes'm."

"North or South?"

Blue eyes stared at her blankly. "Ma'am?"

"North Carolina or South Carolina," Patience explained. "Do you know which is your home?"

Callie's face screwed into a frown, her fingers worried with the hem of her loose shirt as she tried to remember. "No, ma'am, I guess I don't rightly know." Her frown deepened, taking on an edge of distress. "Does it matter?"

Patience covered Callie's hand with hers, stopping the nervous fidget. "It doesn't matter in the least. North or South, both are beautiful country."

"Oh, yes, ma'am, my Carolina is. 'Specially in the morning when the mists lie low in the holler. Why the whole world looks like a fairy land, so soft and gentle-like. The Cherokee call it the land of a thousand smokes, and I guess that's 'bout right."

"You liked it there?"

"I surely did, 'cept when Paw taken the strop to me."

"The strop?"

"You know, the leather that whets his razor."

"He beat you with a leather strap?"

"Most times," Callie answered innocently. "In the field it could be a board, and in the barn, a harness. When there weren't nothing else handy, he mostly used his fist."

Callie's speech and mannerisms suggested the mountains of North Carolina. Patience guessed her home had been one of those few surviving enclaves hidden deep in the sheltering hills, far away from the modern, sophisticated world. A land where time moved slowly, with values that were its own. In one of Keegan O'Hara's fatherly excursions, she had lived for a month in such an enclave, coming to know its people, learning to love the old English flavor of their habits and speech. A land preserved within a land, where quaint and ancient customs still thrived. Yet, in its people, a land like any other, with those who were good and kind, and those of little honor and austere cruelty.

"The Carolinas are so far away, how is it you're with Snake?"

"Further than I ever thought I'd be, that's for sure. Wouldn't a happened atall if I weren't going home from the church social the very minute he was passin' through. He scared me a little then and

I run all the way home, but he follered me. Told my Paw he taken a shine to me. Traded a brand new, genuwine switchblade knife for me.

"My Paw warned him I was weak-minded and given to dreamin', but Snake said that don't matter. Now he hates it as much as Paw did when I sit too long lookin' at a flower weavin' in the sun, or spider webs shiny with dew." A disparaging gesture heaped the blame on herself. "I know it's wrong, and I shouldn't do it, but I can't help gettin' caught up in somethin' pretty. It's like it takes hold of my brain. I use to try to draw the pretties, so I could keep them, but my Paw fed my pencils to the hogs. Hogs'll eat anythin', you know."

Patience listened with growing horror. In dappled shade she watched the younger woman's graceful moves, saw her gentle innocence, marveled at her breathtaking loveliness. Most of all she heard the reverent love of beauty that brought only heartache.

"When your father traded you for the knife, what did you do?"

Callie cast a puzzled look at Patience. "Why, there weren't nothin' to do."

"Did you want to go with Snake?"

"There weren't no choice. A deal's a deal, I had to bide by it." Another languid lift of her shoulders sent silver strands of her hair falling over her breasts in a shimmering veil. "At first I cried a little, Paw was mean sometimes, 'specially since my brothers left and Maw died, but it was still home. I wanted to take my kitty. Snake said no, and Paw did, too. I cried when he kilt it."

Patience swallowed hard, forcing impotent fury down. "Your father killed your cat?"

"Yes'm, he beat Snake to it."

"That must have been terrible." Patience had little trouble visualizing two subhuman men, one as cruel as the other, vying for the chance to inflict another wound to the heart of this exquisite child.

"It surely was. For a long time I was so sick for home and so lonely for kitty that I like to died." A smile broke across her face, dreamy and thoughtful. "A kitty surely does keep the lonelies away. You look like you got the lonelies bad when Indian rides."

Callie's dimples flashed in a delighted giggle. She was a child with a delicious secret. "That's why I brought you a s'prise." She delved into the oversize faded denim bag she always carried hitched over her shoulder. "Somethin' to make you smile."

"Callie, what . . ." Patience stopped in astonishment as the girl laid a tiny kitten in her lap. "My goodness, where did you get this?"

Callie was nearly shivering in her joy of sharing the one thing she loved with Indian's dauntless woman. "Snake stopped at a store in the country, where there weren't nothing else around for miles and miles. There was an old momma cat there with her babies, when Snake went in for some smokes, I snuk one into my bag." Her fingers fidgeted again, a frown creased her unlined forehead. "She had seven, I didn't think she'd miss one. Did I do wrong? You don't like her?"

Patience stroked the kitten, listening to the rumbling purr that seemed too noisy to come from such a tiny body. "I like her very much. I think she's a beautiful kitten."

"You can play with her anytime you feel bad. I was afeared Alice and Eva would find her and hurt her, but I know you won't."

"Callie, the kitten is wonderful. I know you need something that's yours to love, but Snake isn't going to like this."

Callie took the kitten from Patience and buried her face in its fur. "It don't matter what he likes," she said in a rare, small spark of defiance. "Besides, nobody knows 'bout her but me and you." In a rush of new panic she looked fearfully at Patience. "You won't tell? If Alice and Eva find her, you won't let them hurt her?"

"No, Callie, no." Patience stroked the silver hair, soothing the girl with her words and her touch. "I would never tell, and I'll never let anyone hurt your kitty. At least not if I can stop it. But how can you hope to keep her hidden from Snake?"

"She sleeps good in my bag, and when he ain't lookin', I sneak her out for a walk in the desert."

"She'll be too big for the bag soon, and cats don't sleep as much as kittens. She isn't going to be happy so confined, Callie."

"When she's a cat I'll teach her to run from Snake, the rest of 'em, too. Nobody's gonna hurt my kitty," Callie said fiercely. "Nobody."

"Oh, Callie, I hope you're right." Patience's voice was harsh from the sudden tightness in her throat. How could she make the girl understand the impossible task of keeping the kitten hidden? How could she keep her from being hurt again?

"Listen." Callie was suddenly so still she hardly seemed to breathe. "Hear that?"

Patience listened. At first there was nothing, then she heard the heavy thrum of a motorcycle.

PLAY
SILHOUETTE'S

LUCKY HEARTS

GAME

AND YOU GET
★ FREE BOOKS
★ A FREE GIFT
★ AND MUCH MORE

**TURN THE PAGE AND
DEAL YOURSELF IN**

PLAY "LUCKY HEARTS" AND GET . . .

★ **Exciting Silhouette Desire® novels — FREE**

★ **PLUS a lovely Pearl Drop Necklace — FREE**

THEN CONTINUE YOUR LUCKY STREAK WITH A SWEETHEART OF A DEAL

1. Play Lucky Hearts as instructed on the opposite page.

2. Send back this card and you'll receive brand-new Silhouette Desire® novels. These books have a cover price of $3.25 each, but they are yours to keep absolutely free.

3. There's no catch. You're under no obligation to buy anything. We charge nothing — ZERO — for your first shipment. And you don't have to make any minimum number of purchases — not even one!

4. The fact is thousands of readers enjoy receiving books by mail from the Silhouette Reader Service. They like the convenience of home delivery...they like getting the best new novels months before they're available in stores...and they love our discount prices!

5. We hope that after receiving your free books you'll want to remain a subscriber. But the choice is yours—to continue or cancel, anytime at all! So why not take us up on our invitation, with no risk of any kind. You'll be glad you did!

SILHOUETTE'S

With a coin — scratch off the silver card and check below to see what we have for you.

225 CIS AWMF (U-SIL-D-10/95)

YES! I have scratched off the silver card. Please send me all the free books and gift for which I qualify. I understand that I am under no obligation to purchase any books, as explained on the back and on the opposite page.

NAME

ADDRESS   APT.

CITY   STATE   ZIP

Twenty-one gets you 4 free books, and a free simulated cultured pearl necklace

Twenty gets you 4 free books

Nineteen gets you 3 free books

Eighteen gets you 2 free books

DETACH AND MAIL CARD TODAY

THE SILHOUETTE READER SERVICE™: HERE'S HOW IT WORKS

Accepting free books places you under no obligation to buy anything. You may keep the books and gift and return the shipping statement marked "cancel". If you do not cancel, about a month later we'll send you 6 additional novels, and bill you just $2.66 each plus 25¢ delivery and applicable sales tax, if any.* That's the complete price—and compared to cover prices of $3.25 each—quite a bargain! You may cancel at anytime, but if you choose to continue, every month we'll send you 6 more books, which you may either purchase at the discount price...or return at our expense and cancel your subscription.

*Terms and prices subject to change without notice. Sales tax applicable in N.Y.

"It's Snake," Callie said in creeping dread.

"How do you know? How could you?"

"I just know. Glory! When we all got back, and he taken off alone again, I figgered he wasn't gonna be back 'fore dark."

The sound of the engine grew louder, coming at a dangerously high rate of speed.

"I gotta go!" Callie was suddenly frantic. "He's mad, I hear it in the way he's ridin'."

"Callie," Patience began, intending to offer some encouragement, and realized there was none she could give.

"Gotta go, gotta go." The soft voice murmured the singsong phrase over and over as she tucked the kitten into her bag. "You gotta be good, kitty, extra good." Her task done, she was on her feet and half-away when she stopped and turned back to Patience. "Custer said you was a doctor. Not a people doctor, a animal doctor."

"That's true, I am."

Callie swallowed hard, struggling with the unthinkable. "If somebody hurts her, will you fix it? Take care of her?"

"Of course I will, if I can."

Callie nodded as if she understood the qualification, but Patience wondered if she could.

"Her name's Calico, like mine."

"It's a pretty name."

"I just wanted you to know, seein' as how you like her and all."

"I like her a lot," Patience said in a tone filled with sadness for all she couldn't say and couldn't do for this childlike girl. "I'm honored that you wanted to share Calico with me."

"She made you feel better?"

"You both made me feel better."

A smile that would have brought tears to a stone shone on Callie's face only an instant before it was supplanted by abject terror. "Gotta go. Gotta go."

The engine was a howling shriek now, and if mechanical objects could sound mad, it did, indeed. Patience shivered in the burning sun and watched Callie scamper the distance between the two camps. "Please," she whispered, "don't let anything happen to them."

"If she's careful, nothing will." A hard, callused hand slipped beneath her braid to rest lightly at her nape. "Yet."

Without turning, Patience circled the powerful wrist with her fingers, the tips of them lying against a distended vein that pulsed with the rhythm of Indian's heart. Brushing her cheek over the damp heel of his hand, she muttered, "Yet?"

"I'm afraid that's the operative word." He didn't explain that Callie had been with Snake three months, longer than was common. He couldn't explain what he thought would happen to the girl when Snake tired of her.

"Her nose is peeling."

Patience's remark pulled Indian from dark, consuming thoughts. "Sorry, what did you say?"

"You said she never burned, but her nose is peeling," she repeated, wondering where his thoughts had taken him. "In another day or two it will be raw."

"Today was different. We ran into a dust storm, it left us all a little raw and tender and more susceptible to the sun. She had a cap, it must have been lost in the wind."

"I wanted to give her my hat, but Snake would recognize it, and know that she'd been here."

"What you did for her, petting her kitten, promising to help her, was a nice gesture."

"It was more than a gesture, Indian. I like Callie, I wish there was something I could do."

Sliding his arm around her neck, bending it to her throat, he pulled her back against him. "This is a catch-22. She's damned if we don't and more damned if we do."

"She won't survive this. She was meant for cooler climates and kinder times."

"Kinder than where she came from."

"Why?" She turned in the circle of his arm, tilting her forehead to his chest. "Why do we always hurt the gentle ones? Why are we so cruel?"

"There are some who believe it's the nature of the species, that it's a natural and a primitive need for the strong to prey on the weak." His fingers found the knotted muscles of her neck and worked them skillfully, tenderly, probing their tension. "Like Snake, they believe the fragile, like Callie, were meant to be victims, that it's their sole purpose in life."

"Some." She smothered a gasp of pleasure and pain as he found a particularly cramped muscle and ministered to it. "But not you."

"There are others who don't, as well."

Patience raised her head from his chest, considering him curiously. There was an odd ring to his voice, as if he spoke in more than general terms. As if the others he spoke of were more than vague, faceless and nameless beings. "They would help Callie?" She risked the question. "These others who believe as you?"

Indian's fingers grew still. He stared into her eyes, his piercing gaze reaching into her, taking her measure once more, as he judged what he should, or shouldn't, say. After an interminable time he nodded. "They would help Callie and those like her."

"Who are they? Friends?" With a sudden narrowing of her eyes, her gaze probed as deeply as his. "Colleagues?"

"Custer and Hoke, and their sort are my colleagues. For now."

"For now." She repeated, not in question but a glimmer of understanding.

"Yes."

Indian at his frustrating and tacit best, never using two words, or three, or five, when one would do. "What do you mean by those like Callie? Who would help them? When?" If he'd worn a shirt or his vest, she would have shaken him, trying to jolt the answers from him. Instead she tapped his chest with impotent fists. "Indian!"

"Hush." He stopped her inquisition with a finger at her lips. "It's enough that you know there's help. Who they are isn't important. When?" He lifted a naked shoulder glistening with sweat that trickled to the band of low-rising trousers. "The time's indefinite, but soon."

Patience wasn't to be mollified by ambiguous promises. Shrugging away from his touch, she demanded, "How soon, and will it be in time for Callie? She's already pounds thinner since I first saw her. Snake and the desert are sucking the life out of her."

"I'll find her a hat, or something that will serve as a shield against the sun."

"A hat!" Patience looked at him as if he'd gone crazy. "The girl could very well be dying and you think a hat will help?"

"It will keep her skin from burning and preserve precious moisture."

"An ice cube on a third degree burn." She growled the criticism.

"Only that," he agreed mildly, "but a start."

"Damn you!" She moved beyond his reach, her hushed tone only emphasizing the seething depths of her rage. "Damn this. Damn all of you." Her bitter rebuke continued, her voice never rising, the tone never changing. Nothing that would torment innocents like Callie escaped her wrath.

Indian listened without comment as the diatribe ran its course. When she had exhausted her vocabulary and her voice, he caught her by the shoulders, shaking her a little. "I know you're bewildered and incensed by what seems an unnecessary delay, but there's more at stake here than Callie or you."

"Bewildered? Ha! Where did you get the idea what I feel is that simple? I'm a yo-yo vacillating back and forth, and bewildered doesn't begin to say what I feel."

"What you need is to cool down." To prove his point, Indian lifted a moist lock that had escaped her braid and plastered itself to her face.

Patience slapped his hand away. "Don't patronize me."

"I wouldn't think of patronizing you. And I meant what I said, you need to cool down."

"Sure, in a seep that's half a toe high in a flood."

"I didn't say here," he explained with maddening composure.

"Then where?" Even to Patience the demand reminded her of a sulking child.

"I'll take you there." He didn't touch her again as he waited for her to follow his lead. When she didn't respond, he prodded mildly, "Come with me, Patience."

She wanted to say no, to keep her anger, but something in his look wouldn't let her. Something about him would never let her. "All right, I'll come with you."

"It isn't far," he assured her, only then taking her wrist in his grasp, circling the small bones with fingers like possessive manacles. He didn't expect her to run away, didn't expect her to resist. He simply wanted to touch her.

There were saguaro along the obscure trail, but they grew more sparsely now. Walking where only his steps had gone in centuries, he took her deeper into the desert on a course that was hotter than hot, prickly, sticky, and so dry there was no suggestion of the cooling he promised. The trail wandered, sometimes in directionless ways around paloverde, ocotillo, and more cacti, yet ever toward the wall of a mesa of sheer red rock.

Though it appeared a greater distance, they were less than fifteen minutes from the main camp when he led her to the wall and to a fissure that rent it from ridge to ground. Patience had looked out at this towering monolith more than once, even at the fissure. She hadn't once suspected it was more than a fold in the rock, washed in shadow and the natural, darkening mineralized stain called both desert varnish and desert paint.

Even if the shadow had been perceived as fissure, it would have been judged small, dwarfed as it was by the massiveness of the mesa. But it was far from small, and widened at its base to a cave-like opening. When he clambered with her over fallen rocks, and led her through it, Patience expected a cave, and discovered instead a tunnel. Traversing the narrow passage and stepping out on the other side, she found they had come to a small shaded canyon enclosed and protected by its bastion of red rock. Scattered over the floor of the canyon were trees, a glade of aspen, juniper, pinyon pine, and Douglas fir, and tall grasses standing like a small, still sea. Through the center flowed a winding ribbon of water, less than a river, but more than a trickle.

"How did this happen?" Patience asked as she gazed in awe.

"Millions of years ago water flowing over cracks in the top of the mesa found stratums of sandstone among harder elements. It began to dig a crevice, continuing through the yielding stone to shales of finer, harder mudstone and siltstones. Captured, it formed seeps and more springs. Their rare, precious moisture fostered the growth of plants that are the hanging gardens unique to canyon country. Eventually roots of the gardens penetrated where water could not, cracking the stone, allowing another outlet. And the process began again. Over time it was repeated time and again, with water digging deeper and deeper into the body of the sandstone.

"At the same time, by the same process, another trickle ate away at the base of the mesa, pushing farther and farther along its path, finding other crevices, digging caverns and carving caves. Eventually the trickle above became torrents, speeding ever downward. At the base of the mesa, seas gathered, rising and receding, then rising and receding again. In time, the two met, the center of the mesa caved into the caverns." A gallant and graceful sweep of his hand offered the canyon for her pleasure. "And this stronghold was formed."

"No one has found it in all these years," she mused. Remembering the salty, sweat-dried sheen that gleamed over his muscular shoulders and chest, and the distended veins in his arms, instinct told her the boulders at the mouth of the tunnel once guarded this tiny paradise from the rest of the world, until Indian rolled them away. "How did you know?"

"I didn't. I was looking for shelter for the night, sometimes detritus as you saw at the entrance of the tunnel means a cave or small burrow. With a stone as fulcrum, and the limb of a tree as lever, I moved them away and found this."

"How long has it been hidden away? Are we the first to see it?"

"Only the first in a long, long while. Look." Indian directed her attention to a cluster of markings and shapes etched into a wall. "Petroglyphs," he explained. "Figures scratched and carved into the desert varnish. Hundreds, maybe thousands of years ago, those who came before us left this record of their passing. These records in stone can be found in many parts of Arizona. Most of their meaning is lost, yet by them we know a people passed this way and stayed awhile."

Indian pointed higher to a series of indentations scooped from the sandstone and leading mysteriously upward. "Footholds," he explained. "A stairway to their homes." A crumble of stones clung to a ledge high on the canyon wall. There was little surviving conformation, yet the ruin was still too orderly to be anything but man-made. "Their band was small, but they built well, with an eye for defense. No enemy could reach them from above, nor approach from the ground any way but singly by the footholds."

"Who were they?" Patience was fascinated. "Why did they leave?"

"My guess is they were Sinagua. A name that means 'without water,' but it didn't hold true for this band. Not while they were here. There are other cliff dwellings in other places, abandoned as these were. We don't know where the people came from, why they left, nor where they went. We're left with only the evidence of their passing. Preserved as they are by the dry air, without scientific testing we can only guess how long these might have been here."

"Maybe we shouldn't stay." She spoke in whispers out of reverence for an ancient people who had lived, loved, and died, and then abandoned this hidden place.

"Are you thinking of spirits, O'Hara? Ghost from the past?"

"Maybe."

"Frightened?" He lifted a questioning brow, but did not mock.

"This isn't a fearful place. It seems . . ." She looked to Indian, at a loss for words.

"Peaceful?" he supplied.

"Exactly," she concurred. "Too peaceful to intrude."

"They were a peaceful people, good farmers who knew how to live off the land, harvesting the natural plants and animals at their disposal. If they followed the pattern of other Sinagua, this was their haven for a century or better. I don't think their spirits will mind if we make it ours for a time."

"I still don't understand, why did you choose this place of all places to look for shelter?"

"By chance, no more than that."

"Indian, master tracker." She laughed, and for the first time there was a teasing lilt in her voice.

"Only of natural elements, spirits and ghosts elude me." He smiled and it took her breath away. "How about a swim?"

"In that?" She looked at the stream that flowed through the grove of aspen. That it was larger than the seep by the camp, didn't mean it was a river. "Only midget ducks could swim here."

"Don't be so sure. Let me show you." He lifted the brow again, and smiled, causing a flood of strange, unsettling reactions within her. "Master tracker at work." He tapped his chest in a playful gesture totally at odds with the man he'd been till now. "First we go to the stream where only midget ducks can swim."

"That would be a logical move, even for one who isn't the master tracker," Patience observed wryly.

"Ah, but we don't stop there, we follow the trail."

"Let me guess," she interjected. "The trail of the water."

"You've done this before."

"Just a lucky guess."

Suddenly he reached out to cup the side of her face in his palm, a thumb stroked the vein at her temple. "I like you like this, whimsical, a little zany."

"I'm suspecting you're Heckle and Jeckle." She wondered if he could feel the swiftness of her hurrying heart, and hear the huskiness in her teasing retort.

"You mean Jekyll and Hyde."

"I mean Heckle and Jeckle."

"Should I ask who they are?"

"Why not?" Her grin was a dare, as the natural curving of her lips brushed his palm.

"All right." Indian wanted to kiss her, to taste the delight of her laughing mouth. "I'm asking."

"Heckle and Jeckle are television and movie cartoon characters. Two crows to be specific, and as old as Methuselah."

"Before my time. Contrary to what you might think, Methuselah isn't one of my contemporaries." His shrug was becoming a familiar gesture. "We didn't have television or movies on the reservation when I was a kid."

This was the first specific mention of his heritage or his past. Patience wanted more, but dared not push. "Before mine, too.

Some people are old movie buffs, but Tynan, my youngest brother, is an old cartoon buff."

Finding he was hungry for more of her life and history, Indian put aside his stirring needs to walk with her by the stream. "Youngest brother? Youngest of how many?"

"Three."

"Any sisters?"

"One."

"Older than you? Younger?"

"Older."

"Have we reversed roles here? One word answers are my prerogative as the inscrutable red man."

Patience slanted him a mischievous glance. "Bothersome, isn't it?"

"Yep."

"Gary Cooper, right?"

"Yep."

"You're the Indian, not the cowboy, remember." She nudged him in the ribs with her elbow.

"You noticed."

"I had a clue or two." She hoped he would say more, tell her more. Instead he leapt agilely onto a ledge and turned to assist her.

"We have a short climb ahead, but I think you'll find it well worth the effort." Over his shoulder he advised, "Some of the rock is unstable, step where I step, test your position before you shift your weight."

Following the succinct instruction, they climbed single file and in silence. Patience concentrated on the broad, strong back, the lithe sure step as Indian moved again as if he were born of such country, as if he were part of it. Her concentration was so complete, she gave the changing terrain only cursory attention. Quite without her realizing it, they were on level ground, and the still hush of the canyon was broken by the whispering rush of falling water.

Indian stopped short and turned, folding her into his arms as she bumped into him. "O'Hara?"

She wondered how he could stop and turn without her knowledge when she watched him so intently. In the security of his embrace, she understood how taxing the precarious climb had been, how footsore she was, and how tired. "Time to rest before going on?"

"Time to rest." His indulgent chuckle was a rumble deep in his throat. "But we aren't going on." Keeping one arm around her, he swung away, offering a magnificent panorama with a sweep of the other. "Look. See what wonderful secrets my country keeps."

My country. His words were possessive, proud, and the secrets he shared were truly wonderful. Patience was without voice. She simply accepted the pleasure of his embrace as part of the enchantment of what could only be paradise. They stood at the edge of the topmost ledge of another mesa. She'd begun to feel as if she were wrapped in a marvelously intricate Chinese puzzle.

"A mesa within a canyon, within a mesa, within a canyon." She was transfixed by the land in front of her.

"It boggles the mind what time and water and a bit of wind can create." Indian stroked her hair and looked with her at streams that tumbled down a steep slope, twisting, mingling, only to rush apart, finally cascading over mantles of rock to join again. The pool at the base of the falls was a perfect mirror, giving back twofold the richness of clusters of trees and shrubs, and walls of red rock rising tall against the backdrop of a sky as blue as Callie's eyes.

"I haven't seen so much water in days, weeks, a month."

"For this day, it's yours, Patience. Every drop of it."

She almost moaned aloud, thinking of a long soak and the luxury of scrubbing her hair with no thought to conserving limited supplies of water. Indian had never once insisted she be sparing, but innate caution dictated she must. But the pool, a perfect circle carved by the falls, seemed like a tiny, shimmering sea. "A bath. A real bath."

"I would have wagered that would be your first thought." He tugged at her braid and smiled. "I'll make myself scarce for a while. I set some snares earlier, if we're lucky, our dinner is there."

"Dinner?" Patience was surprised at his casual assumption they would be in the canyon that long. "You intend to stay for dinner?"

"I intended to stay the night, unless you object."

"Won't it cause trouble if we aren't in camp by nightfall?"

"Not so long as we're where we're expected to be by morning. I sleep apart like this more often than not. They're accustomed to it."

"What if they come looking for you because I'm with you?"

"Let them."

"But..."

"Shh." He stopped her with the slant of a finger over her lips. "They couldn't find the canyon if they searched for the next ten years. I'm going now to cover our tracks and hide the entrance. You have all the time and water you could wish for. So make the most of it, it may be some time before the odds are so favorable again." With a little bow he backed away. "I leave you to do the things a woman misses most in the desert." Another smile flashed over his face. "Enjoy."

He didn't ask her if she could swim. It didn't occur to him that he should. It was unthinkable that a woman as confident and able could not. It wasn't worry on that score that had him stopping and turning back before he dropped off the side of the ledge. "One more thing. I made camp just beyond the clump of ponderosas past the pool." The ponderosa shouldn't be appearing, not yet, but the canyon within a canyon had a climate all its own. Plants not normally endemic to the locale thrived in comfortable profusion in this enchanted place. "There's a packet of fresh clothing lying by the pit for the camp fire."

Before she could ask him what clothing, from where, he disappeared over the rim. When she was alone, totally alone, with not even a bird in the sky, or buzzing insect for company, she regarded the pool with delicious longing. Then, shedding first her hat, and next her boots, she began to discard the remainder of her clothing one sweat-soaked garment at a time. As she tossed away a lacy scrap of bra and the wisp that was her panties, she tugged the Indian's thong from her braid and worked her fiery hair free of the confining weave. With no worry that her keeper hadn't gone to the floor of the canyon as he said, she stole a moment to bask in the sun. And no matter that its rays were strong and unrelenting, the feel of it was marvelous, penetrating deep into her bones, sending warmth to do battle with a coldness that never seemed to leave her.

Eager as she was to feel the water wash over her, she delayed, savoring the delight of her anticipation. When she could stand to wait no more, and took those steps that would bring her to the edge of the pool, she was surprised to find a thick towel folded and waiting on a flat stone at the water's edge. On it was a small flask of shampoo, and a bar of fine, milled French soap.

A gift from Indian, a man far too thoughtful and kind to play the role of a villainous biker.

"Role?" Patience hesitated at the water's edge. "Where did that idea come from?" Had it been in the back of her mind all along? Did it explain her obsession with knowing who and what he was?

"*Is* this a masquerade, Indian?" It would resolve so many unanswered questions if it were.

Wading at last into the warm, bright water of the pool that had once been sustenance of the ancients, she knew she must have her answer.

"Before we leave the canyon, he *will* tell me his name and why he pretends." The promise lingered in the hush of the canyon and she slipped beneath the surface of the pool, swimming with strong, competent strokes. Surfacing with an explosive, invigorated surge, she flung back her hair with purpose the soothing water couldn't diminish.

"Yes!" she promised. "Before we leave the canyon."

Seven

She swam, basked in the kinder late-afternoon sun, and swam again. Water as delightful as liquid silk caressed her skin, sunlight refurbished her strength. Like a desert sprite, she whiled away the time. Minutes grew into an hour, then two, then slipped away, and she never knew.

Patience was in a world apart, where there were no Blue Doggies, no Snakes, no Evas. A world where there was only she, the sun, the water, and somewhere near, Indian.

The rapidly changing cant of the sun dappled the mirrored surface of the pool with deepening green-gold shades of aspen. Grass and shrub rustled not quite soundlessly with the secret retreat of creatures ceding prior claims. Dauntless hummingbirds came to drink, hovering indignantly, fussily chittering their displeasure with her. Laughing at their antics, she felt a twinge of guilt, yet not enough to leave the pool. It was the scent of food, borne on a drift of wood smoke that pulled her at last from the water.

Smoke rose in a thin, transparent column from the direction Indian had pointed out as their campsite. Glancing at the angle of the sun, reckoning with surprise the passage of time, she knew he'd attended the tasks he'd set for himself. Once he had erased their trail, obscured the entrance to the canyon, and taken the catch from his snares, by a path other than the one that led past the pool, he'd returned to camp.

And thereby lay an unexpected dilemma. Her own clothing was soaked, scrubbed with the fragrant soap and draped over a juniper to dry. The packet of clothing Indian had provided still lay in its place by the camp fire. Unless she chose to cover herself with jeans and shirt still dripping puddles in the dust and squish her way to the fire and food, she had her hat, her boots, and a towel.

Undecided, she stood at the water's edge, her hair streaming down her back, the towel wrapped sarong fashion around the tops of her breasts. Looking from jeans and shirt, dark and weighted with water, to lingerie so delicate it drifted in a breeze she couldn't detect on her damp skin, she made her choice.

Moments later, ravenously hungry, dressed in panties, boots, a hat and a towel, she crossed the grassy expanse that led to the copse of trees and Indian's camp. With what dignity she could muster, she forced herself to walk nonchalantly to the circle of the fire. Something like small chickens roasted over a spit. There was coffee in the dented tin pot Indian used regularly, and a can of peaches lying on the ground. Patience's bedroll was spread over a gathering of grasses, and on it lay a package wrapped in brown paper and tied with twine.

"All the comforts of home," she muttered. "But where is our host?"

"Right behind you, Pocahontas."

Patience spun around as Indian stepped from shadows gathering beneath the trees. "Goodness! You startled me."

"Sorry." The canteen he'd refilled in the nearby stream was forgotten as he let his gaze roam over her from hat to boots, and back again to the towel lapped securely at her breasts. "I have to admit, you startled me, too."

"Oh?" Patience didn't pretend to misunderstand. Her state of undress was unintentionally provocative, but provocative nevertheless. And at the moment she profoundly wished she hadn't left her bra behind. At the time, the thought of the lacy straps revealed above the towel seemed . . . what? More improper than naked breasts? She wasn't quite sure what she thought. When desire flamed in his eyes, she wasn't quite sure of anything.

With a casual shrug of bare, suntanned shoulders, she sought to mask her disquiet with flippant banter. "Are you suggesting this isn't what every good guest wears to the party given by the man who's held her captive for nearly a month?" Then, returning stare

for stare, with the luxurious scent of perfumed soap blending with
the rich fragrances of coffee and food, and with a bed made for her
comfort lying at her feet, she mused, "A man too kind and too
sensitive to be what he would have her believe."

Indian didn't bother with pretending, or not pretending; he
simply ignored her taunt, as he did her banter. A gaze so intense she
could feel it touched her face, her lips, her body, lingered at the
cleft of her breasts and the curve of her hips. She should have been
a comic figure, with her hat perched ridiculously over soaked hair,
and boots stopping just short of the edge of the towel. But if he
found her comical, his laughter was well hidden in the grim lines
of his face and the stillness in his eyes.

As twilight gathered over the rim of the mesa, and firelight
flickered at her feet, with her perceptions heightened by his com-
pelling virility, she was mesmerized by the look of him. Dressed in
the soft, clinging leather of a tunic she hadn't seen before, he was
hard and lean, every ounce of superfluous flesh honed from him,
leaving only bone, muscle, and sinew. His trousers, like the tunic,
were of a lighter fawn-colored leather, the moccasins laced to his
knees were shades darker. With feathers and beads falling from the
thong in his sleek, black hair, and drifting over a broad shoulder,
he was a man stepped from the pages of history.

A man unlike any she'd ever known.

A primitive man, with primitive needs, who knew what he
wanted and took it. And in this exquisite revelation of the savage
need that burned in him, she knew that what he wanted and
needed, and meant to have, was Patience O'Hara.

Her throat was suddenly taut and aching, her heart thundered,
pulsing in every part of her. The air was too thin, her body clam-
ored for more as her breasts rose in a ragged breath. Her face paled
beneath the blush left by the sun. She was afraid, and not afraid.
She wanted to run, she wanted to stay.

Then he was moving toward her in his long, sure steps, and all
she wanted was Indian.

As he paused only a step away from her, flames from the camp
fire leant their brilliance to the dying sun, illuminating the harsh
angles of his face. Drops of water like beads of jet glittered in his
hair and the clean, unadorned scent of him surrounded her. Without intending it, she lifted a hand to the throbbing pulse at his
temple.

The canteen tumbled to the ground, his hand intercepted hers,
closing around her wrist in an iron grip. Tendons ached and veins

were obstructed from the force of it. Tomorrow there would be the beginnings of bruises, today there was bewilderment and pain, for herself, for him.

"You shouldn't look at me like that." His voice was grating, with a subtle edge of tenderness. "Not if you want to leave the canyon as you came to it."

Patience wanted to deny what he stirred in her, what he made her feel. "You're a handsome and distinctive man, surely you're accustomed to women looking at you."

"How I look or don't look has nothing to do with how you look at me. Deny as much as you will, but you know the truth as well as I. I've tried not to see it, but it's there in your eyes in unguarded moments. Even when you struggle against it, it's there. God help me!" His fingers threatened the very bones of her wrist. "I've tried not to see it. Just as you've tried not to see it in me."

He spun away from her, releasing her so abruptly she reeled with the impact of her freedom. He made no effort to reach for her to steady her. He dared not. "Do you know what it does to me?" Each word was harsh, an accusation. In profile, his face was a chiseled mask, his eyes were closed to shut the sight of her from him. "Can you imagine the guilt, when I see the softness, after all I've done to you?"

"After all you've done?" She didn't stop to think how incongruous it was that she wanted to comfort him. He was her captor, the renegade who took her up on his steed of steel and rode with her into the desert. He was her gentle keeper, who offered days and nights like this to ease the hardships he brought down on her. He was nearly twice her size, and more than twice as strong, and she wanted to take him in her arms and protect him from his guilt. "Recount your sins, Indian. Then tell me, what have you done?"

"Enough," he growled tersely. "And today, more than I intended. Almost." He faced her then, in control again, with the curve of his lips a little too tense, the tendons in his throat too taut from the toll of rigid discipline. He bent to take the brown packet from her bedroll. "If we want to keep it 'almost,' for both our sakes, I suggest you change into this."

Mutely, not trusting herself to speak, she took the packet from him and started toward the curtaining shelter of the trees.

"Wait." Indian caught her arm briefly. "Stay here by the fire. I have some things yet to do." His lips tilted in a bleak caricature of a smile. "Don't worry, you'll be changed long before I'm through."

"I won't worry."

Something altered in his face, only a fleeting look, but one painfully vulnerable. His arms hung loosely at his sides, his fingers curled into his palms as he fought a familiar battle. "Maybe you should," he warned in a troubled voice. "Maybe we both should."

Patience only nodded, and folded the package to her breast.

As quickly as it had come, he shook off his somber mood. "This isn't the way I meant for our time in the canyon to go. When I come back, we'll pretend this exchange never happened. We'll have the kind of evening I wanted for you."

He didn't wait for Patience to respond. Turning on his heel, he moved swiftly past the fire and disappeared into the thick brush that fringed the forested area of the plateau.

Long after he'd gone, Patience stood as he'd left her, listening to the silence. As twilight drifted into the canyon like falling snow, collecting in dusky increments that would bring the night, she wondered where he went, what duty he'd invented.

"Where are you, Indian? Where have you gone to ground?" Her words echoed off canyon walls. A lonely sound where once an ancient people had laughed and played and, as she and Indian, simply survived.

"Indian," she mused, and listened to his name whispering through the canyon. Indian, always Indian. Was he to ever be the center of her thoughts?

"No!" The declaration burst from her in rebellion at her weakness. The denial came back to her, defiance dwindling from it at every repetition until it, too, was a tentative whisper. A shiver swept over her as she wondered if the silly little echo could be an omen.

Turning in place, she looked up at an ever-changing sky, at walls carved by water and aeons, with capricious winds adding their unique design. There was a timelessness here, the wisdom of patience, the serenity of acceptance, as the canyon waited for a people that would not return. Within the walled fortress, a world apart from the narrow confines of convention, the only boundary for hopes and dreams was the golden horizon. And in that limitless freedom, she suspected, lay the quintessence of tranquillity.

There was comfort in the canyon night. A soft sleepiness that swept away inhibitions and enticed one to contemplation and reverie. Wisdom, serenity, tranquillity, freedom to dream, these were the gifts of the canyon. If there was an answer for the madness that had descended on her, and ease for the yearning deep inside her, Patience sensed she would find it here.

Fire crackled, sparks spiraled into the dirt at her feet breaking the spell. Realizing it was past time to dress, she extinguished a coal with the toe of her boot and turned her attention to the package and its bow of twine.

When she folded the paper back, she discovered trousers made of pale, supple leather, fashioned like jeans, but with side seams laced with ribbons of brown leather. There was a vest and a jacket of the same leather, with the same lacings. Practical wear intended, she surmised, for the rugged county that lay in the path they seemed to be taking. But there was nothing practical about the blouse that gleamed like emeralds in the firelight.

Threading it over the back of her hand, she reveled in the silky luxury of it. She liked her jeans and sturdy shirts; her work as a veterinarian demanded sturdy attire. But there were times when nothing was a better boost for morale than silk. It was her one indulgence, and explained her penchant for the wispy bits of lace worn under her practical clothing. An indulgence that had nothing to do with wishing to be sexy or seductive, it was simply for herself.

Tossing aside her hat and boots, and then the towel, she slid into the trousers and found them a perfect fit. In all her adventures with her family, she'd worn leather coats and leather vests, and once, a leather shirt, but never leather trousers, and she marveled at their comfort. These skimmed her hips and clung closely to her thighs, yet when she moved she found no restriction. She began to understand a little why leathers were an essential part of a biker's clothing.

"How did he know?" she wondered out loud, as she slipped into the blouse. How could he understand the leather would feel all the better with a cushion of silk beneath it? Wryly, as she tucked the shirt in the trousers and buckled the belt she found last of all, she wondered what woman had taught him the secret joys of silk.

She was still struggling with the belt when Indian halted under a low growing limb of a young aspen. He hadn't intended his return to be an intrusion, and he meant to turn back, but he hesitated, mesmerized by the enchantingly incongruous picture of Patience, barefoot, in leather and silk, with hair streaming over her shoulders like a dark blaze.

Nothing in his life had been so erotic as watching her. Scanty clothing could never have been as beguiling, no deliberate seduction as entrancing nor as complete as her innocent pleasure.

He was no stranger to desire, it had been his constant companion, held carefully in check, for all the weeks he'd kept her. In one nearly disastrous moment lust had virtually shattered the little honor he had left. It had taken every bit of decency and control he could muster to back away from her. And the battle was not yet ended. Desire would not be still. It stirred in him now, licking at imposed constraint, threatening the resolve he brought with him from exile.

Certain escape was the better part of wisdom, he was backing away again, fleeing from an overwhelming force, when her lilting voice reached out to him.

"Indian."

He paused, leaves of the tree catching in his hair, tangling in it unnoticed. He didn't speak.

"Don't go." She extended a hand in a palms-up gesture, a mix of apology and entreaty. "Please. I have no right to drive you from your camp."

"Our camp," he corrected, drawing a long, slow breath, feasting his eyes on her. "I said I wouldn't intrude."

"You aren't, I've finished dressing."

"Your boots."

"Bare feet aren't exactly indecent, Indian." She laughed, and the sound drifted to him like a lazy melody.

Indecent was far from the word he would choose, but he didn't suggest an alternative. "You look grand, bare feet and all."

"Thank you. For the compliment and for these." She skimmed her hands down silk sleeves to leather-clad hips. "I've never had clothing like this." Her gaze returned to his. "I won't ask where you got it."

"Good." His voice was caustic with his conflict. "Then I won't have to lie."

"Would you lie to me, Indian?"

"About some things, yes."

"But not all things."

"But not all things," he admitted.

Patience sighed and raked a hand through her drying hair. "And I suppose it's up to me to know the difference."

"O'Hara?"

She stopped him with a shake of her head. "Never mind. It doesn't matter. Not here." When she looked at him again over the fire, her expression was pleasant but unreadable. "No more questions."

"None?"

"Maybe a trivial one or two."

"Such as?"

Patience laughed again, breaking the tension. "Typical Indian, never a word more than necessary."

Indian inclined his head at her rebuke.

"For heaven's sake! Don't just keep standing there. If one of us doesn't see to our dinner soon, it's going to be a cinder." She looked down at the spit a little perplexed. "Whatever it is."

He laughed then, and even to his ears it was strained. "It's quail. Several of them, actually. After weeks of canned and dried provisions, I think you'll like them."

"At this point, I'll like anything. Swimming makes me ravenous." She sank down by the fire. Sitting with her legs folded, she glanced up at him, inviting him to join her. "From the look of you, you were swimming before."

"I left more than a little of the desert in a pool further down the canyon," he conceded as he sat across from her.

"You clean up pretty good." She grinned to herself at the flagrant understatement.

"Thank you," he replied gruffly, reaching for the spit. "I think."

Half an hour later, Indian set his plate aside and regarded her with honest amusement. "You truly were ravenous."

Patience sipped gingerly of coffee left to brew too long. Taking a page from his book, she said simply, "Swimming."

"So you said. You like swimming?"

She set down her cup and tossed her hair from her shoulder before she rested an elbow on her folded knees. "I didn't, once. For nearly a year I avoided water at all costs. Then I realized what a hindrance it was to my family since so much of our lives are centered around water. We lived by the Chesapeake, and very nearly on it. There were always water sports and fishing. My fear put a terrible restriction on all our lives. Twelve months later, on the anniversary of the day I nearly drowned, I found the courage to return to the same place, and I swam. That day I discovered water could be pleasure again, that it needn't be the bogeyman hiding in my nightmares."

"As simply as that, you came to terms with it?"

"I was too young to understand then, but I know now I should have gone sooner, to spare my family so much concern. Concern they haven't conquered yet. Twenty years later, they still hover, seeing to it that I'm not too quiet, or as introspective and uninvolved as I was that year."

"When this occurred, you say you were too young to understand. How young is too young?"

"It was my birthday, I was seven."

"What happened?"

Patience stared into the fire, remembering, reliving a helpless, claustrophobic horror. But the story she told was short, terse sentences, with no maudlin self-pity. "There was a celebration, with the usual games and contests. The small sailboat I was sailing capsized. We always wore the usual protective paraphernalia, but I was tangled in the lines of the sail and couldn't surface. My brother Kieran and I were racing. He was an impossible distance ahead, or it should have been impossible." The grimness that had crept over her features dissipated. "But for Kieran nothing is accepted as impossible. He came for me. Kieran came." A hint of a smile touched her lips, as if she couldn't say his name too often. "He cut me free."

Indian knew then he would like to know this man whose boyhood refusal of the impossible saved this woman who graced his eyes with beauty and his heart with bittersweet longing. "Kieran." There was abiding respect in the name. "Brother number..."

Patience couldn't remember discussing her family with him, and wondered if his question was simply an assumption there were other brothers. "Kieran is brother number two. Devlin is first, after Kieran there's Tynan, and then Valentina, my sister."

"And last, Patience." Who at eight braved the deep water of the Chesapeake and conquered a year of fear. He wondered again what manner of woman he had claimed for his own here in the desert.

"My mother regrets the name. Because I'm different from the rest of the family, she's convinced she hexed me with it. A boring, placid name decreeing a boring, placid Patience."

"I think not. Different, perhaps, but anything but placid." No man in his right mind would find her boring. But he couldn't let himself dwell on how he felt. Returning to a safer subject he asked, "What part of the bay does your family come from?"

"Virginia, not far from Williamsburg."

"You grew up there, the five of you?"

"There and other places." Before he could follow with another question she clapped her hands together. "No fair! We agreed only trivial questions."

"You agreed, dear heart, not I." The endearment came naturally and seemed right for her teasing mood.

"Dear heart." She smiled at him across the fire. "What a lovely expression."

"It was my mother's name for me." He answered the question in her eyes, the question she'd agreed she wouldn't ask. "Only my father was Indian, an Apache of the Chiricahua. My mother, Sibella, is French. I lived with them in France until I was seven. An age of change for both of us, it seems. My father was gifted in languages—he served as an attaché at the embassy. When he was killed in a terrorist ambush meant for a visiting Middle East potentate, I came to live with my grandfather on the reservations in Arizona."

"Reservations?" The instant she uttered the word, Patience was sorry. She could hardly believe Indian had opened up to her. She didn't want some foolish interruption to stop him.

"My grandfather was shaman to his people, the Apache equivalent for medicine man or priest," he defined for her. "He was Chiricahua, but unique in that he was accepted and revered by all the bands. I lived with him for a time on several reservations." He took his coffee cup from the ground beside him. "That's it, my life in a nutshell." Tossing the last of the black brew into the fire, he watched it rise again as steam. "Any more questions?"

Thousands, Patience thought, but she wouldn't ask. Questions elicited terse one-word answers. He'd volunteered much more. By biding her time, perhaps he would volunteer again. "I have one," she heard herself saying. "How did you do this, the camp? When?"

"Part was done before you came, the rest while you were at the pool. It was simply a matter of bringing the saddlebags from our site outside the canyon."

"The clothing?"

"The leather will be protection in high country."

"You just happened to be passing a shop today on another of the Wolves' mysterious rides, saw them, and bought them?"

"I went looking for them, because I knew you would need them."

A frisson of pleasure drifted through her at this oblique admission of concern. "Why the soap? And why this?" She stroked a gleaming sleeve. "Why do I need another blouse?"

"The soap reminded me of the fragrance you wore the night I first saw you. The blouse is token replacement for the blouses I wouldn't let you bring when we left your car. Call it a small salve for my conscience." He set his cup aside, his gaze across the fire reflecting only its undulating dance, he conceded the truth. "I chose the blouse because nothing matches your eyes as perfectly."

Patience shied away from the tenderness she heard in him. Denying the ache it kindled deep inside her, she began to gather up tin plates and utensils. "I'll scrub these in the stream and pack them back in the saddlebags."

She left him then without daring a backward glance. At the stream, with the light of a full moon to guide her, she crossed a cluster of stones. At a small sandbar, she knelt to scrub the juices of roasted quail from tin plates. She moved by habit, distracted by her thoughts of Indian. When her task was finished and she turned to go, distraction made her careless. Her bare foot skidded over a slippery rock, sending her tumbling in a froth of water and a clatter of tin.

Before the echo of her short-lived cry faded, Indian was racing through the trees, leaping over rocks, and splashing through shallow water to reach her. She was trying to rise, when the pressure of his hold at her shoulders stopped her.

"Lie still," he commanded, and his voice was harsh with worry.

A little dazed by her fall, Patience blinked and struggled to take stock. Her neck hurt from the jolt of her fall, but her head was still on. The fingers of her right hand were half-numb and tingling from banging her elbow. She wondered hazily why that very sensitive nerve was called the funny bone, when there was nothing funny about it. Neck and elbow aside, she decided she would be fine were it not for her toe.

As pain from her fall diminished in other parts of her body, it coalesced and centered in her right great toe. But she couldn't worry about herself now. "The dishes! I lost the dishes in the stream."

As she struggled to rise, his grip at her shoulder tightened. "I said, be still."

"The dishes! They'll be washed away."

"Dammit, O'Hara, I don't give a damn if they end up in China. So, be still," he snarled.

Patience blinked and focused on him. He was so close she could see the muscles in his cheek protesting the clench of his teeth. "You said damn," she murmured. "You only say that when you're angry. Twice must mean you're very angry with me."

"I am very angry, but not with you," he retorted as he buried his fingers in her hair searching for the telltale swelling of head injury. Finding none, he asked, "Does you neck hurt? Your back?" With each negative shake of her head his worry eased only a bit. "Can you sit up?"

"Of course I can sit up," she insisted. "And I would if you'd stop hovering like a mother hen." Proving her point, she pushed against his hold and levered herself upright.

"Not so fast," he cautioned, and continued his deliberate inspection. With a finger at her chin, he turned her face cautiously, first right then left. Nothing. He sighed in relief. "At least you won't have a black eye tomorrow."

"I told you I'm all right." She tried to ignore the sudden rush of her pulse, sought to cloak the shiver of delight his touch ignited in indignation. "I would be just fine and dandy if it weren't for my..." She caught her breath as his hands moved expertly over her ribs, the heel of his hand brushing against the fullness of the undercurve of her breasts. She lost her train of thought and began again. "I would be wonderful if..."

He'd turned his attention to her legs. Competent hands skimmed from her thighs to the long bones of her shins, to her ankles. He was so completely absorbed in his inspection, she was sure he hadn't heard her babbling, and was grateful he hadn't. It was enough that she'd fallen like a clumsy tenderfoot, but babbling like a smitten teenager added insult to injury.

Her gratitude was not to be long lived, as he crouched at her feet, lifting his head to look up at her. The moon showered silver light over him, carving his face in handsome shadowed plains and setting his hair aflame with blue-black luster. His gaze was steady, unfathomable in the dark. When he spoke, his voice was husky. "You would be fine and dandy, and wonderful if it weren't for..." He lifted a brow and waited for Patience to fill in the blank.

"My foot," she prattled, because he was holding her foot, because every sensation she'd ever known or expected to know was suddenly seated there.

"Here?" He brushed a finger over the arch of her instep, and an incredible shock of desire rocketed through her.

"No." She tried to deny what he made her feel. Then again, as futilely, "No."

"Then here?" He turned his attention to the other foot, cradling the instep in his palm. His thumb massaged the highest point of the arch that always seemed slightly sore and sensitive.

Patience shuddered as pleasure laced with a twinge of pain poured through her like wildfire. Biting her lip, she fought to hold back a groan.

Indian looked up sharply. "Does this hurt?"

"Yes. No!" In a thrashing move that tossed her hair from her face, she wondered what was happening to her. In a rush, she blurted, "It's my toe."

"This toe?"

"Yes."

He was instant concern, searching for swelling or a bloodied nail. "Did you stub it on a stone? Or sprain it in your fall?"

A blush flooded her cheeks and burned her throat. She was thankful he couldn't see it. "Actually," she admitted, her voice little above a whisper, "I dropped a plate on it."

Indian's soothing hands grew still. "You did what?"

"You heard me." She tried to pull her foot from his grasp, but he wouldn't allow it. His grin was wicked, the mischief in it prodding her to admit what she hadn't intended to admit again. "All right! I dropped a plate on my stupid toe. There—" she waved a hand, dismissing her humiliation "—are you satisfied?"

His laughter was like a nighthawk on the wing, rising swiftly and strongly, then disappearing abruptly. The remnants still lingered in his voice as he whispered, "You're one of a kind, my love."

It was just a phrase. She told herself that it meant no more than terms like "old friend," "good buddy," or even "dear heart." It was just a phrase, a cliché. Her mind understood, but her heart did not. And when he bent to kiss her instep, that most sensitive part of her foot, she knew she was lost.

"Indian?"

"Shh." He came to her, caressing the plane of her cheek with the back of his knuckles. "I know."

He searched her face, seeking assurance for what he already knew. When she lifted her head, her full lips inviting, he groaned and took her in his arms. His kiss was swift and hard, for the night was short, and his hunger too great, too impatient. Gathering her close he lifted her from the rocks and turned toward shore.

"I'm soaked," Patience protested. "I'll get you wet."

"I've been wet before." His burden light in his arms, he crossed to the trees and the flicker of their camp fire through their leaves became a beacon.

"Wet leather can't be very comfortable." She was babbling like an idiot.

"In another minute, you won't be wearing leather, wet or dry." He set her on her feet by the fire. Without touching her, he looked fiercely down at her. "I intend to make love to you, O'Hara. If it isn't what you want, tell me now, before it's too late."

She wanted to refute desire, and the madness of it but she couldn't. In this place of ancient truths, she couldn't deny her own. "You already know, don't you?" Her voice was level, suddenly serene in accepting. "You've known for a long time."

"I want to hear you say it. I need to hear you say you want me."

Patience wished it were so uncomplicated that it was simply a matter of wanting, of lust. She wished she hadn't fallen in love so improbably with a nameless man, a stranger. But she did love him, and there was nothing that could change it. No way she could deny him.

Even trembling in dread for the payment of pain this night would surely levy, she couldn't deny him. "Love me, Indian." She stroked his cheek, letting her fingertips trail over his lips. "Make love to me, with me, here where we have no past, and after tomorrow, no future. Love me."

There were no words as he swept her to him. No promises, no lies as his mouth raked over hers. But there was truth in desire and passion. Silent Indian, was silent still, as he undressed her. Slipping buttons from wet silk was no chore for his sure fingers. Only his hands caressing her naked breasts expressed his pleasure. Only his tongue curling around a sun-burnished nipple, drawing it to an exquisite bud with his suckling, told of his delight.

Even when she writhed against him and pulled his head closer to her breast wanting more, demanding more, he was silent. When he backed a step away, and she reeled from the loss, he gathered her hands in his, lifting them to his lips. Patience hadn't known that her palms could be so responsive, nor that black eyes watching fiercely what each kiss and each stroke of his tongue did to her, could be so arousing. Her need was exquisite now, consuming. When she thought she could stand no more, that nothing could ever match the pleasure spiraling through her, he moved away again and, with an expert shrug, his tunic, and then his trousers, were falling in the dirt.

When he knelt to pull the last of her wet clothing from her, his lips were warm and soft as they traveled the path of each new revelation. When the leather was kicked away, when there was nothing but the light of the fire to clothe them, he stood, drinking in the sight of her.

With a hand at her hip, he pulled her against him. Molding her to him, he caressed her with the mere touch of his body. Tamping back his desires, he soothed her with his touch and began all over again the delicious, delightful passages of seduction.

There were inches of glowing skin he hadn't tasted, curves and hollows he hadn't caressed, and kisses he hadn't stolen. He had a lifetime of discoveries to make in a single night, but he wouldn't hurry.

With a sweep of his hands he measured the delicate narrow of her waist, his fingers rippled over ridges of her ribs, and curled at the edges of her breasts. Her skin was honey brown with tints of rose. Coloring rare with hair so richly auburn, yet its perfect complement. And with the added blush of the sun, so much like his own in paler hues. As he bent to suckle at a breast that bore no marks of shielding clothing, he wondered if it were a gift of the spirits that the woman he had chosen, the woman he would have, could tolerate the harshest force of his land.

The woman he had chosen. The woman he would have. The words rang like a litany in his mind. With her sigh whispering in his ear, he blazed a trail from her breast to her throat, tallying the erratic cadence of her heart with his lips pressed to the fragrant hollow. Her hair cascaded over him, a gossamer web, seducing him, drawing him to explore the face it framed. Her features were refined and delicate, but with a subtle strength. Good bones, with angular cheeks and contouring hollows, promised lasting beauty. Her eyes were vivid and dreamy, and he could lose himself in them. But it was her mouth that enchanted him. Her mouth he must have.

His kisses were lazy and teasing, his tongue rough velvet as she opened to him. Desire smoldered, and flared, building with each kiss. She was sultry wine to be sipped, and joy to be savored. Slowly his kisses deepened, the touch of his roving hands became more sensual, more demanding. Passions soared and gentleness fled. But gentleness was no longer what Patience needed, nor Indian wanted.

The time for gentleness had long passed when he pulled her down with him to her bed of blanket-covered leaves. Lying over her, his mouth continued its yearning assault, roaming feverishly over her, tasting, learning. Giving indescribable pleasure. Taking it.

As her breath came in long, gasping shudders, and her mouth was ravenous for his, Indian pulled away to feast his eyes on the beautiful wanton he had created. She was his woman, if only for the night.

When she reached for him, he kissed her harder, deeper. Brushing the unruly tumble of bangs again from her eyes, he stared into smoldering green pools, and with a voice husky with passion that would wait no longer, he spoke at last.

His caress found her breast, and the strong, rhythm pounding beneath it. "Brave heart," he murmured. "Dear heart."

Then they were one flesh, one need, one desire as her breasts cushioned him and her thighs parted to receive him. When her body arched to accept his more completely, he met her fierce demands, seeking to ease the sweet torment that spiraled higher and higher, sweeter and sweeter. With a driving rhythm he plunged harder and deeper within her, taking her with him to the edge of a trembling precipice. When the building storm broke at last, and release washed over them, seething, rising, ebbing, rising again, a savage cry of triumph tore from his throat.

Patience answered, giving strength for strength and passion for passion, calling the only name she knew. "Indian."

As flames from their campfire cast dancing shadows over canyon walls, and spirits of a lost and ancient people looked down, he took from Patience the gift of love and gave back the power of life and death.

"My name is Matthew," he murmured into the wild tangle of her hair as he pulled her down to his quiet embrace. "Matthew Winter Sky."

Eight

As evening came early to the canyon, morning came late. Fading darkness lingered in folds of deep purple and washes of delicate gray, when Patience stirred, stretching languorously, waking in delicious increments. Drowsy, lashes heavy on her cheeks, she breathed the perfumes of night-blooming flowers and wood smoke drifting on the wing of a ground-sweeping breeze. With them blended the spicy bouquet of grasses that made her bed. And on her skin, and in her hair, the clean, unadorned scent of Matthew.

Snuggling into the yielding gathering of blanketed grass, she reflected lazily on the joys of love and loving. On drifting into sleep, warm, replete, with her lover's brawny arms around her, his ardent fingers tangled in her hair. And waking to rekindled passion.

In languid grace she turned, her lashes fluttering, anticipating the first sight of him, her mouth curving, yearning for his kiss. With the delicious agony of desire rising in her, she reached out to him, his name a sigh on her lips. "Matthew."

Her seeking hands found only emptiness. No lover slept by her side, no strong arms held her, no wonderfully knowing hands wound in her hair. For an insane moment, Patience thought she'd been drawn into the enchantment of the canyon, creating in her mind a dreamy night of love. A dream lover.

Adamantly, she rejected the notion. No dream of love could be as perfect, no dream lover as magnificent. Her body wouldn't bear delightful memories in the ache of every muscle.

Matthew was no dream.

Matthew!

Patience bolted upright, the blanket taken from his bed falling from her shoulders. Clasping it to her breasts, she turned in place slowly, surveying the camp. It seemed much as it had before. The fire burned above a heap of ashes, the dented coffeepot steamed on heated rocks. Fresh green sticks cut for another spit lay on the ground. But where was he?

"Matthew," she called his name. The only answer given back was the echo.

Folding the blanket around her, she left her bed to wander toward the stream in search of him. Pausing at the edge of the forest she listened as the rising winds of dawn played a game of tag, tugging at the leaves of the aspen, setting them into a gossipy chatter. Over the eastern rim of the canyon the black curtain of night had given way to a purple haze. Her time in the canyon was almost ended, and with it her time with Matthew.

Suddenly she was frantic. Every moment was precious, too precious to be apart from him. Spinning, turning, the cloaked canyon becoming a bewildering kaleidoscope, she wondered where to go. Then she was running, certain he would be at the stream.

Bursting through the trees, her hair streaming wildly at her back, the blanket flapping crazily at her ankle, she halted abruptly. He knelt on the flat plane of a boulder half buried in the sand, lacing a moccasin at his knee.

"Matthew." His name was only a whisper on a drawn breath. Verse and chorus of the lilting song that repeated itself over and over in her heart, in her mind, in every memory.

His task done, he stood with his gaze fixed on the ever-changing sky, a man as one with the solitude of a primordial land. Then, sensing that he was no longer alone, he turned. With a smile and a wave he hailed her from the edge of the stream. "Good morning."

"Good morning." The greeting was a croak emitted from an arid throat. Her heart was pounding, her knees trembled. She didn't trust herself to say more as she waited, transfixed, as a much different Matthew loped across the rock-strewn clearing.

His hair was loose and wet, he wore only breechclout and moccasins. Obviously he'd greeted the dawn with a bath and a swim.

As he approached her, his magnificently formed body agleam with clinging droplets of water, she was assailed again by myriad memories, exquisite sensations that could never be dreams. There had been men in her life, good friends and lasting friendships, but never lovers. Watching him now with desire unfolding like petals of a dew-drenched flower welcoming the morning, she wondered if there would be any who could follow him.

"Patience?"

"Yes?" Aware only that he'd spoken and she hadn't heard, she pulled the blanket tighter, stuttering, "I-I'm sorry. I didn't. . ."

He stopped her with three fingers pressed lightly against her mouth. "You didn't hear me," he finished for her. Then quietly, his voice deep, intimate, "I asked if it is truly a good morning."

"Of course." Her fingers burrowed so deeply in the blanket they threatened the fabric. She looked away, at nothing. "Why wouldn't it be?"

He shook back his hair, impatiently. A muscle rippled in his cheek, his eyes blazed blackly. "Don't do this, O'Hara." With thumb and forefinger, he gripped her chin. "Don't fence with me, don't act as if last night never happened. You aren't a woman who gives herself lightly, then dismisses it in the morning."

His fingers wandered to her throat, measuring the cadence of her skittish pulse, closing around the slender column of her neck in incredibly sensuous possession. "I won't ask you if I was your first lover. Though the thought is sweet." His voice roughened. "Sweeter than I could ever believe. But almost as sweet is knowing that if there have been others, they were few. And none in a *long, long* while."

Her eyes clouded, her breath was lost somewhere inside her. Her mind overflowed with memories, and her heart with love for silent, stoic Indian, her keeper, her sanctuary. For Matthew, gentle Matthew, the maker of her dreams. Her first and only lover. "How could you know? How can you be so sure?"

"You told me." He gazed down at her, so near and yet so far away. "You made me sure, with your unstudied innocence and unabashed delight. You gave yourself to me without reservation, without expectations, dear heart. As if every part of loving were new and wonderful, and enough in itself."

Patience didn't try to pretend, she knew the answer was in her eyes. Folding her hand over his, she turned her mouth into his palm, skimming her lips over the callused flesh, before looking again into his waiting gaze. "It was new, Matthew. New and wonderful."

Matthew forgot to breathe then, he forgot the fish lying by the stream, waiting to be spitted over the fire. He forgot everything but Patience. Then, drawing in a long, starved breath, he asked, "Where were you going just now?"

"To find you." She didn't evade or dissemble, she couldn't. "Because I know you can only be Matthew here in the canyon, and our time is short. Because I was lonely without you."

"Will you be sorry? When this ordeal is ended and you're back with your family in the lush, green world of the Chesapeake, will you regret the canyon? Will you regret me?"

Her heart might break, and her life couldn't be the same, but she would never regret the special moments in this special place, where, for a little time, Indian became Matthew, and Matthew her lover. Shaking her head, not trusting her voice, she managed only two assuring words. "No regrets."

Matthew's hand slipped from her throat to the nape of her neck. Gently, with only that touch, he brought her to him. He didn't take her in his arms, but pulled her head to his chest. "I wish we'd met differently. In some other place, some other time, when I could be myself and you could know who I am and understand what I am, and why." He raked his fingers through her hair, letting it drift over her shoulders in a rain of fire. "I wonder what might have been."

"I know who you are. You're Matthew Winter Sky. Part Apache, part French by blood, but pure Apache in your heart. I know what you are—a gentle man, a man of honor, and far better than those you live among. I know you have purpose, and secrets you must keep." She raised her head from his chest to look up at him. "All that I don't know is, why? And strangely, in the scope of all things, it doesn't matter."

The weight of worry lifted from him. He'd given her so little of himself, yet as much as he dared. By some miracle, with this extraordinary woman, it was enough. "How did you grow so wise in just twenty-seven years? What gene is there in you that gives you such powers of understanding?"

"My mother is Irish, perhaps she's the seventh daughter of the seventh daughter, or my father the seventh son of the seventh son."

"Is she? Is he?"

"No one's ever counted."

"Never?"

"Look!" With a sweep of a blanketed arm, she pointed toward the eastern sky. Purple haze had turned to rose, and the rim of the mesa wore a halo of rubies. As they watched, the color grew more intense. Rose became garnet, and garnet crimson. The sky was aflame and seething and the canyon floor seemed to vibrate with expectation. As the sun lifted like a great ball of fire over the rim, a burst of light rained down, vanquishing the lingering remnants of night. The canyon was garbed, at last, in brilliance.

"Another day," Matthew murmured.

"And soon, time to go."

He caught the hand that held the blanket in place, and pried away her unresisting fingers. "Soon," he said as the patterned square fell to the ground. "But not yet."

"The blanket," Patience cried as he lifted her in his arms.

"You won't need it," Matthew growled in waiting passion. "If you're cold, I can warm you."

"Yes." Patience locked her arms around his neck and buried her face in his throat. "You can warm me."

In camp, he strode past the fire that popped and sizzled in preparation for breakfast. But the only fast he needed to break was the long fast without her. Lowering her to the makeshift bed they'd shared, he paused only long enough to strip away his moccasins and breechclout before kneeling down to her. His kiss began slowly, then changed abruptly. Bittersweet yearning welled within him. He was a desperate man with desperate desires. If she'd been clothed he would have torn every garment from her in his haste. He wanted to possess her, to have her for a lifetime. And the only lifetime they had was the morning.

"Patience, I can't be gentle."

"I know." Clasping her fingers in his hair, she pulled his mouth to her. Her lips brushed over his, teasing, taunting, sending the madness twisting through both of them. Her breath was warm on him as she muttered hoarsely, "Nor can I."

Then the madness was complete, and there was no need for words.

"Matthew, wait." They'd come to the mouth of the tunnel. Patience was dressed in her scrubbed jeans and denim shirt, the leather and silk he'd given her were packed in the saddlebags with the camping equipment. Behind them every vestige of their stay had been obliterated from the canyon floor. If ever the people who had etched their story in the rocks and built homes high in the canyon walls could return, they would find their ancient home unsullied.

She looked out over the canyon, remembering glittering pools and tumbling streams; the fragrance of the morning glory heliotrope, the wild four-o'clocks. And the wonderful evening primrose that Matthew had explained would have flowers of pure white on the first evening, pale pink the second, and dark rose the third morning. She remembered sunset, and twilight, and the softness of the night. She remembered sunrise, magnificent, breathtaking sunrise. She remembered Matthew. First, and last, and always, Matthew.

She would like to come again to the canyon, yet she knew it would never be the same. Nothing in her life would be the same. But neither change nor time could take this interlude from her.

With a tremulous smile she hitched the pack she'd insisted on carrying higher on her shoulder, and turned away from the canyon. Unhurriedly, each gesture deliberate, her back stiffened, her chin lifted, her smile faded. She gripped his arm only briefly, and called his name softly. It was the last time she would ever touch him as she had in the canyon. The last time she could call him Matthew.

Drawing a long breath, she took her hand away. "I'm ready."

Matthew watched her passage through the tunnel, slow and sure-footed. As she stepped into the blazing sun on the other side, he wondered if she realized that with that step rules and identities had changed. He hadn't cautioned her that she must be more than careful with her knowledge. His name would mean nothing to Hoke, but it would be a place to start. It wouldn't lead to The Black Watch, that trail was too deeply hidden. But his history traced to the point he dropped off public records would be proof enough that he wasn't the brigand he concocted.

One word from Patience and everything could crumble around them. As she waited on the other side, in another world, he wondered what he could say to make her understand. The endless questions plagued him. How little was enough? How much too much for her own good? His face was dark with worry as he followed her through the tunnel and into the light.

"I need to close the entrance," he told her as he set aside the supplies he was packing out. "I'd rather the canyon stay hidden from wanderers like the Wolves. It won't take long."

"I'll help." Patience set her pack with his and followed as he climbed the slope of loose shale.

He whirled on her, a glowering frown knitting his brows. "Go back."

"Dammit, Indian." She kicked a rock in exasperation. "I'm not helpless. The blasted rock is so big an elephant would have trouble moving it, much less one very stubborn Apache. It's a miracle you moved it in the first place."

Indian. In all her tirade, he heard only that. A heavy weight lifted from his chest, and on the heels of relief, he felt profound regret. She called the name naturally, with no sense of strain. As if Matthew never existed.

There was bleak anger in him when he caught her by the shoulders. "Listen to me. I understand that you want to help, I know you can. I know you're not helpless, and I don't doubt you can do anything you set your mind to. But not this."

"Tell me why."

Releasing her, he backed away before he shook her or kissed her. Or both. "When I levered it from the entrance of the cave, the rock rested on solid ground. Now it doesn't. This shale is as unstable as thin ice. One unexpected shift and there would be an avalanche. The rock could become a directionless missile. If I have to move, it must be quickly, thinking only of myself. Please." He touched the feather lying over her breast as it fluttered from the tie in her hair. "I can't move as swiftly as I should if you're there."

For long moments she searched his face, seeing the subtle changes in him as he slipped firmly back into his role as Indian. "All right, I won't interfere," she said at last. "But only if you promise to be careful. I don't want the canyon left to human vultures, either. Nor do I want it protected at any cost."

"Worried about me, O'Hara?"

"As much as you worry about me."

"Touché." His teeth were a gleam of white against the darkness of his skin as he flashed the rare and wonderful smile that could charm anything with life left in it. "Nothing's going to happen to me. I can't let it, I have a promise to keep."

A promise to take her home, Patience thought as she retreated to a safer distance. Once that would have thrilled and pleased her. Now she simply felt bewildered. She couldn't see the last of the likes of Blue Doggie, or Snake, and Eva soon enough. Or any of the rest, for that matter. Yet going home didn't seem to be what she wanted anymore.

What do you want, Patience? she mused. *Something you can't have? Someone you can't have.* "Indian," she groaned in an undertone as she watched him work the rock. "What will become of us?"

Contrary to his warning, the rock moved easily and as he wanted after all. He made quick work of the chore, and before she expected it the canyon was securely sealed, perhaps for the next century, the next millenium. Every trace of their trail leading to the opening of the tunnel was erased. Exhibiting little of the strain of his labor, Indian crossed the shale in a slip-sliding dash. The small avalanche that followed him buried the evidence of their passage even deeper.

Standing back to assess his handiwork, he nodded, pleased with the final results. "No one will ever guess we were here, or what lies within the mesa. The small avalanche is common, a natural phenomena, no one will notice. There could be several more before anyone passes this way again. Who knows, there may never be anyone again." Glancing up at the sun, he judged the time. Mid-morning approached, even the laziest Wolf would be stirring.

Catching his mood, Patience settled her pack on her shoulder. "They'll be waiting for us."

"I expect so." Taking up the pack, he walked with her through the desert.

"What will you tell them?" She kept her attention resolutely on the trail, but as he took her along the circuitous route, her worry for the reception that awaited them increased.

"The truth. We spent the night in the desert, what else is there to say?"

"Will it be that simple?" A blooming century plant stood like a sentinel in their path, the tiny inflorescent flowers completing the ageless cycle of blossoms and death. Taking her arm only briefly, Indian guided her around it.

He walked, quietly, contemplatively, for a little distance before answering. "Nothing is simple with the Wolves." Pausing at a mass of plants that seemed to perch atop the soil rather than penetrate it, he plucked a single yellow bloom. "For courage, a reminder that there is beauty in the ugliest of times."

Patience took the wiry sprig from him, hiding her surprise in close examination of it. The leaves were coarse and hairy, the flower bore an uncanny resemblance to one of her favorites at home in Virginia. "This could be the desert's version of sunflowers."

"I'm afraid it isn't quite so distinguished."

"A sunflower is distinguished?"

He chuckled quietly. "If your name were mule-ears, you'd think so."

"You're putting me on."

"There's a latin name, of course, but anyone who isn't a botanist, or versed in horticulture, calls them mule-ears. Actually they're out of their element here, as a rule they grow further north. But I suspect this patch will survive. If the granddaddy of them all was obstinate enough to get here by bird, or wind, or water, its descendants should be stubborn enough to live."

She was so successfully distracted, they reached the perimeter of the camp before she realized it. Patience wasn't sure what she expected, but the last thing was the complete silence.

Conversations dwindled, quarrels ceased, heads turned to watch their pilgrimage through the untidy evidence of another night of cards and drinking. Clutching her flower, she found the cold malice of silence more threatening than open hostility. It was almost a relief when Snake stepped into their path.

"Well, now." He tucked his thumbs into the back pockets of his jeans. A casualness given the lie by biceps flexed and ready beneath their wolf head tattoos. "What have we here?"

"Move out of the way, Snake." Indian's voice was harsh, powerful, with no trace of the teasing of a short time ago.

"Nope. Don't think I will." Snake grinned unpleasantly. "Not before I hear where you've been and what you've been up to."

"I can't see that it's any of your business." Indian was calm, but unrelenting.

"Let's just say I'm making it my business."

"Let's just say you're not." Indian's tone was almost comically polite given the deadly air of his posture.

Patience stood a half pace behind and to the side, directing her attention from one to the other, but always aware of Indian. If it were Snake alone that confronted him, she hadn't a qualm that he could manage. But out of the corner of her eye she saw the others congregating. Six bikers and as many camp followers tightened gradually into an imprisoning circle until Indian, and she with him, were literally surrounded and outnumbered. Stiffly, she edged closer to him, wondering what she could do, how she could help.

Tension crackled, setting keening nerves on end. One wrong move and they would stampede like cattle, erupting into violence as they went.

It was Custer, threading through the circle, who temporarily diffused the tension. "Hey, buddy." His tone was jovial and forced. "You had us worried. Leaving camp like you done ain't right. You know the rules. We check out, we check in, and then only if Hoke okays it. That's the way it was before you came. That'll be the way of it when you're gone."

Indian turned his cold stare on Custer. One not privy to their history would never believe the Apache had walked into the midst of a barroom brawl to knock away a bartender's shotgun aimed point-blank at the back of Custer's curly blond head. It would be easier to believe the tall, black-eyed man would destroy him without an iota of remorse.

Watching him, seeing the coldness and the cruelty, Patience shuddered at the change in him. Which man was he? Matthew or Indian? The metamorphosis was so immediate, was he either, or simply a chameleon?

"Look, man." Custer shook his hands in Indian's face, a strange gesture of plea and threat. If the small man possessed an admirable quality, it was loyalty and gratitude for past favors. "You don't want to do this, you don't want to buck us. What does it matter if you just tell where you were and what you were doing? C'mon, you can't fight us."

Hoke shouldered his way to the inner circle. There was no bluster in him, no plea. Indian knew he was the truly dangerous Wolf. He waited for the leader of the pack to speak. His wait was not long.

"Maybe our good Indian friend has something to hide," Hoke drawled as eyes as empty as death peered up at the taller Indian. "Is that it?" he asked with a careful precision that sent chills scurrying over Patience. "There's something you don't want us to know?"

Indian didn't answer or flinch beneath the riveting scrutiny.

Hoke's empty eyes found Patience. "Is that it, missy? Is your boyfriend into something he shouldn't be?"

Patience didn't trust herself to answer. Catching her lip cruelly between her teeth, she only shrugged.

Hoke took a step closer. "Yes?" The word lingered on his tongue like the hiss of a snake as he gripped her cheeks brutally, lifting her bowed head to glare into her face. "Or no."

Indian's arm shot out, his fingers closed over Hoke's wrist, moving it from Patience's face. "She won't answer you."

Peeling Indian's fingers from his wrist, Hoke stood massaging the pain from it. "Been playing Indian for real and carved away a little of her tongue?"

A murmur of approval rose from the watchers. A gleeful, lascivious growl.

Indian ignored them. His eyes were only for Hoke. "I said won't, Hoke. Not can't. She won't answer because she's been taught to speak to no one but me."

Clamping his fingers at Patience's neck, Indian dragged her to him. The move caught her so by surprise that she stumbled and fell hard against him. His grip didn't ease, and the pain in her neck was excruciating. She almost cried out, but a chance glimpse of Eva's avid grin sealed her lips.

Reaching out to steady herself, she clung to him, and Indian smiled over her head. "She knows she's my woman now beyond any doubt." He pulled her still closer. "A little lesson from our desert classroom."

He turned his head, scanning the crowd, including all of them in his explanation and daring any challenge. "I teach better in privacy." With a yank at her hair, he pulled her head back, his mouth grinned down at her, but his eyes were bleak with sorrow. "Much better, right, sugar?"

"Yes," Patience mumbled through stiff lips.

"I don't believe they heard you." He yanked her hair again.

"Yes!" The acknowledgment exploded from her.

Indian lifted a sardonic brow, and laughed a soundless, chilling laugh. "A thorough lesson you're not likely to forget."

"Yes." This time her response was toneless.

"Tell them who you belong to."

Patience stifled a gasp, her gaze locked with his. Silence filled the circle, and she heard only the sound of his heart. She looked away, waiting for the prodding yank. It never came. She licked her lips and swallowed, but her mouth and throat were dry.

"Who's woman are you, O'Hara?" he asked softly.

Her mind was reeling, the amused stares of the Wolves seemed to touch her physically. One instant they were ravening animals, ready to tear out Indian's throat, in the next it was her blood they wanted as they laughed and cheered him on. She wondered at the sanity of a change so rapid and brutal. But more than that, she marveled at the strength of the man who must tailor his role to fit their whims.

How far would he go to keep his secrets?

Why?

There were Wolves waiting for her answer. *He* waited. "You," she began, and her voice failed her. Gathering her courage, she began again. "I belong to you. I'm Indian's woman."

The relief in the look meant only for her was incredible, but for the Wolves there was no outward sign. Instead he nodded curtly and turned to Hoke. "Any more questions?"

"See?" Custer rushed in. "That wasn't so bad. Shouldn't a been made into something it ain't in the first place."

"Indian broke the rules," Hoke said levelly.

"I didn't leave camp. I simply moved mine for good reason. We were less than fifteen minutes away."

"We searched for you, if you were there, we would have seen signs of your fire," Hoke insisted.

"Would you?" A black gaze swept over the watching band and to Hoke again. "I'm Apache, you see only what I let you see. Use your brain, man. We were on foot, miles from anyone and anything, where do you think we would go?"

"That remains to be seen," Hoke snapped.

"Fine." Indian's voice was quieter but uncompromising. "When you've seen, let me know." He put Patience from him, but keeping her easily within his reach. "If this interrogation is ended, I have other things to do."

"One more thing," Snake addressed Indian as he jerked his head toward Patience. "Will she go with the herd?"

"Maybe." The fringe lying over his chest stirred with his hard-drawn breath, but Indian didn't look at Patience. A new, more dangerous tension infused the air. His attention was so riveted, there was no one in the world but the Apache and the Snake. "That, too, remains to be seen."

"She'd bring a lot."

"If I say so."

Snake grinned. "By roundup it might not be your call."

"You plan to change it?"

Snake lunged forward, curling his hands over the lapel of Indian's tunic. His face was florid with avarice and rage. "Count on it, good buddy. And I promise I'll have fun while I'm at it."

Without so much as a blink, Indian stripped Snake's hands from his tunic. "When you come, good buddy, come loaded for bear. I won't give up what's mine without a fight."

Backing away from Snake, he caught Patience by the arm. There was silence in the camp as the circle parted to let them pass. They reached the site of their original camp before the rumble of voices rose at their backs.

"Tell me about the herd."

Indian laid the last bit of brush on the newly constructed lean-to before he turned to Patience. He'd expected the question. All that surprised him was that she hadn't asked immediately.

"Snake asked you if I would be part of the herd." She pushed a glowing coal back to the fire with a green stick, then leaned back against a boulder, regarding him. "What did he mean?"

Crossing to her, his moccasins making no sound, ruffling none of the dust, Indian considered his answer. She was being drawn more deeply into this than he hoped. He knew now he'd been stupid not to expect it. His judgment had been clouded and poor, he should have cut his losses, aborted the investigation, and taken her to safety.

He'd been a fool. The accusation had whispered in the back of his mind constantly from the first. The perfect vision of hindsight proved it true.

Kneeling on one knee by the fire, he watched the light of the flames play over her questioning features. He wished again he'd met her in another time. "The herd is the name the Wolves have given to the men and women they will be offering for sale along the route we've taken."

"Slavery?" There was horror on her face.

"Their livelihood and their pleasure. On this tour they've literally been taking orders." His tone left little doubt of his loathing for those who not only thrived but relished in dealing in human flesh and misery.

"Where do these men and women come from?"

"Most are illegal aliens who've been enticed to cross the border with the assurance of a golden life in the land of promise. They'll come by truck in the dead of night, packed like sardines, jolted nearly to death over impassable trails, willing to suffer anything for the dream of better days. A roundup of human cattle." He spat the words in growing disgust. "But not all are aliens. Some will be women who were unfortunate in the crossing of paths."

"Women like me."

"I'm afraid so."

"White slavery." She didn't expect an answer. She didn't need one. Thinking of the women of the camp, some she knew by sight, but not by name. Hard women, with a sense of permanence, and as tough as the men with whom they traveled. Only one didn't fit the pattern. Stricken eyes turned from the fire. "Will Callie be part of the herd?"

"If Snake decides he's tired of her, she will be."

Hugging herself tightly, to contain the hopeless despair that knotted her stomach, Patience exclaimed bitterly, "Hasn't she been through enough?"

The sweet face, still fair with its scar, rose like a specter in her mind. What would the life that loomed in Callie's future do to her? How would that netherworld capitalize on her innocence and naiveté? Then, with a prescient understanding she knew. In a cruel, brutal world, helpless innocence would serve as spur for greater brutality and inventive cruelty.

"What can we do?" she whispered, the pain of her vision overwhelming. "Isn't there something?"

He brushed feathers from her shoulder to slip his hand beneath the fall of her banded hair. His fingers moved over taut tendons, soothing the soreness left by his crude performance in front of the Wolves. "I hoped you wouldn't have to know. But I promise, I'll do what I can for her."

Patience whipped her head around, through narrowed eyes she studied his face. "That's what this is all about." She was suddenly animated, the spark of excitement chasing bleak defeat from her face. "The masquerade, the names! All of it was aimed at bringing an end to their unsavory trade. You work with the police. The FBI. Someone."

Taking his hand away, he turned to the dying fire to toss on another branch. Bark had begun to curl and sizzle before he spoke. "Leave it alone. The less you know, the better for you."

"And for you."

Indian turned abruptly from the fire. "I wasn't thinking of myself, I can handle what I must, if there's only myself to consider."

"My blundering into the middle of your investigation has complicated everything for you."

Very carefully avoiding any admission that there was an investigation or an organization of any sort, he settled back down beside her. "You didn't blunder into anything. You had some bad luck and were stranded." He gathered her hand in his. "Bad luck turned worse when we found you."

He used the inclusive "we," but in spite of his refusal to acknowledge her speculations, she knew he was never one of them. "The worst of it is, they're suspicious of you now."

With a small, humorless laugh, he shrugged away her concern. "The Wolves are suspicious of everything and everyone. With only themselves to judge by, its a natural part of their nature."

"Don't make light of it. I'm not obtuse, I saw Snake and Hoke. Blue Doggie was quiet, but even he has his doubts. Before this is done, Custer might, as well."

"I'm not making light of it. But it's simply something I must deal with."

"Can you?" Curling her fingers tighter over his, she studied him again with a probing, laserlike gaze. "So long as I'm around, can you do what you need to do, as freely as you should?"

"You aren't responsible for Snake's attitude, or Hoke's. You can't be blamed for today." His mouth pulled down in a grim line. "When this is resolved, you'll know exactly where the blame lies, and exactly which of us you should hate."

Rising, his body unfolding effortlessly, he towered over her. He was silent, his expression forbidding. "I'll do everything I can for Callie. I'll do it for her, and for you. It's the least repayment I can offer for what I've done." His expression softened. "Last night was not quite what one would call restful, maybe you should turn in. I won't disturb you, but I won't be far away."

"You won't be sleeping in the lean-to?"

"I'll catch what sleep I need out here."

Would he be keeping watch because Snake's threat was more serious than he wanted her to know? she wondered. Or did he regret their time in the canyon so quickly and so much he wanted to avoid further complications? She couldn't bring herself to ask, for fear the answer would be more painful than she could bear.

"You're right, I am a little tired." Moving with deliberate speed she was on her feet before he could offer his usual chivalrous help. She was afraid that if he touched her she would make a fool of herself. Head down, she hurried to the lean-to.

"O'Hara?"

Her heart surged with hope as she turned back. "Yes?"

Indian hesitated, then he smiled. "Nothing, just good night."

"Yes, of course, I forgot. Good night." Ducking swiftly into the brush-covered shelter, she closed her eyes, waiting for disappointment to subside.

"I'm a fool," she decided hours later as she lay sleepless and alone, listening to the sounds of a restless man prowling the camp. "I might as well admit it." The musky scent of mule-ears wafted to her as she brushed a wilted blossom over her lips. "A fool as much out of my element as you are with your silly name."

A fool in love.

Nine

Another day, another camp, the routine that had become the norm in this strange odyssey through the wilds. As she'd gradually oriented herself, Patience realized their path was more meandering and crisscrossing than direct, and far from purposeless. At first the Wolves seemed to have all the time in the world, spending a week in one campsite, two days in another, three in the next. Once each successful ride from camp merited days and nights of revelry.

In the last three days of miles and miles of arduous riding there had been three camps. And in an unnatural quiet a feverish excitement mounted at every turn. Even Indian was not unaffected. He'd grown more taciturn, more watchful, prowling their separate site, sleeping in catnaps and only lightly. By unspoken edict he was no longer privy to the nightly conferences held at Hoke's fire, but she saw that he was never far from the sight of it. Always positioning himself in such a way that he could interpret actions, and gestures, and, with luck, read lips.

The Wolves' trust in him had been fractured, if not broken. Biding time, they watched him, the final verdict undeclared. Patience had questioned why they bothered waiting when any one of

them would maim or murder without compunction. When Snake
or Blue Doggie would relish dealing most violently with Indian.

In the frenetic days of short camps in progressively rougher and
unpredictable terrain, she saw how invaluable he was. Though the
bikers had clearly traveled in this manner before, clearly performed the unholy service of meeting the supply and demand for
human flesh, it was equally clear that once past town and village
and metropolis, Arizona was new and unknown territory. Patience began to realize that it was more than gratitude for a life re-
deemed in a deadly barroom brawl that prompted Custer to bring
Indian to the Wolves. Among them, no one was as at home in the
desert and the high country, no one as adept at finding the best
routes, the more passable trails.

With Indian at the point, no time was lost backtracking around
unanticipated and suddenly looming gorges. No fording wild riv-
ers with fickle currents and treacherous quicksands. No one was
better at finding water along the barren stretches, the pass tucked
among rocks and spires, the natural campsite. Keeping always out
of the sight of civilization, but never far removed from it, he'd led
without error.

Though still immeasurable, his value had been compromised by
Patience and his concern for her. As with the stone that sealed the
canyon, he would deal better with what he must alone and un-
hampered.

Pacing the small perimeter of their camp, she was aware as never
before of the watchful eyes that marked her step. At every turn
there was someone watching. Alice, Eva, Snake, and even Callie.
Callie with her rapidly growing kitten hidden in a knapsack, and a
look of constant fear for it adding to the distress of her mutilated
face.

Everyone was on edge. The excitement of change was in the air,
like a pervasive sickness it spread from one to another. Change, she
suspected, that would most affect herself and Callie, and the man
the Wolves knew as Indian.

"What can I do?" Patience mused as she stalked through her
area of dusty scrub. She couldn't just stand by and do nothing. Yet,
how could she help when Indian was determined to keep her ig-
norant of what he meant to do? In ignorance, how could she help
Callie?

Frustrated, she kicked a stone from her path, and was pleased
at the twinge she felt in her toe. That at least was real, something
she thought she could focus on. Instead she found herself turn-

ing, seeking out Indian on the far side of the adjoining camp. And as she found him, dressed in familiar leather jeans and vest, as always with moccasins laced to his knees, she remembered the clamor of falling tin plates and another injury to her toe.

"Clumsy, silly, and beautiful in the end," she murmured as her heart filled with love. He'd done so much for her at great risk to himself. She hadn't realized how great the risk until the canyon.

The canyon. That nameless place, ageless, yet lost in time, where she'd learned the meaning of love, and the course of her life had been altered forever. Watching as he bent over his motorcycle, it was Matthew's face she saw, Matthew's agile fingers setting right some minor problem. And she longed to set right the problems he faced as Indian.

"Perhaps if I weren't here." The thought drifted from her lips and took root in her mind. Turning abruptly she scanned the hills and cliffs that surrounded them.

In this rougher, greener country grass grew thicker, in unexpected places. For even the least observant without brothers to teach them, there were messages to be read, clues to the secrets held by the land. From Tynan, the survivalist, a rancher in his soul, she'd learned to read the ground and its natural cover as a Gypsy read palms.

It was Tynan's deep voice ringing in her mind, reciting his careful teaching that focused her ranging thoughts. *From a crevice carved in barren rock springs a clutch of green, and the thirsty knows there will be water, perhaps a spring, or fall, perhaps a deep teneja—the natural water basin in the rock. When grass is sparse and the soil unprotected from ravaging winds and rains, the land is poor and shifting, and the hunter knows there will be little game.*

Looking to the rising hills, Patience recalled the land beyond them, murmuring the most valuable lesson Tynan had taught her. "Where the grass is thick and rich, the land and life are bountiful, and there, in the bounty, will be man."

Grass covered the hills rising above and beyond Patience now. If not lush, it was adequate, with messages of its own. The foliage on the west cliff was tall and ragged and undisturbed. On the east, close-cropped and uniform.

"Cattle," she mused. "Maybe sheep." It didn't matter which, either meant people, a ranch or farm. And help.

A farm would be better than a ranch, its range would be smaller, the dwelling nearer. In any case she didn't fool herself that the trek to either would be easy. But, thanks to the vagabond life of her family and their varied knowledge and specific expertise, she was no stranger to arduous travel and harsh terrain.

Not even Indian knew how well versed she was in these circumstances. Even he knew little more than her parents' and brothers' and her sister's names.

There was much he didn't know of Devlin, who could outride and outfight the best of the Wolves on his worst day. Or of Kieran, a jack-of-all-trades and skills, with a penchant for tackling any problem in a heartbeat, solving it logically and almost as quickly, and becoming master of it in the process. He didn't know that Valentina could take a horse where most men would fear to tread, and on the run, shoot a twig from a tree that few could even see.

But mostly he didn't know about Tynan. Ty to the family. A poetic Irishman down to his boots, with the handsome good looks of their father's Black Irish heritage. Yet in skills and temperament and countenance, were it not for dancing blue eyes and the curl in his black hair, he could have been brother to the Indian.

"But Ty is *my* brother," she muttered absently as her feverish plan began to take shape. "And his favorite pupil, his baby sister."

Shading her eyes beyond the brim of her hat, she scanned the skies, judging time and weather. The day was fair and young. The Wolves had risen early, with an important ride ahead of them. They would be gone soon, and only those chosen as her keepers would remain. Patience had already discovered that all were complacent and careless in their surveillance when the others were absent. Slipping away would be no problem. She could be well on her way before anyone knew she'd gone.

There was one thing that must be done. One consideration she owed Indian.

Going to her pack, she searched until she found a small notepad and pen grabbed up without thought in the hurried packing he'd allowed her for this captive journey. The note she scribbled was short and quick. An apology for what she was doing, an explanation, and a wish that without the complication of her presence he could do better and more freely what he'd come to the desert to do.

Reading back what she'd written, flat, inadequate words, little more than a jumble of letters floating on a sea of white, she wished for the power to make him understand that by leaving she was giving him freedom. "Freedom," she muttered, crumpling the paper in her fist. "How can a captive give her captor freedom?"

Torn by indecision, feeling the weight of the danger of what she was planning, she stuffed the note in a pocket. Then, seized by a claustrophobic restlessness that defied the vastness of the land and endless sky, she paced again. An animal on an invisible tether. A lioness locked in a secret cage.

It was Callie's ululating cry that pulled Patience from the abyss of indecision. Spinning on booted heel, delaying what she was certain she would find, she searched for Callie. Callie, with long silver locks and eyes like cornflowers sprinkled with dew, her tear-streaked cheek pressed to the broken, lifeless body of her kitten.

The small distance between the camps didn't keep Patience from seeing how the tiny head dangled, nor the misshapen body that had once been plump and vital. A glance at the soiled and worn knapsack, lying on the ground, then at Snake glowering down at the heartbroken girl, told a ghastly story.

As if he hadn't done enough, and the pain etched on Callie's face weren't sufficiently pitiful, he reached for the kitten again. No one expected Callie's reaction, least of all Snake.

While Patience and even the camp were still frozen in shock by the untenable tableau, Callie's second scream ripped the still air. Time slowed and blurred to monstrous freeze-frame motion as she fought back, desperately, impotently, but fiercely defending the broken creature she loved. Snake's seething rage escalated, turned deadly. Patience sensed the malevolence pulsing through him in black, pitiless waves. Her eyes saw, her mind comprehended, but her body was too leaden with horror to move.

Only Indian moved. Only he was quick enough to stop Snake from tearing the kitten from the gentle hands that held it. Only he dared to stand between a man who'd become a raving maniac and a cowering woman who was only a child.

"Damn your soul," he snarled as a lashing backhand knocked the callous Snake to the ground. Chest heaving, hands fisted, he was the savage Apache as he stood over the still, sprawled form while Callie stumbled to the only one she trusted. Listening to broken sobs muffled by Patience's embrace, he dragged Snake roughly to his feet. With a stare belied by the hush in his voice, he asked, "What more would you do to the child? Haven't you done enough?"

"Enough or not, it ain't your say." Snake was sullen as he tried to shrug off Indian's hold. "She's mine, to do with. Keep her, or trade her, rid her of that pesky cat, or slap her silly, it's nobody's business."

"It is now. I just made it mine." Indian's grip threatened the fabric of Snake's shirt. "Hurt Callie, or anything that belongs to her again, and I'll kick you to death just as surely as you did her kitten." Black eyes narrowed with promise. "The slower you die, the better I'll like it."

When he shoved Snake away, no one in the silent camp mistook his words for idle threat. The truth was etched into the cold savagery of his face. But as he searched for Patience, his gaze colliding with hers over Callie's huddled form, she recognized a familiar sadness, a bitter impotence, lying beneath the glacial mask. Indian felt he'd failed Callie, and in some way, herself, in not protecting a cat. A foolish thought. Indian had failed no one, but how could she make him believe?

It will be easier for him when I'm gone. The words rose unbidden from the deepest recesses of her mind, and she knew her decision had been made. Stroking Callie's hair as the girl cried out her grief, Patience's gaze never left Indian as she committed to memory this last moment. There were tears he couldn't see gathering in her own eyes, for her own grief, when he finally turned away.

The kitten was wrapped in an emerald blouse and flowers from the century plant sprinkled over her grave, and Callie summoned away by a calmer Snake, before Patience took the crumpled note from her pocket. Smoothing the wrinkles from it she read once again what she'd written. In retrospect it seemed even colder and more dispassionate, but could any words say what was in her heart? If she had the words, were they not better kept to herself?

The sounds of a revving engines warned the Wolves would soon be riding, and Indian would come to say goodbye. Scribbling her name, and then, impulsively adding a postscript, she folded the paper carefully and slipped it into the pocket of her shirt.

She was standing with her hand over her heart and the pocket that held the note, when Indian rolled his bike into camp.

"Time to go?" she asked as he dismounted and walked to her.

"Past time." He stopped so close to her the scent of the soap he'd given her drifted through his lungs like sultry smoke, bearing memories of better times. He touched her face, cupping her cheek, brushing his thumb over the fullness of her lips. "What you did for Callie, and the kitten . . ." He lost the thread of what he meant to say, the need to hold her was too strong. But taking her in his arms would only be a beginning, and this was not the time for beginnings. With a shake of his head, putting longing and memories behind him, he continued. "The little ceremony, the funeral, Callie won't forget it."

"I'm sorry about the blouse, I wanted something pretty for Callie's sake."

"It doesn't matter. If it helped, I'm glad."

"What will happen now? I didn't want her to go when Snake called for her. Yet, with what he's done to her, it frightened her more not to go."

"An old habit. In her simple mind they're easiest, even when they hurt."

"Callie shouldn't have to hurt." She caught his hand, lacing her fingers through his. Her lips grazed the first evidence of a bruise beginning to discolor his knuckles. "No one should."

"In a perfect world, perhaps not." With their joined hands he lifted her face to his. "In a perfect world we would have met, but not like this."

Patience was spared the need of dragging an answer from a mind in turmoil by Hoke's demanding call for Indian.

"My canteen." Indian didn't release her. "Have you seen it?"

"I filled it and put it in the lean-to out of the sun." She could have fetched it for him and had it waiting at the first sound of his engine, but then she wouldn't have the diversion she needed.

Squeezing her fingers, he stepped away. "I won't be a minute."

Patience folded the hand he'd held over her breast as she waited for her chance. He moved with the unhurried, ground-eating step, the quiet step that never seemed to change. The supple vest swung with a barely detectable motion around his slim waist, leather trousers clung to his hips and thighs. A bare arm bunched as he grasped the support of the shelter and ducked inside. The moment for which she waited.

Throwing off her distraction, she rushed to his bike. There was a pouch for the canteen attached closely to the base of the handlebars, she slid the note to the bottom of it. He would find it there when he drank the water she'd taken from the swiftest part of the stream that flowed by the camp.

She was still at the bike when he stepped from the lean-to. A brow tilted in question and his lips curled in a half smile. "Hurrying me along?"

Patience shook her head, and when he came near, took the canteen from him. "Warm," she said as heat from it filled her palm.

Carefully, she slipped it into the pouch, shielding the note from his sight, insuring it wouldn't be found too soon.

"Warm, but not boiling as it would be from full sun." Indian wondered why they were speaking of canteens and water at all. He wondered at her strange mood. "What is it, O'Hara?"

The tenderness in him nearly destroyed her resolve. It would be so natural to go into his arms, to comfort and be comforted. But if she allowed that moment of weakness, could she do what she'd planned? Even if it were best for him, could she go if they shared a single kiss? Her mind knew it was senseless superstition, but her heart insisted that the hidden canyon was an enchanted place, where everything had been beautiful, and nothing binding. But here, beyond the enchantment, if her control slipped, could she ever leave him?

"O'Hara?"

Rousing from her concern, she found he'd mounted his bike and watched her curiously. "It's nothing. It's Callie." Both thoughts spilled from her in haste. Raking back the bangs that tumbled over her forehead, she shook her head. "I'm sorry, I'm babbling."

"Four words could hardly be called babbling." He took her hands in both of his, sensing her turmoil. "Which is it? Nothing, or Callie?"

"Both. Neither." She was nearly frantic for him to leave.

"Double talk? To hide what you're feeling?"

She looked into his face, his beloved face. "Double talk," she admitted honestly. "Because I don't know what I feel."

He accepted her excuse, recognizing it as partial truth. "Magda and Lou are staying behind. You'll be all right?"

She knew both women only by sight, but enough to recognize that one was lazy, the other stupid. A providential choice of jailers. Perfect for her plan. "I'll be fine."

"You will, won't you," he said thoughtfully.

"Indian." She was reaching for him, her hands nearly touching him, fulfilling one last need, when she realized what she was doing. With an exaggerated flutter of her fingers, dismissing the gesture, she tucked them firmly into the back pockets of her jeans.

Something about the urgency in her voice, and in the bittersweet gesture disturbed him, but he didn't ask again. Only a frown and a slight narrowing of his eyes expressed his concern.

"I'm just being temperamental and anxious," Patience insisted.

"Are you?" he asked, for he couldn't remember her ever being temperamental. "Anxious about what?"

"Nothing."

"Nothing?" Again the brow arched, he wasn't making this any easier.

Her shoulders lifted inarticulately, her nails scored the insides of her pockets. "You'll be careful?"

"Always." He flashed his smile, accepting the abrupt change of subjects, filing away his questions for another time. "This is a short trip, I'll be back before you know it."

As the increasing tumult of roaring engines signaled their time was done, he smiled again and waved. He was lost in a rising swirl of suffocating dust before Patience turned away to begin preparations for her own venture.

The ground shifted beneath her feet, the small slide threatened to become an avalanche as Patience fought to keep her balance. With a tumbling lunge she caught the twisted branch of a stunted juniper and slowed her descent. Wiping sweat and dirt from her eyes, she peered up at the wall of red rock. On closer inspection it was steeper and more treacherous than it appeared when she'd begun her climb. Now it was clear she couldn't climb it in boots and bare-handed.

"Where are you when I need you, Kieran, you and your bag of tools and sure solutions?" Wearily admitting defeat, and regretting the time lost to poor judgment, she let go of the limb. In a race with falling shale, she leapt and slid down the steep incline. Once on firmer ground, she beat dust from her clothing, and weighed her options.

"You go around, Patience, me girl. There are no other options." Going around the massive mesa, searching for a better way to the top would add hours to her trip. She would fall far short of her goal for the day, but there was no remedy for it. And agonizing over lost time was only more lost time.

Hitching the chafing strap of her pack to another position, she tucked her head down to shield her eyes from the glare of the sun and took the route she should have in the beginning. Though the path was demanding, and her progress slow, there was still time to think. To keep her thoughts from turning to Matthew, she concentrated on Magda and Lou. Had either roused from her lazy stupor to investigate Indian's too-quiet camp? Or realized that the form lying in full sun as shade shifted beneath the tree with the aging day, was only shirt and jeans filled with brush? Patience regretted the hat she'd left tilted over the scarecrow figure as she felt the tight pull of the sun burning her forehead.

If time and distance weren't critical, she would have followed the path of wisdom and rested in the heat of the afternoon, traveling in early twilight and into the first of night. But time was a luxury, and every step would bring her closer to help. As she moved away from water, she drank sparingly from her canteen, and scanned the surrounding terrain for signs of more. A natural tank, a cloistered stream, a *teneja*.

Though the sky was clear, and summer rains rare, she stayed clear of gravely dry washes. A sudden gathering of thunderheads, a cloudburst, and a wall of water would roar down the chasm, filling it, taking with it anything and anyone in its path.

The land she crossed was wider, less confined, with rocks and boulders scattered among the eroded rubble of millenia. Shrunken cacti in need of water marked her path, and a Gila woodpecker eyed her suspiciously from a hole carved in the highest saguaro. Overhead a scavenging, wide-winged vulture waited for something to die. If not the peculiar biped so rare in his territory, there would be other prey. There always was.

As the day wore on, the trail grew rougher and began to climb, while her feathered companion kept his vigil. He shouldn't have disturbed her, but he did. She caught herself glancing up when she should be watching the trail. After she'd stumbled for the second time, and her canteen tumbled down the precarious slope she'd just climbed, her temper flared. Snatching up a handful of loose stone and shrugging from her pack, she lurched to her feet.

"Go away!" A stone sailed into the sky, then plummeted harmlessly to the ground. The vulture swooped and circled, arrogantly unconcerned.

"Shoo!" Another stone flew. "Scat!" An angry huff sent her sweat-soaked bangs from her forehead. "One last chance." The largest stone was drawn back, threatening, desperate. "Do you hear me, bird?"

An arm hooked through hers, the stone was taken from her hand. "I don't think he does."

"Matthew?" She blinked, wondering if the sun had baked her brains and the wilderness stolen her sanity. Then as her vision cleared, she whispered, "Why are you here? I thought . . ."

"You thought I would be miles away by now, foolishly believing you would be in camp when I returned." He tossed the stone away and pulled her roughly to him. "But that's the extent of your thinking, wasn't it? You didn't think once that you might die out here, lost and alone, did you?"

"I didn't plan to be lost or to die."

"Your feathered friend doesn't agree."

"My feathered friend is in for a long wait." She pulled away, only then questioning how he'd come here.

"You could have fallen, or been caught in a slide." He was angry and fierce, and implacable.

"Don't forget raging coyotes and hairy tarantulas, or an attack from a mad saguaro." Frustrations forgotten, with her feet planted firmly now, her chin rose to a fighting angle. In the unforgiving light, with red dust caked to her shirt and leather jeans, and her face flushed from heat and exhaustion, she was magnificently furious. "Why did you come here?"

"Why?" Matthew's face was ashen beneath its normal coppery hue. His gaze heated and his mouth stark. "You wander into the hills alone, and you ask why I came after you?"

"I didn't wander anywhere," Patience snapped. Something in his stance warned her that he was at the end of his control, but she goaded him anyway. "I made it clear in my note that I wanted nothing so much as to get away from you, so why *are* you here?"

"I haven't read any damnable note," he said in a voice so quiet it sent shivers through her. Before she could dodge away, he locked his fingers at the back of her neck, letting her feel the pressure of each pad as he pulled her back to him. "Perhaps this will explain why I'm here."

His mouth covered hers, ravaged hers. She stood woodenly beneath the assault, but as the passion beneath the anger touched her, a shiver of response fluttered up her spine and the flush of desire swept her own anger away. She'd feared one kiss beyond the canyon and she would be lost. One kiss, and she was.

Abruptly, without warning, he lifted his head to stare down at her. "What the hell do you mean, why? You know why. You know it was this."

When his lips reclaimed hers, it was more than a kiss; he staked a claim, branded, persuaded, possessed. The ground was unsteady, the world tilted on its axis. When his tongue traced the softness of her mouth, she lost her hold on reality and tumbled into a vortex of sensations. She was hot, and tired, and dirty. He was overbearing and a little cruel in his anger, but none of it mattered as he plundered and caressed with a savage pleasure.

When she pushed away, to breathe, to think, he smiled down at her and her world tilted again.

"That's why I came." With no further word, he bent to pick up her pack. Hefting it in his palm, his smile turned grave. "Traveling light?"

"Light enough." The rush of her heart was just returning to normal and her breath still came in gasps. When he turned down the trail, back the way she'd come, she blurted, "I'm not going back. Nothing you can do or say will make me."

Swinging around, he caught her face in his palm, his thumb brushed over her lips in a familiar gesture. "Nothing?"

Patience shook free of his touch and stepped beyond his reach. "Nothing, not even that."

"That?" His voice was low, calm.

"The kiss." Slipping her thumbs in the belt loops of her trousers, she tried to match calm for calm. "That's what it was about, wasn't it? To persuade me to go back."

"No, it wasn't. In fact it was never my intention that either of us would go back." Leaving her gaping, he retraced his path to the floor of the canyon. His own pack was there, where he'd thrown it when he saw Patience fall. As the canteen slipped over the edge, and in the moment he thought she would fall with it, he'd lost all reason. As Matthew Winter Sky, the impassive Apache, had never done before.

He'd charged up the rocky track, losing sight of her through its twists and turns, cursing and praying, and damning himself with every step. When he found her flinging rocks and shooing away a vulture as if it were a troublesome barnyard fowl, he wanted to throttle her for frightening him, and kiss her for being the irrepressible O'Hara she'd always been. In the end, he'd channeled every conflicting emotion into his kiss.

Slipping his own pack over his shoulder, he realized he'd punished both Patience and himself with the kiss. Why? he wondered. Did he need to push her away even as he pulled her close? Was it guilt? Or simply that she made him feel things he'd never expected, or wanted?

Wheeling around, he stared at the hillock where Patience waited. "Do I want this now? Is there room in my life for a woman?"

He had no answers. All that was clear was that he had to take Patience out of the desert before the Wolves found her again.

He covered the distance between them at a slower pace this time, making a detour down the slope to rescue her canteen. It would be needed before they reached a safe house and civilization. At the top of the rise, he found her resting under the broad-leafed shade of an ancient Arizona oak. Pulling free the hat he'd clipped to his pack, he set it rakishly on her head. "I thought you might need this more than the lady you left behind."

"She was a good likeness, wouldn't you say?" Patience adjusted the hat, and was grateful for the protection she'd missed.

"A few inches bigger than you, but a number of pounds lighter." He matched his tone to hers as, by intuitive consensus, they skirted the real issue between them.

Patience pushed back the brim of the hat she'd adjusted to look up at him. "You didn't read my note?"

"No."

"Then how?" She sighed, not understanding. "How did you know? What brought you here?"

"I turned back. We were halfway to the ranch where we were expected, but the sense that something was wrong was so strong I had to come back to camp. When I discovered your ruse, I followed your trail."

"Just like that? The Wolves let you leave them, as suspicious as they've been of you?"

"It wasn't a question of letting me do anything. I did what I had to, and no one was going to stop me."

"What about your investigation?"

His face was bland. "What investigation?"

"We're playing that game again?"

"None of this is a game."

Patience shrugged aside his comment. It did no good to argue with Matthew at his most obstinate. "What about Callie?"

"She'll be okay for a while. There are snags at the other end."

"Across the border, with the illegal aliens?"

"I'd forgotten that you knew." He questioned what else he might have told her in a weak moment and then forgotten. It wasn't like him to talk, and even less like him to forget. Patience O'Hara was a dangerous woman. Dangerous, indeed.

But dangerous or not, they needed to move. Assessing the path she'd taken, he found he approved. She'd chosen wisely and with thought. She would do well in his country.

"We need to move on." Gruffly, he sidestepped new needs and new desires. It didn't matter how well she suited his country or him, when she knew all the truth, nothing would matter. Taking her hand, he pulled her to her feet. "We've a lot of ground to cover. The more distance we can put between ourselves and the others, the better."

"They'll come looking?"

"With a vengeance." He pondered telling her the complete truth, deciding quickly that she should know. "The penalty for escape is death, Patience."

She paled beneath the shading brim of her hat. "For both of us?"

"Yes."

"Is that the reason you aren't taking me back? Because you can't?"

"We aren't going back for a lot of reasons," he answered cryptically. "We need to move. Now. To make the most of the daylight we have left."

"What about your bike?"

"I ditched it in a canyon a mile from here. When your trail was fresher and I knew I was close, I didn't want to draw any more attention to you."

"I tried to cover my tracks."

"You did."

"But not from you." Indian, master tracker, she should have known he would find her, no matter where she went. Without another word, slinging the pack over her shoulder, she turned to continue her climb over the small hillock, with Matthew only a pace behind.

They halted in a small clearing, one of nature's surprises. In a rocky realm that seemed shrunken with thirst, suddenly there was water. First, it was the sound of only a trickle. But as they'd drawn nearer, the trickle became a quiet fall spilling over algae-draped rocks, then slipping into a quiet pool. Vertical cliffs cast deep shadows, hurrying the night. A breeze channeling through this small corridor danced among the limbs of a huge sycamore and rattled the daggerlike leaves of a sotol. And as the sun glided beneath the west ridge, dusk fell over another canyon.

"This should serve," Matthew decided as he listened to tree frogs just beginning to croak. "We'll stop here for the night."

Patience sank down on a boulder, letting her pack slip from her shoulder, too tired and too thirsty to comment.

"I'll check the grounds, then make camp." Matthew set his pack aside as he watched her in concern.

Patience got to her feet, trying to shake off her fatigue. "I'll help."

"Stay. Sit." His hand at her shoulder stopped her from a purposeless, headlong rush.

Anger flashed in her eyes, and the spark restored her spirit. "Sit! Stay! Next you'll pat me on the head and call me Rover. I can help. I *will* help."

"You're tired, O'Hara. You've walked a long way."

"No further than you."

"It isn't the same. The Apache was born and bred to survive where others perish of hunger and thirst and sunstroke. It's no great feat of my own, simply part of my heritage. If you'll rest, I promise not to pat you on the head."

Patience smiled then. "I'll rest when you do, Matthew, and not before." Taking off her hat, letting the breeze cool her sweat-soaked head, she looked around. "Firewood?"

Even an Apache knew when he'd met his match. He knew as well that the smallest light shone for miles in this lightless land. The Wolves hadn't found their trail yet, he'd covered it too well and it was too soon, but caution was not easily put aside. "We'll risk a small fire, so long as the fuel is dry and the flame is shielded well."

"The deadfall by the pool should be dry enough to make little smoke."

"We'll make camp there." Then he could save her a few steps.

Making camp was simple when one traveled fast and light. Matthew had the chosen area cleared, a pit scraped out for the fire, and their blankets spread by it before Patience finished with the wood. Deciding he would wait until the fire was lit to prepare the little food they had, he went to join her in her chore.

As he crossed to her, a sound, one that couldn't be mistaken, sent fear roiling in the pit of his stomach. "Patience!" She didn't answer, didn't move. The rattler coiled at her feet buzzed angrily. Coils tightening, rattles moving faster than the eye could see, its head pulled back, weaving, ready to strike. "For the love of God, Patience, don't move."

"Matthew?"

He heard the panic, the abject terror, in a second she would bolt. His handgun was still in his pack. He reached into the lacings of his moccasin for his knife, it wasn't there. Cursing, he remembered it lay on a stone by the fire pit, with the sticks he'd cut to fashion into lances. There was no time to go back.

"Matthew!" Terror was shrill in her voice.

"I'm here." Sweat beaded his forehead and trickled in his eyes. In an agonizing journey, he put one foot carefully in front of the other as he eased in a half circle. If he could just reach the dead-fall and a branch.

Rattles buzzed, coils loosened, the triangular head stopped weaving. In a blur the snake struck. Matthew's lunging interception was quicker. As her frenzied scream reverberated from canyon walls, fangs meant for Patience buried deep in his forearm.

Shaking free, catching the recoiling snake at the back of its head, he flung it away. Patience was safe from it when he turned to her, blood welling from twin wounds in a distended vein, the pain and vertigo already beginning.

"O'Hara?"

Ten

___

"I'm here." Patience acted quickly, with a cool head, every shred of terror obliterated by fear for Matthew. "Don't move."

Guiding him to the ground, she lashed her belt around his arm a few inches above the bite, pulling it tight enough to impede circulation, but not enough to block it completely. "Your knife!" she cried when she found the sheath inside his moccasin empty. "Where is it?"

"By the fire." The venom had gone directly into his bloodstream, the shock and sickness moving swiftly.

"Do you have antivenom?" She felt his gaze on her, losing its focus. "Matthew." She touched his face, drawing his attention back to her. "Do you have a snake bite kit?"

"Kit." He drifted away, then, with agonized effort, refocused. "Not for me."

"Are you sensitive to the serum?" If he were, to inject it would cause immediate death. "Matthew." She called his name again, keeping him with her. "You can't take the serum, can you?"

"No."

Patience slumped with the burden of her fear for him, but an instant later she was straightening, calm and clinical, the professional. "Then we'll do it as it has been done for hundreds of years."

Racing to the camp he'd made, she searched through his pack for the kit. With it and the knife, she hurried back to him. Kneeling by him, with suction cups for extracting the venom, and antiseptic to clean the wound, she made the first cut.

Matthew muttered and thrashed. Patience was instantly by his side, gathering him in her arms, holding him tightly, keeping him from doing greater injury to his grotesquely swollen arm.

"O'Hara?"

"I'm here. I'll always be here."

He subsided against her, his breathing erratic. "Sibella?" He frowned, his eyes moving rapidly beneath bluish lids. Then in French, *"Ma mère?"*

Sibella. Mother. Matthew's mother.

In the hours of the night, Patience had come to know them all. His Apache father, Daniel Gray Sky, the dashing attaché of the American Embassy in France, who died in a terrorist attack; Sibella, the very young, the very spoiled, the very winsome daughter of a wealthy French scholar; Robert Morning Sky, shaman, teacher, beloved grandfather, Matthew's family from the age of seven.

There were other names, Jeb, Mitch, Jamie, finally Simon, and then The Watch. From guttural half sentences, and frantic warnings, she walked with him through vivid recreations of a dangerous, clandestine life. Putting bits and pieces together, she deduced that The Watch was a secret, investigative government agency. Simon was its commander, Jeb and Mitch, and Jamie, like Matthew, were fellow agents. More than that, they were trusted friends.

In his delirious ramblings she heard the names of places, familiar and unfamiliar. Places where he'd spent his life after the reservations and the University of Arizona. In the passage of night marked by fever and agony, he grew oddly preoccupied with faces. The hurt, mutilated faces of Callie and someone called Jocie. In rare moments of respite, it was impotent concern for them that ultimately disturbed his feverish stupor. Their names tumbled repeatedly from cracked lips until in Patience's mind they were one with his agony.

It was her name that sent pain lancing through her. O'Hara, the name that had become dear to her, called time and again. Always with mutterings of guilt for what he'd done to her by keeping her prisoner in the desert. Pleading that she not hate him.

Keeping her vigil through the night, tending the fire, holding him when he grew restless, she listened to the life of Matthew Winter Sky.

"Winter Sky," she murmured as dawn broke over the rim of the canyon. A strong name for a strong man. An uncommon name. A man of uncommon honor.

When he fell into normal sleep, fearful she would disturb him, she left his side at last, going wearily to her own blanket. Lying across the fire from him, she watched as the light of the blaze flickered over his ashen features. Tears streaked in glittering paths down her face for a keen mind wandering in a blacker darkness than any night, for a silent tongue that babbled intimate thoughts. For the magnificent body made suddenly gaunt by shock and raging fever, and for an arm once powerful, bloated and discolored.

If Matthew survived at all, he could lose his arm to the venomous destruction of the walls of blood vessels. Then to atrophy, the withering of the strong to useless monstrosity. He'd known the consequences. Matthew was too in tune to this formidable land not to understand the risk he took. Yet he hadn't hesitated.

"He knew." She watched him through the flames. Indian, Matthew, lover. In the balance—the little freedom he'd taken, the care he'd given, the love, the life—she questioned how, even in hallucination, he would believe she could ever hate him.

Stirring, stretching, shaking feeling back into a shoulder constantly numbed by his weight, she reached for the coffee, her only sustenance through the night. The murky brew warmed her, but she found little comfort in it. She was watching the morning star fade into dawn when she felt Matthew's gaze. His sooty eyes glittered with fever and were lucid.

"Have to move." His throat strained with the effort of coherent speech. "Too open here, they'll find us."

Patience acknowledged his alarm, he'd put into words the thoughts she'd avoided. "There's a ranch or a sheep farm somewhere out there. When you're better, I'll go for help."

"No!" He struggled to sit up.

Patience flew across the fire to stop him, her tin cup clattering against a stone. "Be still. If you want to live and keep your arm, be still."

He was too weak to fight as she pushed him carefully back to his blanket. "Can't take risk. They're everywhere."

The Wolves' contacts, patrons in their unholy commerce. They could be anyone, rancher, sheep herder, farmer, shopkeeper. A wrong choice and she could deliver Matthew into a murderous grasp. There was another way, the only way. As she soothed him, her assurance that she would abide by his wishes becoming a mindless chant, she made desperate and agonizing decisions.

It was still very early, but with the sun fully risen and temperatures soaring, when she ceased her labors and appraised the result. The already obscure trail was blocked by a fall of rock, one nature had been readying, hurried along by one propitious shove of human hands. Every lingering mark of the campsite had been obliterated, brushed clean of any tracks and with ashes buried. She'd wished for more and better, another landslide. Nature hadn't cooperated a second time. Backing away from her handiwork, stepping on carefully positioned stones, she made her way across another, wider expanse to a hidden shelter formed by a jutting overhang and thick vegetation.

When she knelt by Matthew's side as he leaned against a stone, she was gratified by the coolness of his skin, the clear concentration in his steady gaze. Moving the filled canteen nearer to his good hand, she queried, "Can you manage alone?"

Matthew nodded. "The worst is ended."

But only the worst. Patience knew this was a reprieve, a testament to his monumental strength. There would be hours of agony when she'd gone. Lonely hours, with no one to comfort him. No one to care. For just one moment she questioned the wisdom of her venture, but only a moment. Touching his cheek to keep his attention, she promised, "I won't be long."

Matthew's hollow-eyed gaze held hers. "If there's nothing, keep going. Due north to Sedona. Call McKinzie, Simon McKinzie." He searched for a telephone number, a coded password, both were buried too deeply in a glazed mind.

"I won't be going to Sedona or calling Simon," she assured him. "When you're better, we'll do it together."

"No!" He tried to argue.

"I won't leave you behind, Matthew." Brushing loose tendrils of fever-dampened hair from his face, she tried to smile. "I'll be back before you know it."

His eyes fluttered as he tried to keep them open, but the effort was too great. He'd slipped into comatose sleep when she kissed his forehead and rose. One last check on his supplies and her own, and she had no reason to delay.

By her reckoning it was just past seven when she moved from the overhang in a slow jog. From a safe distance, she scanned her back trail for signs that could lead a clever Wolf to Matthew. There were none readily apparent, but time and a lucky guess could nullify her best effort.

Time was precious. Wasted time was her enemy.

"I'll be back for you, Matthew." She repeated the promise as she set out on her solitary quest.

An unmerciful sun was high, defeat and despair a heavy weight in her step, when she virtually stumbled over a well-worn trail. There were hoof marks in the dust. Shod hooves. A band of horses had passed this way often and not so long ago. On a hunch, she altered her course to follow where their path led. Just when she was sure she'd made a costly error, that she was destined to traverse this wasteland forever, the trail turned down into a hidden ravine carved by the waters of a raging river. For now, in the driest summer on record, that same river was a peaceful, meandering stream, the riverbed a lush oasis. Best of all, tucked close against the opposite wall, out of the path of all but the highest waterline, was a small shack fallen into disrepair.

A line shack, a relic from the early days of ranching, before trucks and planes and helicopters became the norm? A luckless miner's claim? A squatter overpowered by the stronger landholder? Or a greenhorn farmer who'd watched his crops wash away in torrential floods, leaving disaster in its wake?

Whoever built it, for whatever reason, it was abandoned. It could be godsend or deathtrap. She couldn't know until she took a closer look.

Taking the path of the horses, she'd only begun the little descent when she found the fresher tracks of a single horse. From her vantage, she searched every uncloistered inch of this natural fortress. "I know you're here, horse. I'm going to find you, and when I go for Matthew, you'll go with me."

She found him in the narrow chasm of the north end of the ravine, grazing in grass that flanked a towering waterfall. He was big and rangy, a sturdy workhorse. Judging from the marks worn into his coat by saddle and bridle, part of a cowboy's winter string. Able and hard used, then turned out on the range to rest. He started in surprise, twitching nervously as he caught sight of her, but he didn't bolt. "Easy, boy," she crooned. "I'm not here to hurt you."

He backed away, rearing and dancing, his eyes rolling. Still he did not bolt.

Gathering all the forbearance at her command, Patience inched toward him, the soothing patter never ending. "Found yourself a nice, lonely place, boy? Are you the vanguard? Will the others be along later, or are you always solitary?"

She wasn't sure what she said to him beyond that. Words didn't matter, only the tone. She must have him, the trip to the ravine would be more direct than her fanning search, but Matthew would never make it. In the exigency of need, she moved carefully. Gradually the horse relaxed with her constant, lilting chant, and stepped a little toward her. As she offered a leaf plucked from a sycamore, he stretched his neck to nibble curiously at her hand. From then it was a simple matter to discover he liked to have his nose rubbed and his ears scratched. He was a pet. One of those rare, loyal creatures more in tune with his human than his kind.

As she scratched and stroked, he whickered softly. If he'd been a kitten, he would have purred. He nuzzled at her neck, she laughed and dodged away, but only to pet him again.

When she went to the shack, to put it into what order she could for Matthew, the horse was her shadow. He would have followed her into the cabin if the door hadn't been set so low. "If you'll wait, like a good boy, I shouldn't be long." When she assessed the little that was possible in the tumbled-down cabin, she sighed, amending, "I *won't* be long at all. An hour at the most."

She was wrong, failing to take into account her own degree of exhaustion. It was two hours before she rode bareback from the ravine with her canteen refilled, but her short supply of food depleted. Dread that she'd been gone from Matthew too long, was answered by a need in the horse to please her. The journey that had taken five hours of difficult hiking was accomplished more directly in two, as he picked his way among the rubble of fallen stone and dry earth with the sure-footed confidence of a mountain goat.

The day was waning, but twilight was hours away when she pulled the horse to a halt a little way from the shelter. Denying the urge to rush to him, she waited and listened, half expecting the Wolves would be there. But there was no sign of trouble. All was as she had left it. Quiet. Still.

Too quiet? Too still? Had his condition worsened?

"Matthew." She was dismounted, running, bursting through clawing shrub to the shelter. His bed was empty. "Matthew?"

"Here." With tottering steps he moved from the gloom far from his bed.

"What are you doing? You shouldn't be moving around." She was poised at the entrance, frozen in fear for him.

"I heard the horse," he explained hoarsely.

It was then she saw the knife in his left hand, and the little strength with which he held it. In an instant of empathy she lived the horror of a vigorous man stripped of strength, waiting for an unrecognized enemy. Going to him, she took him in her arms, supporting him as much as holding him. She didn't bother with apologies as she led him to his blanket, for she knew he would have none of them. "I've found a place where we can be safe for a while. Long enough for you to regain your stamina. There's water and shelter."

"And horses?"

"Just the one, for now." She gathered supplies as she spoke. "We'll need a little more than two hours riding double. It will be near dark before we make it, but the horse knows the way."

Matthew didn't contest her plan, he didn't question. The simple act of moving from his bed had taken too much out of him to allow him to do more than sit and listen. But the deadly fatigue didn't cloud the realization that she'd done well. Again.

When they were packed and mounted, with the horse standing tolerantly, Matthew murmured in her ear, "I'd like to meet the man who trained this horse."

Her original plan for a travois with herself as beast of burden was discarded with the acquisition of the horse. They could travel faster and the way would be less jolting riding double. Patience was engrossed in lashing Matthew's good wrist to her belt, if he fell, they would fall together. If she could, she would break his fall. When his comment registered, she replied grimly, "I'd like to kiss him."

Before their trek was done, with darkness closing in at the end of a long day of summer, and with Matthew a deadweight at her back, she knew nothing would be thanks enough to the person responsible for this horse. Lucky, as she'd begun to think of him, stood firm in front of the forsaken hovel as she undertook the impossible task of releasing Matthew and dismounting, trying all the while to keep him astride the broad, bare back. In the end they tumbled together to the ground, Patience scarcely managing to cushion his body with her own.

He was deadweight again when she recovered the breath knocked from her in their fall and shuffled with him through the sagging door. Letting him crumple to a heap on the crude bed she'd cleaned and made for him, she started a small fire in the crumbling fireplace. Making him more comfortable and assuring herself that he was sleeping normally, she went to see to Lucky. The horse had been rubbed down with handfuls of foliage from nearby junipers, watered, and hobbled by a length of fabric torn from her spare shirt when she returned to the shack.

Faced with the dilemma of food, with her charge sleeping like the dead and every muscle in her body bearing its own witness, she determined that rest was the sustenance needed most by Matthew and herself. Rolling into a blanket on the floor in front of the fire, she slept immediately and as deeply as he.

Matthew was lucid and ravenous, his hunger inflamed by the scent of stew bubbling in a pot over the fire. Shifting in bed, lifting his body on one arm when he found the other nearly useless, he inspected the cabin. He'd only vague recollections of the grueling trip into the ravine, and nothing of the cabin itself, yet he knew he'd been in this small room and in this bed for days. As if it were a dream, he recalled the tender embrace that held him when he thrashed in delirium, and the competent hands that bathed him in cooling water when his body was consumed by the inferno that raged inside him.

He remembered the rattler, coils loosening, its head lifting into an S-shaped loop, ready to strike. He remembered a woman with hair like flame working furiously over the oozing, burning wounds in his arm.

"Patience."

There was no answer to his whispered call. He was alone. Throwing back the blanket that covered him, he stood, threatening to bang his head on the low ceiling as he rose to his full height. He was as naked and weak as a newborn babe. His mouth was dryer than the desert, and his arm a leaden weight. But he was alive, and thanks to Patience's knowledge and care, in time he would have two vital arms.

Striding to a wooden bucket he found the water he needed. First he drank deeply, then splashed the cooling liquid on his face and head. Nothing had felt so good in all his life. Except Patience's caring touch. Her kiss.

He wanted to see her, wanted to know what she was about. With water trickling over his shoulders and chest he looked for his clothing and found his leather trousers cleaned and hanging on a peg. He slipped into them, won a clumsy, weak-handed struggle to close the snap, and was pulling on his moccasins when the door opened and Patience stepped in.

"Matthew, you're awake." Her voice was warm in pleased surprise.

"Yes." He was absorbed in her. She wore the leathers he'd given her, over one shoulder rested the tied carcasses of two Gambel's quail. In her hand she held a bow and one arrow. "You've been hunting."

Setting the weapon aside, she lifted the quail from her shoulder. "I thought you might be ready for more than broth made of the dried provisions from our packs."

"You shot those?" He crossed to the bow, hefting it in his palm, appreciating its balance. "With this?"

"A lucky couple of shots." She shrugged aside her expertise.

"Which brother taught you to shoot?"

"All of them had a hand in it. Each is an accomplished bow hunter." She didn't add that her father and mother were, as well. Or that only Valentina didn't like the bow.

He strummed a thumb over the bowstring made of fishing line and estimated the tension at thirty pounds. "You made the bow."

"The line was here. It isn't the best of substitutes for a proper bowstring, but it serves."

It did more than serve, he thought as he drank in the wild disheveled hair, the flush of her cheeks, the triumph of a successful hunt sparkling in her green eyes. She was so exquisitely alive, one could as easily believe she'd just left a lover's arms. He yearned to be that lover, and wondered if he would be again. Steeling himself against willful desire, he set the bow aside. "Is there anything you haven't been taught, or can't do?"

Her laugh was low and melodious, prettier than he'd ever heard it. "Quite a lot, but I've been fortunate in that my family has tried its collective hand at a smattering of everything. What they've missed, they're still aspiring toward." She laughed again. "Our motto should be So Much To Do, So Little Time, But We're Trying."

"Time for adventure, time for travel," he muttered. "When was there time for normal family things? When did you go to school?"

"We didn't. We had no formal education. Wherever we went, whatever we were doing, Mother saw to the basics. She proved a gifted and inspiring teacher, and an uncompromising taskmaster. Beyond that the world was our classroom, our instructors the best it had to offer. As each of us found our own area of expertise—" she gestured to the bow "—we learned from each other."

He moved closer, looking down at her, recalling how adept she'd been from the first, seeing how she adapted to living off the land and thrived. "Among your strengths and many talents, what is your field of expertise? What special thing do you bring to the family?"

"Special? Me?" Preoccupied with his question, she took the quail to the yard and absently began plucking feathers from them. Matthew lounged in the doorway, watching, waiting for her evaluation of her place in her family. After a while she looked up from her chore. "You've found me out. I suppose I could best be called jill-of-all-trades, but unlike Kieran, master of none. I bring very little to the family."

He left the shade of the cabin to join her in the yard. "Could it be you bring the example of courage to the family? Courage to face your fears, and finally to be different?"

"Maybe," she said thoughtfully. "Then again, maybe not."

"I think your family would agree with me."

"You've never met my family. You don't know them."

"I don't need to know them in this." Before she could say more he moved away toward the stream. "I'll walk for a little now."

"But not too far?" Worry lines formed between her brows.

"Not too far," he agreed mildly. "My heart rate is regular now, there are no hemorrhages into the skin. The cuts at the wound and those you made later at the advancing edge of the edema are healing." The precise account of his condition finished, he smiled. "There's no reason a little exercise shouldn't be beneficial. I promise not to go one step more than feels comfortable."

"I'll hold you to that promise."

"I thought you might." He smiled again and walked with a surprisingly steady gait over the uneven ground to the stream.

Patience studied him guardedly. He was amazingly better. Either the snake hadn't injected a full measure of venom, or Matthew commanded incredible powers of recuperation. If she had to choose the source of his fortune, she would choose Matthew. Always Matthew.

When she was certain he would not push too hard, too fast, she turned her attention to the sky, her second greatest concern. She kept a constant watch. At the first sign of rain in the north, they would have to ride as if they raced the devil to beat the wall of water that would come raging through the narrow chasm. Staying in the ravine had been risky, but without its shelter would Matthew be as strong? Would he have survived?

"I can't think of that." Casting one more glance toward the stream, and another at a sky that held no threats, she returned to her task.

A week passed, Matthew grew stronger each day. His right arm would never be as strong again, but he was already working with his left, mastering new skills, compensating for the loss. Patience went about her chores with guilt heavy on her heart, but no mention was made of her paralytic fear of reptiles. No finger was ever pointed in blame.

As she hunted, she was rarely far from the entrance of their walled fortress, while Matthew ranged farther and farther in the opposite direction. Horses moved in and out of the area, displaying no concern for their presence, as they came to drink and graze. At first she was anxious about Lucky, but he showed no sign of wanting to run free. After days of observing, Matthew chose a handsome bay, cutting him from the herd with astonishing expertise. If he was hampered by his weakened arm, only one who knew him as well as Patience could see.

A second week passed. Matthew was restless and working harder to strengthen his right hand as he increased his left-handed dexterity. The more he worked, the greater Patience's guilt, the more she stayed away from the shack. Soon she was coming in only for meals, or in time to huddle resolutely on the floor, wrapped in her blanket for the night. On the morning she woke in the narrow bed, while Matthew slept on the floor, she knew he'd settled an ongoing debate in his own incontrovertible way.

A second concern weighed heavily on her mind. If the Wolves still searched for them, as Matthew assured they would, then time and the odds were in the bikers' favor. Sooner or later one of them would find the horse trail and the ravine as she had. When they sensed his weakness as ravening animals did, what would become of Matthew?

Guarding the entrance of the ravine became an obsession, until the night she stopped coming to her bed to sleep.

The moon was full, and from her vantage afforded a perfect view of the trail. She was curled inside the blanket she'd brought with her, warding off a night chill made more cutting by the contrasting heat of the day. Her eyes burned, and her stomach protested the meal she hadn't been able to choke down. In her loneliness her body longed for the touch of the only man she would ever love.

She shivered in the chill and watched. The hand that shot out of the darkness, gripping her shoulder was hard and uncompromising. Not a lover's hand. "Dammit, woman!" With the curse, a guttural voice demanded, "What the devil do you think you're doing?"

Stifling a startled cry, Patience whirled around. Matthew crouched over her, a grim silhouette. "You startled me." She grabbed at the blanket as it tumbled to the ground around her. "I didn't know you were coming up from camp. I didn't hear you."

"You're sure as hell going to know when I go back, because we're going together." Taking his hand from her shoulder, he scooped her from the ground. If there was weakness in either of the arms that held her, it was masked by anger.

"Matthew, don't." She pushed against him, trying to pull free. "I have to keep watch."

"No," he growled. "You don't need to keep watch. No one does. When they come, we'll have plenty of warning. Their bikes will announce them."

"Not if they travel the last on foot, if they seal the mouth of the ravine!"

"Fine. Let them." He was moving implacably down the trail, unhindered by darkness or his burden.

"We'll be trapped!"

"We won't be trapped." He'd reached level ground, and moved with a comfortable stride to the shack. "We won't be leaving the way we came."

She struggled in earnest now, insisting that he put her down. When he complied, she swung around to face him. "What do you mean?"

"There's another way out."

"There can't be. The ravine is too steep and rough. The north wall is impassable and narrows until its only wide enough for the waterfall. We can't go over, and the horses certainly couldn't."

"We aren't going over, we're going through."

"Near the falls?" At his nod, she asked, "Another tunnel?"

"A fissure would be more apt. The horses will be cramped, but they can make it. Then we'll have several hours of hard riding to Sedona. We'll go tomorrow."

"Tomorrow." She looked out over the ravine, a study in moonlight and shadow. Tomorrow she would be leaving, returning to her life. Where was the elation? What sorrow tempered relief?

"We'll go at first light. Passage through the fissure could be dangerous in darkness. Even so, we'll need to start our day early. But first, this." His hands at her shoulders were light now, tenderly turning her, pulling her back to him. First his lips brushed over her forehead, then her temple, and her cheek in a soft, seeking kiss.

When he found her mouth, Patience swayed against him, her arms circled his neck. A moan whispered through her parted lips, his name lost in his kiss, love unspoken.

His kiss was long and lingering, his mouth teasing, demanding, persuading, his tongue a welcome caress. There was leashed passion in him. She felt it, as she felt her own. Suddenly it no longer mattered who waited beyond the ravine or why. She didn't care who he was, or what secrets he kept. Here he was Indian and Matthew, the best of both. Her fingers brushed over his hair to frame his face, and as her lips parted for his, the rest of the world disappeared.

"O'Hara," he groaned as he kissed her again, deeply. His breath shuddered in his chest as he lifted his mouth from hers at last. Slipping the tie from her hair with impatient fingers, he buried his face in the gleaming tresses, damning a need that couldn't be gentle. So little of the life he'd forced upon her had been gentle, he wanted it for her now.

Bewildered by the stillness belied by the ragged rush of his heart, she held him, wanting him, knowing he wanted her. Turning her face only a little, she kissed the pulse at his throat and felt the blood pounding through him. With her tongue she tasted the saltiness of his skin, breathing the unadorned cleanliness of him. Pulling her hair from his grasp, she lifted her head, her gaze colliding with his as she pulled his mouth back to hers.

Her kiss was ravenous, insatiable, her wordless, muttered demand for more fanned his fevered skin. Passion and desire spiraled beyond control. In a swift move he swept her up against him. His arms were tight, possessive, as he stalked to the shack.

There was only the fire to light his way, there had never been more. No candles, no lanterns, only this small, careful flame. But it was enough as he lay her on his blanket spread in front of it in preparation for the night. Enough that as he removed her clothing, slowly, deliciously, every desirable inch was revealed by the rosy glow of fiery coals. Enough that when he took her, the woman with hair like fire and bathed in the light of fire, became fire itself. And he was consumed in her, by her. Possessed.

With desire spiraling from one plane to another, he took her with him to the brink, and then further, into the unthinking madness that magnified every exquisite caress, every touch, every stroke of his body. When she cried out, arching to meet him in mind-shattering rapture, it was he who possessed. He who held the flame in his arms.

In the aftermath, in sweet fulfillment, he held her, refusing to think of yesterday or tomorrow. And when the fire burned low, and the night was wine dark, he made love to her again. This time gently, but no less passionately. The last of love, for which the first was made.

She was the warrior's woman. His woman. In his heart she would always be.

Eleven

By sunrise, their day was hours old. Working sometimes together and sometimes apart, they set out to return the ravine to the condition in which they'd found it, removing every trace of their weeks of habitation. Neither spoke of the night they'd shared, but neither forgot. The memory lingered in the haunting softness of Patience's eyes as her gaze followed him. In Matthew's light, wistful touches when he was near.

An hour ticked by. The shack and ravine were scoured of the last clues. The mood changed. Patience became aware of Matthew's increasing distraction. Time and again, she saw him lift his head, his brow scored by a frown, his stare unfocused. Each time she waited for an explanation, each time he was silent. He'd begun the day being quietly attentive, now he was scarcely aware she existed. As he lapsed deeper into an absorbed silence, Patience kept her own counsel as quietly.

"Not that." For the first time in a while he spoke, taking the bow from her before she could dismantle it. "There's no need to destroy the bow, I'll take it with me."

"We have no more need for it, why weigh ourselves down with useless baggage?"

"Don't argue, O'Hara. For once, just don't argue." He stepped to his waiting horse.

Patience was surprised by his outburst. She hadn't argued, neither of them had. Abruptly it all made sense. His solemn quiet, the watchfulness, the edgy irritation. "They're out there," she whispered. "The Wolves have found us, haven't they?"

Matthew finished tying the bow to the pack draped over his horse's rump before he turned back to her. "They're out there, but they haven't found us." Returning to her, he looped an arm around her shoulders and pulled her close. "They won't find us. We'll be gone long before they're that close."

Patience strained to hear, to feel what he'd felt. There was nothing. "How did you know?"

"I'm not sure I can explain." But with an eloquent shrug, he tried. "It's a lot of little things. Taken alone, they mean nothing. Together, they add up to trouble. A vibration in the earth, a feeling in the air. A snatch of sound in a silence too great. A skittish horse." He looked out over the ravine. "The birds and animals have gone to ground, they know something is coming. I know it will be the Wolves."

"How soon?"

"We have time, but only a little now. As soon as you're ready, we'll move out."

Stroking his hand as it lay on her arm, she nodded. "I need a minute more."

"Take your minute," he said quietly. "I'll see to the horses."

Moving from his embrace, Patience went to the door of the shack. It looked as she'd found it. Order had been turned to chaos, it was a derelict again. But in her mind, it would always be a tranquil refuge, a haven where, by the light of a flickering fire, she had loved and been loved fiercely in return.

Trailing her fingers over the uneven stone of the fireplace, she said goodbye to a moment that would never come again. Head down, she hurried from the shack. Eyes blinded by unshed tears looked to Matthew. "I'm ready."

The way through the fissure was difficult as Matthew had warned. The passage was narrow and climbed steeply. Water trickled from jutting boulders, the temperature plummeted, the air was dank, and darkness nearly complete. Twice the way was so constricted Patience had to dismount, for horse and rider could not pass through together. Twice more she had to stand at Lucky's head, taking him where he was afraid to go. Every sound seemed to reverberate, magnified by a hollow quiet—water drumming over stone, the brush of clothing against craggy walls, the steady clop of shod hooves. Above it all, Matthew's disembodied voice encouraging, leading the way.

Like an unexpected scream, a deluge of sound swept over them. A battering, throbbing timpani with no direction and no end. Patience bit back a cry. In the disorienting pandemonium, she quieted her terrified horse with the hopeless certainty the Wolves were ahead, waiting for them. Her first instinct was to turn back, to flee, but the space was too close for the horses to turn. And on foot what chance had they?

"O'Hara!" Matthew called, his voice threading through the tumult. "Listen to me. This isn't what you think. Sound carries through the ravine, the passage distorts it. The bikes sound as if they're right at us, but they aren't. I would guess they've just found the entrance to the ravine. They may never find this way, and if they do, we have time. We're almost there now, almost through."

He coaxed her along, above the roar of engines and the more frightening silence that followed. As Lucky plodded on, iron shoes striking fire against stone, she closed her eyes, waiting for a stealthy step at her back.

Heat and light burst over her without warning, and Matthew's hands at her waist lifted her from Lucky's back. "We made it." Then he was laughing as he kissed her. "We really made it."

"Have we?" Patience couldn't share his elation. If they could traverse the fissure, so could the Wolves. "They found the ravine, Matthew. They can find the way behind the waterfall."

"What they'll find will be a dead end." When she looked at him in question, he explained, "In a land of balanced rocks destined to fall, in a hundred years who's to know or care that we hurried more than a few along?"

"How can you?" The boulders that flanked the fissure were massive, and precariously stacked. One would think a gust of wind could send them tumbling, but she knew they'd withstood much more for countless years.

Taking a length of rope from his pack, he pointed to one tall, slender column. "We play dominoes."

Patience didn't understand until he looped the rope around the spire and tied the other to a braided leather collar he hooked around his horse's neck. The leather she recognized as strips cut from a spare tunic, the braiding had been his exercise in dexterity, both now turned to useful purpose.

The stone spire fell with one long, hard pull from the powerful horse, bringing others down with it. Dominoes.

When the sound and fury ended and the dust settled at last, the back of the fissure had disappeared. Sealed as if it had never been, by tons of stone. It all seemed impossibly easy, a spur-of-the-moment solution, but she knew he had been planning and preparing for this for more than a week.

In the wake of clamorous sound, the plateau to which their climb had led them, was quiet and pastoral. A stream danced willy-nilly along its way with no hint that soon it would tumble off the face of a cliff in a thundering waterfall. When Patience spoke, it was in bittersweet awe. "It's hard to believe it was ever there."

"It was there, the ravine exists, the days we spent there really happened." He held her close, but only for a moment before he took her arm to guide her to the horses. "It's time to move on. Your nightmare is almost over, O'Hara. You'll be home before you know it."

Riding bareback for hours through terrain that grew rougher with each mile was an experience. One of many Patience hoped she would never have to repeat. The little farmhouse with shabby equipment, a shiny TV antenna jutting like a single porcupine quill from its roof, and obviously too poor to be part of the Wolves' cabal, was never a more welcome sight. The farmer, an ancient widower of Mexican descent, could barely speak English, but he understood enough that Matthew could make a few telephone calls. Persuading him to let them leave the horses as collateral for the use of his truck, was another matter.

"I've decided you're a warlock," Patience observed through clenched teeth as she scrambled back into her seat after the farmer's "most precious" truck jolted her from it in the negotiation of one of a million potholes. "In a thirsty land, you find water. We need horses, they appear. We must escape, you find a way. We need communication and transportation, and the only farmhouse for miles offers both. Though, at the moment, I think I prefer the horses to this 'most precious' truck."

Matthew fought the steering wheel as the battered vehicle bumped over a small wash. "He was a shrewd old codger. This is a '55 Chevy, hard used and neglected for nearly forty years. Before being consigned the honorable title of 'most precious,' naturally. I've a feeling we were lucky the battery still had power and there was gasoline.''

"It had nothing to do with luck, you're a warlock, plain and simple."

She was teasing. Even her complaining was done in good spirit. But the closer their return to civilization, the surer he became that the truth would destroy what she felt for him. Grimly, losing the lighthearted spirit, he muttered, "What warlock in his right mind would put a woman accustomed to a Corvette, aptly called Beauty, in a heap like this?"

"Beauty was my parent's idea, not mine. The name, Black Beauty, was part of an ongoing joke when I insisted a horse would be more practical for a journey in the west." She looked at him curiously, seeing tension in the way he gripped the wheel and the grave set of his features. "You're disturbed about something."

He managed an apologetic smile. "Just tired."

Patience was instant concern. "Does your arm hurt? Should I drive?"

"My arm's fine." A stretch of road rougher than any before it made further comment impossible. When they were past it, they found nothing more to say.

The bone-jarring ride ended when Matthew turned onto a paved road. They sped through the magnificent red rock country, and neither found reason to comment. On the outskirts of Sedona, Matthew turned the truck onto another road, this one narrow and graveled and quite smooth. They were climbing, and the mountainous view grew more spectacular.

"The calls I made . . ." Matthew began in a peculiar hesitancy. "One was to Simon McKinzie, the man I work for. The other was to Patrick McCallum, a friend. His villa is at the crest of this mountain. He and his wife, Jordana, aren't in residence now, but there's a permanent staff. You'll be safe with them until Simon comes."

There were other calls he didn't explain, and Patience didn't question. She recognized Simon McKinzie's name, she knew who and what he was. Patrick McCallum hadn't been part of the delirium. As she pondered this new twist, Matthew was pulling to a halt in front of a sprawling Mediterranean-style villa. A man much like Matthew lounged at the steps leading to the house. His face was lean and saturnine, his hair black as night, but as he approached the truck, his green eyes flashed with laughter.

"Matthew!" He opened the door at the driver's side, laughing again as it creaked and sagged. "I won't ask how you came to be in possession of Jesus's 'most precious' truck."

"Rafe! No one told me you were here." Matthew was out of the truck, first shaking hands with the man whose genuine amusement was at odds with his looks, then clapping his shoulder. "I take it you know Jesus."

"Everyone knows Jesus and his truck. They're local characters." With the negligent grace of a stalking cat Rafe crossed to Patience, opening her door with a gallant bow. "Rafe Courtenay, at your service, Dr. O'Hara."

She heard the hint of a soft Southern accent, and recognized the courtliness of a Creole as he took her hand, helping her from the truck as if it were a limousine and she were dressed in a Paris original rather than stained and dusty leather and cotton. "New Orleans, Mr. Courtenay?"

"Is it that obvious?"

"Only because I lived there for a while."

"Then you know I'm guilty as charged." Rafe Courtenay smiled again, and she saw that he was really quite handsome and very kind. Tucking her hand in his arm, he led her to the stairs, leaving Matthew to follow. "Your rooms have been made ready for you. I imagine the first thing you'd like is a long soak and nap before dinner."

"How did you know, Mr. Courtenay?" Patience laughed up at him, as at ease as if she'd known him for years.

"Sisters, Dr. O'Hara. I have a few."

The interior of the house was lovely and relaxing. It proved to be a unique maze of uncluttered pathways, terraces, and gardens that flowed in and out of charming living areas without any sense of interruption. It was a house of textures and contrast, an experience for the senses. Nothing was carelessly placed, yet there was no sense of rigid order. Living in this house would be easy. There was serenity here, a joyful enhancement of life.

"How wonderful," she exclaimed as she saw how perfectly the house blended with its surroundings.

"It is, isn't it?" Rafe agreed. "Patrick had the house designed for Jordana. Tomorrow someone will tell you the bricks used in the walls are handmade, burnt adobe, and the beams and headers hewn of dead, standing spruce out of Colorado." The solemn mouth barely hid a grin, green eyes smiled down at her. "But that's tomorrow. For now, your bath and a long rest await you."

He opened a door to a room as gracious as those she'd seen. A woman dressed in peasant blouse and a gaily printed broomstick skirt came forward to meet them. Taking her hand, the woman fussed over her as she shooed the men away.

"Go!" She tossed her head with all the arrogance of an aristocrat. "Discuss whatever men discuss over brandy on the terrace. Maria will see to Dr. O'Hara's comfort. Jordana is busy with her boys." Then in an aside, "Little League, you know. The woman is amazing. They tell me she knows from the crack of the bat if it's a home run. So, because of the season, it is a long time since her Maria has someone to fuss over." Turning Patience in place, the housekeeper continued happily, "Look well at her before you go, gentlemen, you will not recognize her when next you see her."

Patience was swept along with the tide, with nothing more from Matthew. As the door closed behind them, she heard his expression of surprise at Rafe's presence, and Rafe's explanation that he was only passing through and would be leaving on a midnight flight. Their voices were fading when she heard Rafe asking what Matthew found in the desert. She didn't hear his answer.

Dinner was served on the terrace. There were regional dishes served in colorful, glazed stoneware, vintage wine sparkling in crystal, and servants unobtrusively attending. In the background the slow strum of a guitar spun its web of musical magic and Patience felt she'd literally stepped from the desert into paradise. No place had ever been so lovely, and she'd never felt more beautiful in a flowing gown of jacquard silk in deepest amethyst. Maria had put up her hair, securing it with matching combs, deliberately letting it fall in curling tendrils around her face.

"Irresistible. Our stolid Matthew won't know what hit him when he sees you," she'd promised.

Indeed, Matthew's gaze rarely left her. But she was no more irresistible than he. He wore black, stark, nearly unrelieved. Only the white of his open shirt broke the somber lines of jacket and trousers. Yet on Matthew they weren't somber. His hair was combed back and tied, but without adornment. He held the wineglass with a sophisticated ease, as if he'd held it so thousands of times. There should have been no trace of Indian in the man who sat across from her, but he was there, the man of the desert, lying beneath the debonair facade.

He lifted the glass to his lips. As he watched her over its rim, savoring the finest wine, she hadn't a glimmer of what he was thinking, nor what intentions lay behind his dark, solemn gaze.

Rafe was the perfect host. Dinner was unhurried, the wine endless, and the night air seductive. Despite the long nap she'd taken at Maria's insistence, Patience found herself nodding, hiding yawns behind her hand. She barely roused when Matthew lifted her from her chair, chuckling as he thanked Rafe for a pleasant evening and bade him good-night for both of them.

"Matthew?" she asked drowsily as he lay her on her bed.

"Yes, love?"

"Is this my room?"

"It is, for now." He took the combs from her hair.

"What are you doing?"

"Putting you to bed, dear heart, only that."

"Do you like the dress?"

"Very much." His fingers were busy with the tiny buttons that marched stubbornly from neckline to hem.

"Did you know it was bought especially for me when you called to say we were coming?"

"I know." The last button was conquered. The dress fell away from her naked breasts and with it every good intention, and he feared he was lost.

"Matthew?" Her hand curled around the nape of his neck, her lashes fluttered over her cheeks.

"I'm here." He ached to taste a rosy nipple and feel its bloom tighten to a bud on his tongue.

"Are you going to leave me?"

With a low, lamenting groan he came down to her then, gathering her to him. And into his waking passion there was woven a thread of regret. "No, love," he whispered into her hair. "Not tonight."

Something was wrong. Patience knew it before she opened her eyes. In a room so beautiful it should be shared, she was alone.

"Matthew." She knew before she called that he wouldn't answer. The answer she didn't want was scrawled on the note lying by her pillow. Tearing it open she held it in trembling hands, finally gathering the courage to read it.

It was the mea culpa she anticipated, accepting all the blame for what had happened and none of the credit for her survival. "'I wish you happiness, O'Hara,' " she read the last out loud. " 'Forgive me, Matthew.' "

Rising, she paced across the room, then wondered where she was going. Bleakly she crumpled the note in her palm. "How? How can a man who knows me so well know me so little?"

She was still standing, lost and alone, when Maria knocked and bustled in with fresh flowers. "Ah, you wake early. That's good, there's nothing prettier than sunrise in Sedona. Have you looked out?"

Patience pulled herself from her thoughts. "I didn't think of it."

Maria stopped arranging the flowers. "The letter, it is unexpected? It is bad news? From Matthew?"

"From Matthew, but not unexpected."

"Perhaps it is a mistake?"

Patience looked up at her in surprise.

"Forgive me for presuming, but I have known Matthew for a long while. He is a regular and favored visitor. The clothing he wore to dinner, he keeps here along with others, for unexpected visits. I know him both as Patrick's guest, and as a friend. More than that, I know him as only one Apache can know another. I see that he looks at you as he's never looked at a woman before. Yet it makes no sense what else I see. Love is in his eyes and sorrow in his face. Then this morning he was leaving for the desert."

"You saw him? He was returning to the desert? You're sure?"

"Of course. He conferred with Simon in the study quite some time before he left."

"Simon McKinzie is here?"

"He arrived by helicopter just at dawn." Maria set the flowers aside. "He asked that I convey to you his invitation to join him for breakfast in half an hour."

"Accept for me, please, Maria." She glanced at the beside clock. "Tell him I'll be there, precisely at eight."

"Good." Maria smiled. "Now if I may be so kind as to suggest an ensemble." She flung open a closet, extracting a riding skirt of soft brown, and with it a black jacket with collar and lapels laced with matching brown leather.

Patience was reminded of the leather trousers Matthew had given her in the canyon. "It's beautiful, Maria, but I doubt Jordana would appreciate a stranger wearing it."

"Jordana has one similar, one she likes because she can see it in its textures. But this was purchased for you, also, in the little time we had before your arrival. I bought it myself on Matthew's instruction. He remembered the other from a recent visit. He was quite taken with it when Jordana wore it," Maria explained. "He felt that if I were fortunate in fulfilling his instructions, this would suit you and he hoped you would like it." Letting it register that the ensemble was Matthew's thoughtful choice for Patience, she asked, "Shall I put it away? Would you prefer to choose something else?"

Patience crossed to Maria. Stroking leather like satin, she shook her head. "Leave it. I won't be choosing anything else. But, if you don't mind, I'd like some time alone."

"Surely." Maria bowed in graceful consent. "I shall tell Simon to expect you."

As she turned to go, Patience stopped her. "Maria, you said Jordana sees in textures. What does that mean?"

"You don't know?" Maria observed more than questioned. Then, softly, "Jordana's blind, she sees through the other senses."

"I'm sorry." Patience felt a stab of heartache for a woman she didn't know. "I should have guessed." She recalled the uncluttered paths, the gardens, the sunlight. All of them a veritable banquet for the senses.

"There was no reason you should know, but neither should you feel sorrow. Never for Jordana."

"Patrick loves his wife very much, doesn't he?"

"More than his life. He shows it in everything he does."

Patience blinked back a gathering of tears. "It must be wonderful to know you're loved so completely."

"It is for Jordana. She wouldn't trade a second of Patrick's love for a lifetime of sight." Maria hesitated, then suggested, "Isn't such love something you know, as well?"

Patience didn't respond. How could she make Maria understand what she didn't herself?

After a moment Maria smiled sadly, murmuring, "If there's nothing else?"

"Nothing, thank you."

Then Patience was alone with her thoughts of love and Matthew.

"Dr. O'Hara." Simon McKinzie slid back his chair, rising with an old-fashioned gallantry as she stepped onto the terrace. He was a bearlike man with a shock of closely clipped silver hair. Behind him stretched a timeless landscape in varying shades of red. "Allow me to introduce myself, I'm Simon McKinzie." He offered his hand. "I'm very glad you consented to join me."

Patience touched his hand only briefly as she took the seat a servant pulled out for her. "I know who you are, Mr. McKinzie." She folded her hands in front of her and turned a cold, green gaze toward him. "I know what you are. I know that Matthew works for you, and for The Black Watch. What I don't know is why you sent him back to the desert knowing that he'd been ill, and that the Wolves will be waiting for him."

Simon pulled his own chair back to the table abruptly. His eyes narrowed, the warmth was gone from him. "I think you'd better explain what you know about The Watch, and how."

"Do you really want to discuss The Watch here, Mr. McKinzie? Would you like for me to discuss Jeb and Mitch, and Jamie McLachlan? Should I begin with Jamie's hands? The hands of a gifted pianist, broken and crushed in the line of secret duty?"

Simon's caustic suspicion eased a bit. He was pleased by her discretion and surprised by her spirit. Leaning back in his chair, he appraised and reevaluated. "No, I suppose I wouldn't."

"You're wondering if Matthew told me what I know," Patience continued with an angry edge still in her voice. "The answer is yes. Matthew told me quite a lot, but he didn't intend it."

"Matthew does nothing without intention," Simon growled. "Nothing!"

"He was delirious, Mr. McKinzie. People say things they don't intend in the throes of delirium. Even Matthew." She saw the sudden change in Simon's face. A poker face that only the greatest shock would crack. She drew a long breath and rescinded her first opinion of the leader of The Black Watch. "You don't know," she said at last. "He didn't tell you about the rattlesnake, and the bite he took for me."

"Good God!" Simon's hands folded into massive fists, his voice was strangled. "Where was the bite? When?"

She answered each question as succinctly as it was asked. "His right forearm, just above the wrist. Nearly three weeks ago."

"He can't tolerate antivenom."

"No, he can't." In that blunt statement she conveyed the agony and the loss Matthew suffered.

Simon flung back his chair to stalk to the terrace wall. In his effort for control, his grief was apparent. When he turned away from the panorama that reached to the horizon, his face was ashen, his eyes bleak. "He went to salvage what he could of the investigation. Just before he left he said time was running out for someone called Callie. She was his strongest reason for going back." He paused and drew a long, harsh breath. "He went back to bring her out."

"Of course." Patience understood then why he'd left so hastily. "Callie."

Simon approached the table again. "Do you know her? Is she part of the Wolves' operation?"

"Callie's a teenage girl with the mind of a child. She's too uncomplicated and too honest to be part of anything so ugly. And too beautiful to bear the scar she must."

"Scar?" Simon watched Patience closely. "What kind of scar? Physical, mental?"

"Both, but the most evident is physical. A man called Snake carved his initial across her cheek. A raw, ugly S, slithering from eye to chin."

"Jocie," Simon growled not quite under his breath. "In his delirium did he speak of her?"

"Only the name. In his rambling she was linked with Callie."

The massive head tilted thoughtfully. "From what you've said, I can see that she would be. Jocie was a young girl in much the same circumstances as Callie. Her face was scarred, too. It was repaired, but every time she looked in a mirror she still saw it and was reminded of other horrors that had been done to her." A square, hard hand raked through silver hair that shone in the sun. "She drove her car off the side of a mountain in North Carolina six months ago. It might have been an accident, but Matthew doesn't believe so. He blames himself."

Patience was bewildered. "Why would he?"

"Jocie was a runaway and he was searching for her. He's convinced that if he'd found her sooner, if he'd helped her more later, she would have recovered. Jocie was not involved with the Wolves. Nevertheless, she is the reason he pretended to turn renegade, and why he wants so desperately to stop them."

"Failing in that, to expiate his sins, he's gone for Callie."

"How is he? What didn't he tell me?"

Patience knew then that she liked this gruff, overwhelming man. "He was very ill for some time. But his recuperative powers are nothing short of miraculous. He'll lose some tissue in his right arm, and some strength, but he's already compensating for it with his left. He'll be all right if..."

Simon was at her side, lifting her face in his huge palm. "If he comes out of the desert?"

"Yes." She wanted to turn away, to hide the pain and fear she felt. Simon's bearish hold wouldn't allow it.

"He'll be back, and he'll bring Callie out."

"How can he?" Her cry was frantic. "There are too many of them. They usually carry only chains and knives, but there are other weapons. An arsenal of them."

"Their weapons won't matter. Matthew isn't stupid, Dr. O'Hara. He isn't going to stroll into their camp announcing he's come for the girl, and he isn't alone. Rafe had a sudden and convenient change of plans. Believe me, there isn't a man alive I'd rather have at my side."

"Rafe is part of The Black Watch?"

"No, but if I had a dozen like him, I could conquer the world." Simon smiled and released her face, but only to take her hand. "Since neither of us has any appetite for breakfast, why don't we take a stroll and become better acquainted. It's my guess that once Matthew resolves a few problems, he'll come for you. And I like to know the ladies in my agents' lives."

Patience caught her lip between her teeth and shook her head. "You're wrong, Mr. McKinzie."

"O'Hara." He pulled her from her chair, tucked her hand in the crook of his arm and patted it affectionately even as he scolded her. "It isn't just rattlesnake venom that loosens our wily Apache's tongue, and you must believe me when I say Matthew isn't stupid."

He led her from the terrace and onto the grounds. Before the morning ended she knew more of Matthew's sad childhood and his rebellious teen years. She knew of the great influence his grandfather had played in his life. And though he dismissed his own influence, by reading between the lines, she knew that Simon had been instrumental in Matthew's reconciliation with the mother he thought had abandoned him.

"When he understood that she'd only done what was best for him when she left him at the reservation following his father's burial, he stopped hating Sibella and the part of himself that wasn't Apache. Without that hatred, he found he could live in both worlds," Simon finished.

"In the end, he came to work for you."

"He has for years. In some things I know him better than he knows himself." Simon led her to a curve in the path they followed. "He'll be back, O'Hara." He used the name Matthew had given her naturally, as if he'd heard it many times in the hours before Matthew had left for the desert. "Give him a week. Patrick and Jordana always welcome anyone from The Watch, for any reason, and Maria would be delighted to have someone to fuss over.

"Stay," he urged. "Rest. Call your family, tell them you're all right." He looked out over towering spires and rich red walls of rock. Beyond them lay the desert. "But above all, if you love him, wait for Matthew."

Patience waited.

In the luxury of Patrick McCallum's villa, she rested, and read, and walked. She arranged the return of Jesus's truck, and for the horses to be kept at the villa stables until they could be returned to the range. She called her family and discovered that as accustomed as they were to various members being out of touch for indefinite times, they hadn't thought to worry. She glossed over the adventure and mentioned Matthew only casually. She read some more, and walked some more.

Simon called regularly from Washington. Once to say the information Matthew had gathered in the desert was enough to bring in the Wolves. They would be arraigned on a variety of charges. Some of their contacts were lost, but there would come a day, he promised. Matthew, he told her, continued to recover. The renegade who had never been had resigned from The Watch. And when a particular problem was resolved, and he stopped being hardheaded, he would surely be along. If she would wait.

Maria fussed happily.

Patience waited for Matthew.

On a bright morning of the second week, at the sound of the car stopping in the drive, Patience closed the bag Maria had reluctantly supplied then insisted on filling with clothing bought for her stay. Her goodbyes and her thanks had been expressed to the staff, so there was nothing left to do. "My ride waits. It's time to go home."

Sinking into a chair, she folded her hands tightly in her lap. "I'll miss this." She didn't speak of the luxury, or even the beauty. She'd fallen in love with the stark land as she had with Matthew. "But there'll be another place for me. Somewhere."

But never another love. Never another Matthew.

The melancholy refrain rang in her thoughts as she stood, smoothed down the brown skirt, adjusted the black jacket, gathered up her bag, and stepped from her room.

The house was curiously quiet and, oddly, no one was around as she made her way to the front entrance. She was closing the heavy door behind her while she juggled the bag when a hand lifted it from her shoulder.

"Going somewhere, O'Hara?"

Patience spun around, her hands going to her mouth. She could hardly believe it was Matthew standing in front of her. He wore a rancher's dress clothing, a tailored jacket, tailored trousers, handmade boots, and, incredibly, a hat. All of it magnificent on him. She realized then that he wore everything, or nothing at all, magnificently. "Matthew!" she managed when she found her voice. "What are you doing here?"

He set down her bag and moved closer. "My question first."

Lacing her fingers behind her back, she leaned against the carved door. "Home." She opened her mouth to say more, but nothing came to mind. "I'm going home."

"Callie has a new home." Seemingly apropos of nothing, he followed the thread of a single word, not ready to deal with the answer he'd demanded. "A place in North Carolina called Stone Meadow. A halfway house established not so long ago for young people who've suffered through what she has." A flicker of sorrow crossed his face. "Some have been helped at the house, others not. I stayed there with her for a time, and I think she'll be one of the lucky ones.

"She has a new kitten. She can have dozens, if she likes. The barns at Stone Meadow are populated with mousers who reproduce with astonishing regularity. They're undoubtedly the most pampered mousers in the world, for the kids lavish the love they've never had on them."

"Does Callie hate me?" Patience asked. "For leaving her?"

"Callie doesn't hate anyone, it isn't her nature. Even so, she would never hate you." A smile ghosted over his face. "Would you like to guess the kitten's name?"

"Calico?"

Only the slightest move of his head told her she was wrong. "What do you think of Patience? Doctor Patience, in fact."

Patience laughed softly, even as she blinked back tears. "A cumbersome name for a small kitten."

"She'll grow to it, Callie will see that she does. They're safe, O'Hara. Callie's safe, and so is her kitten."

"Thank you for that, Matthew."

He didn't acknowledge her gratitude, he hardly heard it, his mind and heart were too full of Patience, and his need too great to wait a moment longer. He took a step toward her, closing even the little distance between them. "Simon told me you would be here."

He was so close she could feel the heat of his body, yet he didn't touch her. His gaze beneath the brim of the Stetson was unfathomable. Patience waited.

"He told me why, O'Hara."

She didn't respond, she couldn't.

Levelly, as if he were discussing the weather, Matthew continued, "I could have picked up the telephone and called, but I didn't think I had the right. Simon named me six kinds of fool, and I guess I have been." With the tip of his thumb, he tilted the brim of his hat, and out of its shadow his face was grave. "I've never loved anyone before, and no one's loved me. Until I found you in the desert, I didn't know how forgiving love could be, or how much I needed both."

A tingle of shock rushed through her, were it not for the support of the door, her knees would have buckled. Matthew had said what she'd wanted desperately, yet what did it mean? What did he want from her? Hope and fear roughened her voice. "Why are you here?"

"Isn't it obvious? I came for the woman I claimed long ago. The woman Simon said would be waiting because she loves me." He brushed a fingertip over her cheek, catching a tear that trembled on a lash. "Was he wrong?"

Patience leaned her head back against the door, closing her eyes for only a moment. But when she opened them again, the last of her doubts were resolved, her gaze was serene and direct. "He wasn't wrong. I love you, Matthew."

He held himself motionless. "And Indian?"

She nodded, never taking her gaze from his beloved face. "And Indian."

He drew a labored breath, letting her see the hunger in him, not so contained, no longer controlled. "What I'm wearing now, it's who I am when I'm not on assignment. I'm a rancher. My spread is a couple of hours from here. Can you live with that?"

"Apache, white man, warrior, warlock, spy, rancher. Indian, Matthew." Breathing a sigh she shook her head in mock exasperation with herself. "Just like an O'Hara, so many to love, so little time."

"That's a yes?"

"Most definitely a yes." She reached out to him, touching him, and was pleased with the low sound of delight her touch drew from him.

A sudden frown creased his forehead. "Do you like my hat?"

She was startled by the abrupt question. "Of course I do."

"Good." Before the word was finished the hat was spinning into the yard.

"Matthew! Why on earth did you do that?"

"Because I'm going to kiss you, and I don't want anything in the way." His hands were at her waist, bringing her body to his. "After I kiss you, I'm going to make love to you. After I make love to you, I'm going to ask you to marry me. Then I'm going to take you home. My home. Our home. Where there are lots of critters that need a vet, and a man who needs you more."

Patience was laughing as she went into his arms. "In case you're too busy later to hear my answer, it's yes. Again."

His laughter was a growl in his throat. As his mouth took hers, she knew she'd found the true wolf in the desert. And with the wolf she would abide in love, and make her home forever.

* * * * *

COMING NEXT MONTH

#961 ANGELS AND ELVES—Joan Elliott Pickart

The Baby Bet

November's *Man of the Month*, Forrest MacAllister, is the MacAllister clan's most confirmed bachelor, as well as its Baby Bet Champion. But winning bets is nothing compared to maintaining his bachelor status around sexy Jillian Jones-Jenkins!

#962 ONCE IN A BLUE MOON—Kristin James

When Michael Traynor took off years ago, Isabelle Gray swore she'd never fall for him again. Now he was back—and she had to keep a ten-year-old secret she'd hidden from him since he left....

#963 WHATEVER COMES—Lass Small

Sean Morant was used to having beautiful women draped on his arm, but that was *before* he met Amabel Clayton. She was as determined as she was feisty, and somehow Sean had to make the stubborn woman his!

#964 COWBOY HOMECOMING—Pamela Ingrahm

Cowboy Steve Williams came home to find Tegan McReed claiming she owned *his* land! But getting the beautiful woman off his ranch—and his mind—wasn't as easy as it seemed!

#965 REBEL LOVE—Jackie Merritt

Cass Whitfield was devastated when Gard Sterling couldn't even remember the wonderful night they'd spent together! Could Gard convince her that he wasn't the same bad boy who hurt her years ago?

#966 ARIZONA HEAT—Jennifer Greene

When Kansas McClellan asked Paxton Moore to help her find her missing brother, she knew she was in trouble. Not only was the man stubborn, but he was sexy enough to make her heat rise to a dangerous level!

Take 4 bestselling love stories FREE

Plus get a FREE surprise gift!

Become a Privileged Woman,
You'll be entitled to all these Free Benefits. And Free Gifts, too.

To thank you for buying our books, we've designed an exclusive FREE program called *PAGES & PRIVILEGES*™. You can enroll with just one Proof of Purchase, and get the kind of luxuries that, until now, you could only read about.

BIG HOTEL DISCOUNTS

A privileged woman stays in the finest hotels. And so can you—at up to 60% off! Imagine standing in a hotel check-in line and watching as the guest in front of you pays $150 for the same room that's only costing you $60. Your *Pages & Privileges* discounts are good at Sheraton, Marriott, Best Western, Hyatt and thousands of other fine hotels all over the U.S., Canada and Europe.

FREE DISCOUNT TRAVEL SERVICE

A privileged woman is always jetting to romantic places.

When <u>you</u> fly, just make one phone call for the lowest published airfare at time of booking— <u>or double the difference back!</u>

PLUS—you'll get a $25 voucher to use the first time you book a flight AND <u>5% cash back on every ticket you buy thereafter through the travel service!</u>